The Break-Up Test
Rose McClelland

"sweet, heartwarming...witty and humorous. I absolutely loved it."
Sara Palacios, chicklitplus.com

"delightful...a page turner...an author to watch out for"
Rea Book Reviews

"Funny, witty and thoroughly enjoyable"
Eleanor Jordan

"A debut novel that keeps it real...you will love this"
Yasmin Selena

The Break-Up Test: 978-1-908910-32-5

Printed for Crooked Cat by Createspace

First Red Line Edition, Crooked Cat Publishing Ltd. 2012

Discover us online:
www.crookedcatpublishing.com

Join us on facebook:
www.facebook.com/crookedcatpublishing

To Rhoda
for years of encouragement,
and to Joe -
without whom this book
definitely would not have happened

The Author

Rose McClelland lives in Belfast and writes chick-lit/women's fiction.

Her kindle version of 'The Break-Up Test' received lovely reviews on Amazon including: "Rose McClelland's voice reads like the younger sister of Marian Keyes with a more streetwise but vulnerable edge."

Rose wrote a short play which was directed by Rawlife Theatre Company and performed in The Black Box Theatre, Belfast. She writes book reviews for 'Judging Covers' and writes a mixture of author interviews and articles for her blog.

Her second novel, 'How to Look Like You' is also available on kindle and in paperback.

Rose has been writing creatively since her twenties. She started writing her first novel six years ago and is currently writing her fourth book.

Acknowledgements

Thanks to my sister Rhoda for all the proof-reading, encouragement and constant 'more please!' comments.

Thank you to Laurence and Steph of Crooked Cat for liking the book and for being so easy to work with. Thank you for the fabulous cover!

Thank you Ger Nicholl of The Book Bureau for the tips about the Irish voice and the Northern Irish settings. Thank you for your support and encouragement.

Thank you to my brother Dave and his girlfriend Dee for the chat around the dining room table that day. Everyone should have a life coach like you!

Thank you to all my friends on Facebook and Twitter for the massive amount of support and encouragement. Thanks to Lisa, Lynsey, Mary-ellen, sister Ruth, Audra, Shauna, Colin and my Mum – you are like a little cheering squad!

Thank you to all my family and friends who have shown so much support – I have kept a note of every single message of encouragement.

Thank you to the Writers Circle, particularly to Yasmin Selena Butt and Janet Brigden.

Thank you to Joe F who told me to stop worrying about what people think and just go for it!

Thanks to Martin McSharry and Lynn Harris of Rawlife Theatre Company for directing my piece "The Box of Tissues". Thank you Julie McCann for performing it and making people laugh – I never intended it to be funny! Thanks to Martin Toland for encouraging me to write a short play.

And finally, thanks to you for liking the look of the book and deciding to buy it. I hope you get as much fun from reading it as I got from writing it.

Rose McClelland
Belfast, September 2012

The Break-Up Test

Chapter One
<u>AMY</u>

Amy lay stiff and motionless, staring at the ceiling. He had left the room, his bare buttocks walking away from her as he clutched his mobile phone to his ear.

Was that a woman's voice she heard from the other end?

The sunlight was screaming through the pale yellow curtains. Clothes were scattered on the floor.

Amy looked at the digital clock on the bedside table. 15:09. An afternoon romp. That was a first. Her heart sank.

I've been had. Again.

It had started off so romantically. A walk around the park, the autumnal leaves kicking underfoot. Squirrels scurrying by. Couples walking hand in hand, wrapped up in gloves and scarves, usually accompanied by a cute puppy on a lead to finish off the picture.

For a brief moment, there she was, part of one of the Sunday morning couples, sitting on a park bench, talking to her man.

This time he said he'd be away for ten weeks. A production job that would take him from music venue to concert hall, town to town.

"Maybe you could come visit me one time?" he asked, with that flirty smile on his lips and the twinkle in his eye.

"I'd like that," she smiled shyly, secretly hoping, secretly knowing, that once those ten weeks were up, things would be different. He'd be there, all the time. They'd do this Sunday morning thing, all the time. They'd be together, forever.

"Do you want to go to mine, for coffee?" he asked.

She supposed that to anyone else, it would've have seemed a strange 'date'. Meet at the park at mid-day, go back to his for coffee, be naked in bed by 15:09. But that was the way they were. Different. Creative. Original.

Back at his, he made me a peppermint tea. In a ceramic mug. The kind of mug that belonged in a cosy farmhouse.

On the coffee table, there was a book.

Looking back, was it placed strategically?

She flicked through it while he was in the kitchen.

Pictures. Pictures of naked women. Pictures of two naked women. Posing together. In the shower, in the bath. Quite tasteful really.

"Oh, you've seen the book," he chuckled, lightly, when he returned with the two mugs of herbal tea. All healthy here. No shots or wine or mid-afternoon getting sloshed for them.

"Yes, interesting."

Why did I say that? Trying to be cool? Stuck for something to say? Wanting to appear like the independent open-minded modern female that I am?

"Yes, a friend bought me that. She thought I'd appreciate it."

There should have been alarm bells at that point. Loud, clanging alarm bells.

Who is this girl buying him intimate books?

But the bells were more like a soft tinkle than a loud clanging.

"There's a dvd to go with it."

"Oh?" she replied. More of at a loss of what to say than anything else.

"Shall I put it on?" he jumped up from the seat hardly waiting for her response, and fiddled with the dvd player.

Was the dvd already in the player?

I think so. Well-prepared, if you think about it.

She noticed the line of his back as he bent over to fix the dvd player. Toned, athletic, manly. A pale blue t-shirt lightly

4

skimming over his back.

He returned to the sofa and sat next to her. His hand rested on her leg. As though they were girlfriend and boyfriend. As though it were territorial. It felt as though a buzz of electricity ran from under his hand and up her leg.

That sounds stupid and corny I know, but that's what it felt like.

The young women on the screen paraded in-front of themselves, showering themselves, bathing themselves. It was quite erotic really. They weren't porn queens either. Just normal girls with rounded tummies and decent sized hips and average faces. Not threatening. And they were enjoying themselves and there seemed nothing wrong with it. Like this is normal, animal instincts, and we should all do it. And suddenly her groin was pulsing and she was wanting to do it too. And that's how they ended up in bed at 15:09.

He said he had arrangements for that night, that a group of them were going out for a reunion. He didn't invite her.

Afterwards, when it would've been 15:05, his mobile rang, and he said, "I better take this" and when he answered, she could hear a girl's voice, and she couldn't help but wonder if that was the same girl who'd bought him the dvd and the book of the naked girls.

I just wondered, that's all. You can't blame me for thinking that.

So he padded out of the bedroom, his bare buttocks walking away from her, and that was at 15:09.

She needed to pee, so she slowly began to extricate herself from the bed. She gently pulled her top to her, covering her exposed breasts. All of a sudden, she was an over-sensitive, vulnerable mass of thin skin. When earlier she had arched her back to him in wild abandon, now she felt raw and exposed, as though someone had stripped a layer of skin away and left her empty.

She tip-toed out of the bedroom and down the corridor. She could hear him downstairs, still talking on the phone, laughing.

In the bathroom, a girl looked back at her in the mirror. Her face was flushed, her eyes dilated, her cheeks and lips red from his lips and bearded skin, her eye make-up slightly smudged, her hair wild. She could hardly recognise herself. And all at 15:09.

When she dressed and tidied up, she went downstairs.

He was fresh and chirpy, as though he'd gotten something out of his system, as though he was relieved.

"Well, I must get down to the shops and get some food in before heading out tonight," he smiled. "I'll walk you home on my way."

He made it sound like a compliment, as though he was doing her a good deed.

On the walk, they struggled for something to talk about, trying to clutch words from mid-air.

"Nice day," she mused.

Earlier they were naked together, now there was nothing to talk about.

"Yeah."

Thankfully, they were nearing her road.

"Well…" he widened his eyes. "Keep in touch."

Keep in touch!

Keep in touch!

What does that mean?

See you in two weeks time? Five weeks time? Three months?

Keep in touch!

She nodded, hoping tears wouldn't spring out and splash themselves all the way down her face and onto the ground.

He gave her a half-hug, half-kiss and trundled off to buy his groceries.

And she walked home, berating herself.

I've been had, again.

Meet at the park at mid-day, back to his for a herbal tea and a dodgy dvd, quick romp, and all over by 15:09.

6

Chapter Two
<u>BETH</u>

Beth sat at her desk at work, resisting the urge to stare at her mobile phone. It was on her right hand side, next to the keyboard, waiting to light up like the Blackpool illuminations. If only he would just text. It'd been five days. It was usually five days, so perhaps one was due? (If you looked at it from a law of averages point of view, that is).

Of course, she had hoped for a text sooner than this. The last date had been different. Special. Lots of compliments. So why? Why? Why? Why?

Why was her phone lying dormant? Waiting for a sound to bleat out like a lamb?

She ran his list of compliments through in her head.

"You've such great skin. You've such amazing eyes. You have lovely lips."

All the compliments were physical, granted, so perhaps he was only after sex?

Her heart sank at the thought of it.

The washing machine fixated within her head started on its cycle, churning ideas round and round like the clothes in the drum.

What if he's bored 'cos he didn't get sex? What if I seemed too keen? Too nice? Too 'something'?

"Do you have that report ready?" her boss asked, emerging out of his office, peering at her over the top of his glasses which were resting halfway down his nose.

"Erm.. yes.. I'll just be a minute," she broke out of her

reverie and tried to concentrate.

Concentrate! Concentrate? How could she concentrate when her thoughts kept lapsing back to Karl? The way he snuggled up close to her on the sofa. The way he looked at her lips and then pulled her to him so he could kiss her? The way he ran his hand under her top and softly across her back? How could she concentrate on reports when her eyes kept veering back towards the black screen of her mobile? Waiting for it to spring to life?

The waiting flipped to frustration.

Just what on earth is keeping him anyway? This is just plain rude! What does he take me for?

He can't just pick me up and put me down whenever he feels like it!

I am furious! Even if he does get in contact, I don't want to have anything to do with him anyway!

If this is how selfish he's gonna be, I don't want him!

The report had nearly finished winding its way out of the rollers. The paper was still hot.

Super secretary in the corner was chatting away with ease to a client. Her head totally on the ball. Her engagement ring twinkling in the light as though winking at Beth. No head trouble for this lady. Her hubby waited for her religiously everyday. He even phoned her a couple of times during the day to see how she was. And he sent her emails. She knew for a fact that they also chatted over the dinner table every night. And he pushed her trolley around Tesco every week. How could some women get it so right, when she was getting it so wrong? Why not even one text in five whole days? Especially after the whole, "You've got great lips, great eyes, great legs" combo? It didn't make sense.

"There's your report," she set the bundle of paper on her boss's desk.

"Thanks," he replied, not looking up from his work.

She turned and closed the door quietly behind her on her

way out.

And when she returned to her phone, she saw that one crisp, little white envelope had magically leapt onto the screen with the lovely words emblazoned across it:

"One message received: Karl."

Chapter Three
<u>SARAH</u>

He said he'd be there by eight pm and it was now nine.

He said he couldn't get away on time and he had to get the next train.

By nine pm, Sarah had drunk a full bottle of wine to herself and she was opening bottle number two.

She was sitting with her flatmates. They were watching Sex and the City and it was the one where nobody turned up for Carrie's birthday.

It was like life imitating art.

After his phone call, ("I'm running late honey, I'm on my way"), Sarah was furious and when she returned to the living-room, she accidentally knocked her glass of wine over and that made her even more angry and she cursed. Her flatmates looked at her quietly as though they weren't sure what to say and they didn't know what to say in case she burst out crying.

She decided to walk to the off-licence to get more wine.

Ten pm came and her phone lit up and it was him and he was outside her flat.

She buzzed him in and he arrived up the stairs and for the first few minutes, she was huffy.

They went straight to her bedroom. They didn't even go in to the living-room to make small talk with her flatmates because she knew they didn't like him.

"Your breath stinks of wine," he crinkled up his nose in disgust.

"That's cos I've been drinking wine," she retorted

sarcastically.

He did that 'sigh' thing, which meant he didn't want to argue, as though that would be the waste of a perfectly good Saturday night.

She wondered what excuse he had to give this time.

She wondered whose 40th, 30th, engagement party, or christening he'd had to invent.

She wondered if "She" doesn't wonder about how many celebratory friends he has?

He was skinny.

He smoked his cigarettes at three drags one after the other. Which she found annoying.

He did this with coffee too. Three slurps one after the other.

Perhaps this is a good sign. Perhaps it means I am going off him.

That would be a good thing.

It would make my life a whole lot simpler.

He offered her a chewing gum.

She declined.

He poured more wine for her.

They listened to music.

He never argued back.

Perhaps that's why she liked him.

He did this quiet thing where he waited for her bad mood to ease.

He plied her with more wine.

The wine started to trickle down to her toes.

She often wondered how wine could do that – get down to her very toes.

He put an arm around her and they lay there, listening to music, with the wine sloshing around her toes.

And there was this unspoken chemistry between them.

As though, if he'd just move his face slightly to one side, then his lips would be on mine, being all tingly and electrifying.

And suddenly it didn't matter what excuses he'd given.

Because anyway, even though he shares a bed with Kat, they don't sleep together.

I know that because he told me.

Now any woman would say, "Don't be silly, that's the oldest line in the book."

But right now, with him lying quietly beside her, and the wine sloshing around in her toes, and his lips so close to her that they're tingly and electrifying, she believed him.

Chapter Four
JAMIE

<u>Facebook</u>

To: Amy
From: Jamie
Subject: Long time, no chat!
Message:

Hey Aimes! Jamie here! How the hell are you??! I'm sorry I haven't been in touch for a while – but you know the score – work, life, bumming about! What are you up to these days?? I had a browse through your photos – looking good hun! VERY surprised to see that you're not showing off three sprogs and an uber-gorgeous husband yet. What's going on?? Tell me all your news.

Oh… and one other thing… I have a small favour to ask… Okay, it's quite a large favour actually… Okay, I'm just going to spit it out… Can I come and stay with you for a while? It'll only be for a few weeks… I know I have a real cheek contacting you out of the blue like this… but work are sending me up there (usual boring computer stuff – you won't be interested) .. and well… because they're such skin flints, they're not gonna pay my hotel expenses. (I know – don't ask – I'm raging too – there have been words, believe me) – so I need somewhere to stay – and I'm not flash enough yet to put myself up in a hotel for a few weeks so…. Can I stay Amy? I promise I'll pay you back in cooking favours (I have moved on

from my beans and toast days at Uni – honest!)
Please? Pretty please?
(Oh, and if you say no, I'll understand, I SWEAR).
Much love,
Jamie x

To: Jamie
From: Amy
Subject: re: Long time, no chat!
Message:

Hey Jamie! What a lovely surprise! Of course you can come and stay! It'll be just like the Uni days all over again! Although I hope you're not still as messy!!
As for the cooking – I am impressed! I seem to remember you setting off the smoke alarm on more than one occasion with your beans and toast efforts!
And sprogs? You're joking?! I know, everyone from Uni seems to be married with kids by now. It makes Facebook immensely sickening. Me and sprogs? Ha! Don't ask! In fact, let's have a good chin wag about it all when we meet. When are you coming?
Aimes x

To: Amy
From: Jamie
Subject: You are an angel.
Message:

Aimes, you're a life-saver – honest to God.
Right, I'll be up on Saturday.
Richmond station isn't it? I'll be there by 4pm. Get the beer goggles on.
Hey – do you remember that time we had that drinking competition at Uni??!

Jamie x

To: Jamie
From: Amy
Subject: Drinking competition?!
Message:

Drinking competition?! Are you kidding?! I don't remember a
single thing.
I had a total black out that night.
All I remember is waking up next to your sweaty armpit.
I've never drank tequila since.
See ya Saturday!
Aimes x
PS. I'll invite Beth and Sarah too! It'll be just like Uni days!
PPS. Will you be okay getting the train from Brighton all the
way to Waterloo and then Richmond on your own?? Haha

To: Amy
From: Jamie
Subject: Touché!
Message:

Touché missus! It wasn't much fun lying next to your snoring
either I can tell you!
See ya Saturday!
CAN'T WAIT!!
Jamie x
PS. Yes, I think I can manage Brighton to Richmond all on
my own. Independent man of the world or what??

Chapter Five
JAMIE

"What are you thinking about?" Stacey asked him.

Jamie turned to face her. Her curly mass of hair was strewn behind her on the pillow. Her pupils were dilated with post-coital bliss. Her left breast was leaning to one side, like a lop-sided pancake. The right breast was tucked under the duvet.

She had a little smile on her lips; flirtatious, teasing, expectant. As though she wanted him to say something romantic, gushy, sappy.

Of course he couldn't tell her what he was really thinking.

That he was thinking about Saturday. That he was thinking about Amy. That he was thinking about how they hadn't seen each other in such a long time. That, judging from her facebook photos, she hadn't changed a bit.

She was still the same Amy.

The one he'd fancied for three years at Uni. The one he'd house-shared with. The one he'd lusted after. The one he'd kissed.

Of course, the slight problem was that Amy had forgotten the kiss. Or rather, the kiss was in a blackout. A tequila blackout. And the next morning, it was forgotten.

The graduation robes were returned to their vendor. The front door key was given back to the landlord. The bags were packed, and the big old house they'd all shared for three years lay empty. Their voices echoed off the walls as they'd said goodbye.

Three years of fun, of independence, of excitement.

Glorious student days.

But that was years ago now. Now there were suits. And jobs. And nine to five schedules. And a woman lying next to him in bed that he'd only met two weeks ago.

He directed a pensive stare towards the curtains for a moment, as though he was straining to compose the depth of his feelings.

The curtains were pink with a flowery design.

I'm thinking... He wondered silently in his own head; *I'm thinking ... that I need a coffee. I'm thinking... that we probably had sex far too soon. I'm thinking... I feel guilty but I don't think this is going to go anywhere.*

I'm thinking that I need the loo, followed by a fry, following by a couple of paracetamol to wash down my hangover.

Her eyes were still expectant. Her head was leaning on her hand and a faint smell of morning breath was escaping from her mouth.

"I'm thinking about London on Saturday," he replied. "I guess I'm thinking about everything I need to organise before I go."

Stacey tried to hide it, but her face fell with disappointment.

"So," she said, sitting up and pulling her top to her breasts. "Who is this Amy girl again? Remind me about how you know her?"

Jamie sat up in bed and reached for the glass of water on the bedside table. He took a long glug and then wiped his mouth with the back of his hand.

"She's a mate from Uni."

Stacey nodded.

"And you're staying with her for how long?"

Jamie shrugged his shoulders.

"A few weeks. Depends how long the project goes on. Could be longer."

Stacey abruptly pulled her top over her head, covering her breasts. She found her knickers, which were lying on the floor next to the bed. With one toe, she navigated the knickers off the floor and into her hand, surreptitiously sliding them on underneath the duvet.

This amused Jamie. Earlier she was on top of him naked. Now she was covering her body with unnecessary shyness.

"And… erm… what's she like?" Stacey ventured, as though fishing. As though standing on the river bank, huge fishing pole in hand, waiting for the sharks to come along and gobble her wooden stick.

Jamie shrugged. "She's cool. She's a good laugh."

Stacey nodded. "Pretty?"

The fishing line was digging deeper.

Jamie shrugged again. "Yeah, I guess…"

Stacey picked up her jeans which were crumpled on the floor next to the laundry basket. She yanked them on with extra force.

"Right," she said, crossly.

She disappeared into the bathroom, closing the door abruptly behind her.

Jamie sighed. This is when he would have needed a cigarette. When he could have reached into his bedside cabinet, pulled out a big hefty box of twenty Marlboro Reds, flicked a lighter, listened to the comforting tinge as the flame met the nicotine, inhaled deeply and let a puff of smoke escape from his lips in a release of tension.

But no.

Having bowed to the pressure that is 'anti-social behaviour,' he'd thrown his last pack of cigarettes away two months, two weeks and two days ago.

Not that he was counting or anything.

After the sound of running water and a flushed toilet, Stacey emerged from the bathroom.

Oh shit. Had she been crying?

Her eyes looked decidedly red.

Oh holy crap, surely not?

18

But we've only been seeing each other a couple of weeks. In fact was it even that long?

Jamie couldn't remember.

He remembered the night they met, yes. It was at a party. There was a coffee table strewn with beer cans. There was music playing. There were people chatting. Low lighting. He was pleasantly drunk. And then this girl just appeared next to him on the sofa. Smiling, chatting, putting her hand on his leg, leaning in to kiss him. It was all so fast really. And he was so drunk. And yet they'd found a bedroom upstairs. There was a romp, underneath the pile of coats.

And that was that. She'd shoved a piece of paper with her number into his jeans pocket. Then she'd said, "On second thoughts..." She'd fished through his phone, stored her number in his contacts list, made a note of his number and texted him there and then.

It was a joke, granted. They were drunk, and it was funny.

But the next day, she texted him again, and they just happened to meet up again, and she just happened to be here next to him in his bedroom. He knew it was all too fast. He knew it didn't feel right. But well, he had been pulled along for the ride.

Why not go along with these things?

Why not?

She regained her composure and her face lit up again. "So, I was thinking..." she began energetically. "We could go and get breakfast somewhere, and then maybe go for a walk down along the seafront... and if you're interested, I have a few people coming over for dinner tonight – it'd be cool if they got to meet you."

"Amy...er...listen Stace, I'm really sorry but I can't... I've got loads of stuff to sort out before heading off this weekend..."

Her face fell even further than the last time, except this time she couldn't hide it.

"Oh Jamie!" she sighed, almost in a two-year old tantrum type way. "It's a Sunday! It's chill out day!"

He shrugged helplessly.

"I know Stace, I'm really sorry."

He tried to ignore the guilt-inducing tears-about-to-well-up-in-the-face type look that she had adopted. She sat right beside him on the sofa until her taxi arrived. She folded her arms tightly, as though trying to hug herself. She stared at him too, as though if she looked at him long enough, she'd keep a picture of him in her head.

The taxi beeped mercifully. He walked her to the door.

"Text me later on tonight," she instructed. "And let's meet up again before you go."

Jamie nodded. "Sure," he gave her a peck on the cheek. "Have a good day."

She looked at him quizzically, as though to say, "How am I supposed to do that when you're not going to spend the day with me?"

The taxi-man waited patiently. Stacey retreated down the walk-way, got into the car, stared at him through the window pane with puppy dog eyes and waved goodbye.

Chapter Six
<u>AMY</u>

The train station was busy. People scurrying by, hurried expressions, a spring in their step.

Amy sat on one of the steel chairs at the train side coffee shop. She hugged a cardboard cup of Americano, steam rising up, curling around her face in a comforting embrace.

The large clock hanging from the ceiling pointed its hands at 3:45pm. Typical of Amy to be perfectly on time.

She pulled her mobile phone out of her handbag, checking it again for what was probably the tenth time that day. Even though her phone was on LOUD VIBRATE. Even though she would have no chance of missing the sound of a text despite all the hustle and bustle surrounding her.

She was hoping for a text from Gav. Just one measly text. Just one "Hello how are ya? x"

But of course, nothing.

Probably up to his eyes shagging one of those dancers from the production tour he was on. But no, she didn't want to think about that.

She watched the people around her.

Mothers. Toddlers. Babies.

Couples having post-coital Saturday afternoon lunches together.

Making her want to vomit.

"Aimes!" A loud voice broke her out of her reverie. Jamie.

He came bounding through the barriers with energy and enthusiasm, holding his arms out to give her a big hug.

She set down her coffee cup and jumped up to hug him back.

"Jamie! Look at you!" she grinned. "Don't you look great?!"

"Do you think?" he asked, surprised. "Well, thanks! And look at you! Tanned!"

Amy smiled sheepishly. "Out of a bottle I'm afraid. I wish it was from foreign holidays but no such luck!"

He stood, grinned, and seemed to stare at her for what felt like ages. In a moment that had slowed down to a complete pause. In a moment where all the hustle and bustle careered around them effortlessly while they stood, paused, silent, taking each other in.

Jamie broke the pause. "Drink?"

Amy nodded. "Yeah, come on. There's a pub across the road."

They headed up the steps together, Jamie lugging a bag over his shoulder, Amy swinging her handbag effortlessly, and the two of them falling into quick, easy chit-chat.

"So much to catch up on..."

"What have you been up to..."

"Oh.. you first..."

"No you..."

"Wait..." Jamie said, as they had approached the entrance of the train station.

He rummaged into his jeans pocket, pulled out a pack of Marlboros and ushered Amy over to the low wall so he could sit and smoke a fag.

"Oh Jamie..." Amy began disappointedly. "You're not still smoking are you?"

He nodded, flicked the lighter and inhaled deeply.

"God yes."

She shook her head. "Dear oh dear oh dear."

She noticed, briefly, that his hand was slightly shaky as the cigarette balanced between both fingers. She noticed it, but shrugged it off.

"I did however…" Jamie began, "….stop for two months, two weeks and two days…so.. on my reckoning… I'm allowed one thousand, five hundred and forty fags to play catch up for all that lost time."

Amy looked at him wryly.

"I suppose that's what you were working out on the train on the way up?"

Jamie smiled. "You know me too well."

They sat on the low wall, with the Saturday shoppers passing by, people queuing for buses and taxis whizzing past.

"So what made you crack?" Amy asked. "What was the big defining pressure that made you inhale again?"

Jamie rolled his eyes. "God, let's get a drink... I'll fill you in…"

Chapter Seven
<u>JAMIE</u>

Cigarette smoke curled up in front of Jamie as he watched the three women sitting opposite him.

Amy, with her vibrant hair - a mass of beautiful red curls. Beth, with her poker-thin limbs curled around themselves as she crossed her legs neatly. Sarah, with her full lips and curvy hips, sipping from her pint glass.

They were sitting in the beer garden, surrounded by overhanging flowerbeds, half-empty pint glasses in plastic mugs and low jazz music filtering through an overhead loudspeaker.

"I can't believe I haven't been up to see you guys sooner," Jamie sighed.

"I know," Sarah piped up. "It's a disgrace! Call yourself a friend?" she winked.

"To be fair, you guys haven't been down to see me in Brighton either."

"No, that's true," they agreed.

There was a silence then as they stared into their pint glasses, reflecting.

"What happens?" Sarah asked. "You have this great big graduation day and you promise you'll all be best friends forever and then..."

She trailed off.

"Work happens," Jamie shrugged his shoulders.

They nodded.

"Yup. Good old nine to five," Amy quipped.

"Well..." Jamie raised his glass. "Here's to reunions... and picking up where you left off."

"I'll drink to that," Beth said.

"So tell me everything..." Jamie began.

And so they did.

They talked for three hours, five drinks (each), ten cigarettes (Jamie), four bags of Salt & Vinegar (Jamie), four loo-breaks (Sarah), one eyeing up of the bouncer (Sarah), and one eyeing up of the barmaid (Jamie).

Jamie listened in horrified amazement as he heard one story after the other. Amy, then Beth, then Sarah – all broken-hearted over men who were treating them like dirt.

What had happened to them all since their uni days? Those young, carefree girls who went out four nights a week regaling him of their latest conquests and carry-on? They might not have changed physically, but they were a world apart from the three girls he had flat-shared with in his uni days.

The three girls with their funny Irish accents. The three girls who'd met over the dinner table in their student halls and clicked immediately because of their backgrounds. Amy from Dungiven, Sarah from Belfast and Beth from Derry. All cuddling together like little lambs. Bracing the big bad world of London.

Of course, it wasn't long until they had settled into student life well. Amy, and the way she used to career round the campus, her red coat billowing out behind her, turning heads wherever she went. Beth, winning awards left, right and centre for her artwork and being head of her class. And Sarah, bringing home one hapless victim after the other, never short of a man to keep her company.

"Well that's just nuts," Jamie let out a low whistle. "I'm disgusted with all of you."

The three of them sat in shock.

Where was the tea and sympathy?

Where was the 'there, there, everything will be okay'?

Where was the 'well he doesn't know what he's missing. One day

25

he'll wake up and smell the coffee' chat?

"What about 'treat 'em mean, keep 'em keen?'" Jamie asked. "Men can spot a wet blanket a mile away." He said his comment flippantly, flicking his lighter open and inhaling his eleventh cigarette.

In response to the sea of annoyed faces watching him, he replied defensively, "What? I'm just saying."

"You need to live in the real world…"

"Wouldn't you rather I told you the truth…"

"You should be glad I'm letting you in on all these secrets…"

On and on he went, lacing his monologue with drunken advice. 'Advice' he knew he was only spewing out because of his inebriated tongue.

'Advice' he was only retorting as a knee-jerk reaction to Stacey's puppy dog expression treatment.

'Advice' he was only hoping would wean Amy away from the arms of Gav's and into his.

'Advice' that was, for a momentary while, making him sound knowledgeable and purposefully steering the conversation away from clothes, shoes, shopping and 'do you remember so-and-so from uni?' chat.

'Advice' that somehow ended up with the four of them drawing up a list of commandments. A list written over the space of three napkins, using a combination of Sarah's lip-liner, Amy's eye-liner and the creative inspiration plucked from the bottom of four plastic pints.

Chapter Eight
<u>AMY</u>

"Are you ready yet?" Jamie called from the hallway, as Amy was in her bedroom pulling a top over her head and jutting her feet into trainers.

"Give me two secs!"

She grabbed the jeans that was strewn on the floor and threw them into the laundry basket.

That was when she noticed the napkins, poking out of the back pocket, reminding her of the night before.

She picked up the napkins and smiled wryly as she read through the list.

A collection of all their handwriting, a smudge of eyeliner, dodgy spelling in places and definite drunken writing.

<u>The Break-Up Test</u>
<u>The Ten Commandments</u>
1. Do a hobby U love. (Beth)
2. Pamper self once / week. (Beth)
3. New clothes (Retail therapy ALWAYS works!) (Sarah)
4. Girlie nights – wine, chocolate and chin-wag (Sarah)
5. YES to as many invites as poss. (Sarah)
6. Open mind about other fellas. (Jamie)
7. Date s with other guys – just for the laugh. (Jamie)
8. Non-Dates – i.e.. time for yourself! (Sarah)
9. If a bloke says he's not interested, just accept it and move on. (Jamie)
10. Let the guy ask you out. (Sarah)

Amy rolled her eyes.

God, it's amazing what crap we come up with when we're drunk.

She screwed the napkins up and chucked them in the bin.

"Just coming!"

After a stroll around Richmond Park, Jamie and Amy found a quiet coffee shop on top of the hill that looked down onto the river.

It was quiet.

Quiet because everyone else was probably still sleeping off hangovers, curling up in bed, having long lazy sex.

"Remind me why we're up so early?" Amy asked, stirring her cappuccino and watching as the froth smoothly licked round the side of the mug.

"Blows the cobwebs away. Stops you from sitting around feeling hungover all day," Jamie quipped, slicing a knife through his scone and slathering a hefty wedge of butter on top.

Amy smiled. "And since when have you turned into mister get up & go?"

She took a sip of her cappuccino and grinned at him. "I seem to remember you being the laziest trollop at Uni!"

Jamie smiled mischievously. "Well – maybe there's a lot of things you don't know about me Miss Amy. Maybe you're going to have to get to know me all over again."

She smiled, albeit in a kindly way. And there it was. That smile. That smile that was meant to be for a kid brother. That smile that meant, "Thanks, you're so endearing." As though she should be petting him, like a puppy dog.

Amy sank back into the sofa, staring out the window, listening to the comforting music playing throughout the café. Enjoying that it was devoid of crying babies, or over-enthusiastic teenagers, or gossiping women. Just peaceful.

She supposed in a way, that she and Jamie could have passed for one of those Sunday couples. That for some reason they would have prised themselves from the love nest that would have been their bed, and they would have deposited themselves here instead, into this peaceful capsule, into this quiet café.

Amy would be peaceful, if she could. If she could shut off the nagging thought that was Gav. If she could stop wondering why he *still* hadn't texted her. Not since that dreadful dodgy dvd day. Not since the time he'd said, "Keep in touch."

She supposed she could have texted him first. She supposed she could have sent something simple like, "It was great to see you again x." But she wouldn't.

If she'd learned enough from the myriad of "How To" books, she knew not to do that.

But his very absence of any communication whatsoever stunned her.

Had he really no intention of ever getting in touch with her again ever??

"Remember that time we had the house party?" Jamie asked, breaking her out of her reverie.

Amy chuckled. "Oh God yeah! Do you remember that?! That was a disaster!"

"Because of all the mess?"

"No!" Amy laughed. "Because I jinxed myself! I was so freaked out at the thought of two random strangers using my bed for a romp, that I put a poster on my bedroom door –

"STRICTLY NO ENTRY ALLOWED."

"And… did you find someone in it?" Jamie probed.

"No! There was no-one in it! In fact there was no man in that bedroom for the rest of the year! I totally jinxed myself!"

29

"Ha! ha!" Jamie laughed. "Well jeez Amy, if you were needed romping services, you could have asked, I was only down the hallway."

"Ha! ha! Very funny."

Slight twinge of pain.

Why is the thought of me being a romping partner so hard to comprehend?

"Or the time we got burgled," Jamie grimaced, trying quickly to change the subject.

"Bloody awful!" Amy winced. "I remember thinking – 'Poor Sarah – they took all her gorgeous clothes'. And then thinking – 'Poor Beth – they took her lap top'. And 'Poor Jamie – they took his dvd player'. I remember feeling relieved that I'd got off so lightly. They'd obviously looked through my stuff and thought nothing was worth taking."

"Yeah, I remember that. That was when you discovered they'd stolen your food from the freezer."

"I know! My ten pound weekly Iceland shop! I was raging!"

Jamie chuckled.

"They were the days."

"Do you miss them?" Amy asked quietly, watching him, as though sensing something, as though there was some sort of nostalgia, for another time, when things were easier, when they had the world at their feet and time on their hands. As though he was sad that things hadn't turned out as he'd expected.

"Argh... yes and no..." Jamie shrugged. "God, of course it'd be great to be the eternal student. That freedom. That lack of responsibility. That constant social life..."

"Sounds like you're still like that to be honest."

"You think?"

"Yup!"

There was a silence then, as they stared into their cups, contemplating.

Amy picked up her mobile phone absentmindedly and

flicked it open.

No messages.

"Phone watching again?" Jamie asked.

"Hmmmph?" Amy looked up, surprised, as though she had no idea what he was talking about.

"You. You're phone watching," he persisted. "You've done it constantly ever since I've arrived."

Amy was surprised at his tone. He seemed annoyed, offended even. As though his company wasn't good enough and that was why she had to keep hoping to hear from Gav.

"Have I? I didn't realise. Sorry."

Except that she didn't know what she was apologising for. If she wanted to stare at her phone all day long, she was entitled to, wasn't she?

"So what about Stacey?" Amy asked, changing the subject quickly. "Have you texted her since you've come up?"

Jamie looked down into his cup and stirred his coffee again, even though it was half empty.

"Erm… no…"

"Tsk, tsk. So you've been away from her for how long and you haven't sent her a measly text yet?"

"No…"

Amy shook her head.

"What?!"

"Look, all I'm saying is, she's missus nice and you can't be bothered with her. I bet if she was a bitch you'd be all over her."

"No I wouldn't." He took a sip of his coffee, draining the remnants of the cup. He looked across at her. Her hair was piled up on top of her head in a messy ponytail. She was wearing a tight white t-shirt and faded blue jeans. She was sipping the last bit of froth from her cappuccino and biting into a heart shaped biscuit. She looked, despite only wearing jeans and a t-shirt, breath-taking.

"I think there are just people for people," he looked at her squarely. He was trying to emit vibes to her. He was trying to tell her by brainwave that some people are just meant to be. He was trying to tell her that she was meant for him.

She screwed up her face. "This biscuit's rotten," she grimaced. "D'you want it?" She absentmindedly handed the biscuit in his direction.

He took the biscuit out of her hand and rotated it with his fingers.

"Great. A broken heart biscuit," he said. "She gives me a broken heart."

Amy looked up at him and laughed. "You're nuts."

Then she looked serious.

"So do you think Gav thinks that too – that there's just people for people – and that I'm just not for him."

"Well if he does, then he's mad."

And there it came again. The affectionate look. The look for the kid brother.

"Aw thanks Jamie."

Still too early to ask her out then, he noted to himself.

"So have there been any texts from Gav at all recently then?" he asked, hoping she would say no. Hoping she would say, 'No, I suppose it's really about time I moved on and forgot about him.'

She shook her head.

"No."

She shrugged her shoulders.

"He's probably just really busy, he'll have a lot of work on.. and I'm sure he'll be in touch when he's next coming home and… "

On and on and on she went, with excuses, explanations and reasons to keep hanging on for him.

Jamie watched, feeling his heckles raise.

What an absolute bloody waste.

A gorgeous girl like her waiting around for that ungrateful twat.

His patience, which had been simmering away on a low heat suddenly rose to a bubbling crescendo.

"Oh Amy, for feck's sake!" he blurted out.

Her eyes widened in surprise.

"When are you going to wake up and smell the coffee? He's a twat! Are you really trying to tell me he's not shagging half the country as we speak? Are you really trying to tell me he's off on some production job and he's not shagging half the dancers or actresses or whatever it is he's doing?"

Amy's eyes widened further.

But it was too late. Jamie was on a roll. The bubbling pot had started to overflow.

"And you're trying to tell me that the only reason he's not texting you is not because he's not thinking about you but because he accidentally forgot?"

That was when the tears started. Quiet droplets of tears that had begun to well up in the corner of her eyes and threatened to squeeze out and plop their way down her cheeks.

"Oh shit," Jamie said, suddenly realising he'd gone too far. "Oh jeez Amy – I'm so sorry – I really don't know what came over me – Oh my god, I'm so sorry."

He reached over to put a hand on her arm but she recoiled away.

"It's okay," she snivelled, raising a napkin to her eyes and hurriedly trying to mop up her tears.

"I'm just... I'm probably just tired... and hungover..."

She picked up her bag and began putting her things away – her phone, her hand cream, her nail file.

"No... no it's not okay... look, now you're going to leave..." Jamie said, running a hand through his hair in exasperation. "Oh God, I feel like such a twat... Oh Amy, I didn't mean it honestly... it's not of my business... I just don't want to see you getting hurt, that's all..."

She nodded, briskly, as though trying to prevent any more tears falling.

33

"I know – its okay, honestly – look, I'm probably pmt'ed – I'm gonna head home – I just want to be on my own for a while."

"Shit," Jamie said, under his breath, hanging his head.

"I'll see you later," she said quietly, walking out of the coffee shop and looking as though her insides had crumpled away to nothing.

Chapter Nine
<u>AMY</u>

Amy left the coffee shop, defeated. The woman behind the counter gave her a curious look, as though she'd noticed her crying. As though she'd presumed that Jamie and Amy were a couple having a Sunday morning row. A look as though to say 'Aw come on now – he looks like a nice fella – don't give him such a hard time.'

She wanted to go up to her and tell her to mind her own business. She wanted to tell her that actually she and Jamie weren't a couple. She wanted to tell her that it was okay for her with her comfortable life and her wedding band on her finger and her husband to go home to.

But that some of us in the world are less fortunate. Some of us are being mucked around and we don't know whether we're coming or going.

She wanted to say all that, but she didn't. She just turned on her heel and walked out.

She went home, got to her bedroom, collapsed on her bed, and started crying.

Loud, sobbing tears. Tears that she wasn't sure where they were coming from. Tears that seemed never-ending. Tears that seemed to wrench themselves from her very gut and work their way up her torso and out of her soul. Tears that made her face red raw. Tears that seeped through one tissue after the other and even drenched her pillowcase. Tears of anger. Tears of release. Tears of self-pity.

She thought of everything Jamie had said. She thought of

the look on his face, as though he felt sorry for her, as though he thought she was a fool. She thought of how harsh he was, and that just made her indignant and angry all over again.

How dare he give off to me like that! After me letting him stay here out of the goodness of my heart!

She thought about what he had said.

Was he right? Was I mad to keep waiting around for Gav? Did Gav have no interest in me whatsoever?

She felt like her heart was bleeding. Literally bleeding. As though she wanted to sit down with Gav and plead, "Please... tell me... What's wrong with me? Why aren't you texting me? Why aren't you interested? What is it I'm doing wrong? Am I not pretty enough? Funny enough? Something enough?

It was as though she had a metaphorical stick which she was beating herself over the head with, saying, "You're not good enough yet, you're not good enough yet, you're not good enough yet..."

She began to count the times she had been here before, in this exact same set-up. Heart-broken over some guy who wasn't interested. Unrequited love. Hadn't she spent her entire twenties suffering from it? If only there was some miracle cure for it. Like a bottle of calpol, or a monthly trip to the chiropractor, kneading it out of her. She wondered if there was an element of Jamie's words that were truth?

She thought about the time a counsellor had tried to tell her the same thing in the past. She had been sent there for something else – a burglary and a break-up, but somehow the counsellor had brought everything back to her father. She said something about abandonment, and him running out when she was six, and not being able to trust, and something about her spending her whole life trying to bring him back again, through other men.

But she had shrugged it all off at the time. She thought that that kind of chat was reserved for American chat shows, or self-help books, but not for her. She thought it was all co-incidence, or hearsay, or a lot of gobble-de-gook to try to make a rhyme out of reason.

The clock had ticked, and then the counsellor had mechanically said, "Time's Up," and the box of tissues had sat between them, untouched. She had set a couple of ten pound notes on the table, got up, walked to the door, said "Thank you" very formally and politely, and she had left. There had been a few tears that day, in the toilets afterwards. But she had quickly wiped them away, spread on a layer of make-up, like icing on a cake, and she had gone to the pub and got drunk.

That was a long time ago. So even that day, there was no quick fix. There was no bottle of calpol, or chiropractor trip, or even a one hour counselling session that would do the trick.

She wondered how many times she had been in this position, and how many more times she'd find herself there. Like history repeating itself over and over and over. Like a broken record jumping, jumping, jumping. How many times had she fallen for a guy who was distant? Physically, emotionally, mentally, metaphorically? It made her head swim to actually contemplate it. And again she wondered, was there an element of truth in what Jamie had said?

And then she caught herself on.

All the tears were cried out of her. She had none left.

She looked at herself in the mirror. Face red-raw.

She splashed water on her face and dried it off.

She felt wonderfully … cleansed. As though she'd washed her soul out in soapy water and wrung it dry.

She was exhausted, as though released of all her tension and angst and frustration. She wondered if she did have pmt.

She decided that chocolate was in order. A large mug of comforting hot chocolate with marshmallows on top. She tucked herself up in bed with the hot chocolate. She threw all the tissues away and put the wet pillowcase in the laundry basket. She climbed into bed, relaxed and ready to sip her hot chocolate. She told herself that this too would pass, that tomorrow was a new day, and that what seems awful today would be less dramatic tomorrow. She made a list of all the things she was grateful for; her job, her home, her friends.

She thought to herself, *What was I doing letting Jamie upset me so much? Sure wasn't he just an ignoramus anyway?*

She decided she was being too harsh on herself. That she was getting far too deep and analytical. That the only thing that was wrong was that she fancied a guy and he happened to be working away from home at the moment – simple as that.

She decided there was no point in analysing her past and her previous choices and all that carry-on. All that was wrong was that she fancied Gav, there was chemistry with him, and she missed him. Simple as that.

And that was why she decided to text him.

"Hey Gav, Amy here, just thought I'd drop you a wee hello to see how you are x "

SEND.

Sit back.

Think, "Feck! I've texted him!"

Phone bleeps.

Reply!

"Hey Aimes… Good to hear from ya. All going well here. I'm home this weekend if you fancy meeting up? Saturday night – mine? 8pm? X "

She gulped.

This weekend!

Hurrah!

And then,

Why didn't he tell me sooner?! So I'd have time to immac, and shave legs, and fake tan, and pluck eyebrows, and plan outfit, and condition hair, and most importantly, to have been able to look forward to it!

Have just had one wasted cry-fest night for nothing!

Am full of plans now.

Lots to do tomorrow. Busy schedule ahead.

Her phone beeped again.

This time it was Sarah.

"Hiya! Just wondering if you all fancy getting together this weekend? The four of us? I'm thinking this Saturday night? My house. 8pm. Drinks and nibbles? Sar x x "

Shit.

Feel a real plunge of guilt and remorse and conscience but know I'm not going to go..

The trouble would be how to think up a feasible lie to get out of it. I know there's no point in telling Jamie, Beth or Sarah what I'm up to. It just wouldn't be worth the hassle. So the next best thing to do would be to lie.

Damn having to answer to people and be accountable to them!

She didn't feel so guilty about lying to Jamie, especially since he was the one that induced the cry-fest in the first place. But Beth and Sarah, she did feel guilty about lying to them.

However, her adrenalin and serotonin infested mood incurred by the thought of meeting Gav again cancelled out any feelings of guilt and conscience.

I DESERVE this night with Gav goddammit!

This night could be one step closer on the road to us being an item.

"Oh Sarah! I'm so sorry!" Amy texted, "I can't this Saturday night. I've to go and visit my mum – she needs the company – you girls go ahead and I promise I'll make it to the next one. Aimes x x "

In Amy's convincing lie construction, she nearly believed herself. She nearly thought she *was* going to visit her mum, passing by Gav's on the way for a quick shag.

"Aww!" Sarah texted back, "It won't be the same without you! Keep up the good work and see you next time! X x "

Good work?

Indeed.

Amy slept soundly that night, cushioned in romantic dreams about Gav and how he'd put his arms around her and they'd cuddle up on the sofa.

When she awoke the next morning and went downstairs, there was a huge bunch of flowers on the dining room table. With a note from Jamie.

"I'm so sorry. J x x x"

"How was school today?" Amy's mum asked. She held her hand as they walked up the street towards their house, towards their big red door.

"It was good," Amy smiled, skipping along next to her mother's longer strides.

But when they got in through the big red door, the house was different than normal.

There was no Dad.

Usually he was in his armchair, the one beside the window.

Usually she would jump up on his lap. ("Shoes off first, missy!")

She would settle into the crook between the comfy arm of the sofa and his warm lap. She would put her head on his chest and feel the up and down rhythm of his breathing.

"Read to me," she'd say.

"But I'm reading the newspaper. It's too old for you."

"I know, but read to me."

So he'd read, and she'd listen to the soft lulling sound of his voice, and mum's cooking smells would waft in from the kitchen.

She'd place her head on his chest, with the scratchy feel of his jumper on her cheek.

It felt like home.

She couldn't remember if his smell was a mixture of cigarette smoke and manly aftershave.

She could only remember sitting on his knee, and him taking the time to read to her, and her feeling special.

She had found it strange that night when he hugged her

extra tight before bedtime. She'd found it strange that he said 'goodnight' many times; that his eyes seemed to well up with tears.

And then there were the raised voices again. Voices that frightened her. Voices that made her feel as though it didn't feel like home anymore. Voices that sounded as though something was very, very wrong.

"Where's dad?" Amy asked, when she saw the empty armchair. "Has he gone out for a walk without us?"

"No love, come and chat to me."

They sat in the other room – the one for special visitors, the one with the big table and the hard chairs and the lacy curtains that hung in the window and drowned out the light. They sat in the dark, dingy room.

There was orange juice and biscuits on the table. The special biscuits with chocolate on, as though she had been a good girl.

"I have to talk to you about your dad."

Amy looked at her, expectantly. Her mum had a shaky voice.

"He's had to go away… for a while… and I'm not sure he'll be able to come back…."

Amy's brow furrowed.

They sat in silence for a while.

"Has he gone away with Cassie's dad? Has he gone away with the angels?"

Mum's eyes flitted downwards. As though she was struggling. She was squeezing the tissue in her hands very tightly.

"No.. no love… he's not gone away with the angels…"

Another silence.

"Well.. where then? And why didn't he bring us?"

Her mum looked confused, as though she didn't know how to answer, a bit like Cassie's face in school when the teacher asked her hard questions.

"Well, maybe we'll know that one day," mum finally replied.

But that didn't feel like enough.

There was no screaming or shouting that day. No crying. No more words spoken.

Mum just got up from the table and said, "I'm going to put the dinner on. I'll make your favourite – fish fingers. You can watch whatever you want on TV."

But somehow Amy didn't feel like eating fish fingers. There was a funny feeling in her tummy – one she'd never had before.

Her mum looked at her plate, looked at Amy's down-turned mouth, and said "Try to eat something pet."

Amy shook her head. "I don't feel like it."

"Okay," her mum said softly. "Just leave it. Let me know later if you want some toast."

Amy left the table and went down into the basement to play with her dolls house.

Later, when she poked her head around the living room door, she saw her mum, sitting in Dad's armchair, with a cigarette in her hand. She had never noticed a cigarette in her mum's hand before. The wisps of smoke curled up around her face and her eyes looked sad, as though there wasn't any life in them.

And somehow, somehow, that day, the world seemed very grey.

Chapter Ten
SARAH

Sarah had no idea what was in store for her on that Saturday sunny day. Of course she didn't. It appeared a day like any other. She spread her marmalade on her toast like any other. She sipped her coffee and watched the morning news like any other. She put her make-up on and made herself presentable to the world. And then she stepped outside.

It was only supposed to be an average Saturday shopping trip. A stroll around Covent Garden, rifling through the sale rails to see if any miraculous bargains would jump her way. Clothes that flattered her figure and made her feel sexy and desirable. She settled for a black skirt with figure hugging material that made her look curvaceous and womanly. She wondered, briefly, if Stephen would like it; if it would be the piece de resistance to entice him towards her.

She spied an Ann Summers shop. She had never set foot inside an Ann Summers shop. She didn't know why. Fear perhaps? Or embarrassment? The notion that she could re-emerge carrying trillions of bags with "Ann Summers" emblazoned across the front – which might as well have been a slogan to say, "I've been naughty. I've been buying whips and vibrators and lube oil and all sorts of mischief. I am a BAD GIRL" – was too daunting for her.

She was convinced that she would be the one unfortunate enough to emerge from the shop and bump into her Great Aunt Josie, or mum's elderly friend Maisie, or ever worse, the old man from across the street.

To hell with it. I'll just have a look. There's no harm in looking. Life's too short.

She stepped inside the shop, passing the sexy negligee and the women looking at bras and the boyfriends standing behind them, nudging their preferences. She passed boxes of sex toys and lube cream and novelty games. And then she found herself in front of a wall of vibrators. She couldn't help looking, of course she couldn't. Rows and rows of colours and sizes and different styles.

"Can I help you?" a voice appeared beside her. Two voices in fact. Two bright-eyed, teenage-like sales assistants. They were smiling broadly, with over-enthusiastic grins, as though she were in a toy store, hoping to purchase a teddy for a child.

"Erm… no …. Thanks… I'm fine."

She felt flustered, embarrassed, hassled.

Shouldn't this be a private thing? Do you really think I want to discuss sex toys with a total random stranger?

Sarah left the shop then, hurriedly, wondering why she felt so aggravated.

Am I that much of a prude?

It was in that flustered, aggravated state, that she bumped into Stephen and Kat.

Literally, bumped into them.

"Oh hi," Stephen said, as Sarah's face met his and Kat's full on.

"Hi" Sarah found herself saying.

Stephen cleared his throat, dropped his hand from holding Kat's and suddenly started performing his hands in a frantic dance gesture instead.

"Erm.. Kat… you remember Sarah… Sarah… you remember Kat…"

The hands danced energetically, which was ironic, because Kat's mouth and Sarah's mouth dropped wide open and they stood still, as though someone had pressed the pause button.

"You've met before right?" Stephen asked, as though words

were tripping out of his mouth without his control.

Sarah nodded, closed her mouth and found herself saying, "Yes…. I remember."

This is the part where I'm supposed to be crying and screaming, Sarah thought calmly.

This is the part where I'm supposed to make a scene, right here, in the middle of the street, in the middle of all these Londoners, even though no-one would take any notice.

This is the part where I'm supposed to have a melt-down.

But Sarah was calm. Far too calm. It was almost as though she was standing above herself, watching herself. As though she was observing, "Now there is a calm and mature woman if I've ever met one."

Kat's face was gloating. A full blown, obvious gloat. She raised her left hand to her ear, fiddled with her ear, and rested her hand on her neck, just so Sarah could spot the twinkling engagement ring.

"Your ring?!" Sarah said, falling into the trap; stepping onto the land mine that Kat had so effortlessly set up.

"Yes" Kat smiled, looking at Stephen and perfecting her gloat even further, if that was possible.

"You're getting married?" Sarah asked. This question was directed at Stephen.

Stephen nodded, apologetically, with a look as though to offer his condolences. With a look as though to say, "Yes, I'm sorry, I know this is really going to break your heart and you're going to be crying on your pillow for weeks on end but yes, it's true I'm afraid, we're getting married."

"Congratulations," Sarah said calmly, with a look as though to say, "Don't be so fecking UP YOURSELF! I won't spare you a second thought!"

Kat waffled on about rings and engagements and wedding dresses and churches and people to invite but all Sarah heard was "BLAH BLAH BLAH BLAH BLAH."

"That's wonderful," Sarah said calmly. "I'm very happy for

you. You're very lucky."

Again, where was this script coming from? Who was this actress who had stepped in for her today?

"Well, I must crack on," Sarah continued, as though they'd been standing on the street corner, discussing the weather, or the latest news, or general chit-chat. "See ya later."

Kat smiled her sickly smile. The smile that said, "I am so cushioned in happiness and romance at the moment that I am practically drifting along on a cloud."

Stephen was giving Sarah the guilty glance. The glance that said, "Shit, I have really broken your heart here, I am so totally responsible for your happiness."

That was when Sarah walked away.

Walked through Covent Garden.

Walked towards Leicester Square.

Walked past the Empire building.

Walked through the busy throng of people.

Walked through the hustle and bustle of noise and voices and movement and clutter and angst and...

.....Arrrrrgggggghhhhhhhh!!!.....

She needed to scream.

A very, very, loud, heart-wrenching, gut-busting scream.

Or cry.

She needed to sob big fat tears but she knew if she started she wouldn't be able to stop.

Concentrate on getting home.

Concentrate on getting the tube without crying.

Concentrate on not drawing attention to yourself.

But it was too late. The first tear had plopped out. The man opposite her on the tube was too engrossed in his book to pay any attention.

The tears rolled effortlessly down her cheeks.

"Oh God Jamie! I feel like such a fool!" Sarah snivelled. She'd found herself on Amy's doorstep instead of going home. She couldn't be alone. She needed a very firm shoulder to cry on.

"Where's Amy?" she asked, squeezing past Jamie and walking towards the living room.

"Erm... I think she's at the hairdressers... God Sarah! What happened?"

Sarah plopped herself onto the sofa, whipped a tissue out of the box on the coffee table and dabbed at her eyes.

"If I tell you what happened.. promise you won't say 'I told you so'?"

He quickly joined her on the sofa and put a hand on her knee. "Of course not.. God... what's going on?" He'd decided he'd done enough damage with being too honest with Amy, it was time to start trying to be a more sympathetic listener.

So Sarah told him everything; from Kat's sickly sweet smile, to her gloat, to the ring, and back to Kat's sickly sweet smile again.

"Hmmm..." Jamie pondered.

"What?"

"Well, do you really think she has much to be sickly sweet about? Would you want to marry a guy when you knew fine rightly he'd been having a fling with another woman?"

Sarah took a deep breath and expelled a gust of breath.

"I mean.." Jamie went on, "It doesn't sound like this Kat one has much to gloat about if you ask me. In fact, I'd say she should be running for the hills."

Sarah kicked off her shoes, lifted her feet up onto the sofa and hugged her arms around her knees.

"I know... but I just feel like such a fool... I really honestly believed him... I really honestly believed him that he was just friends with her... how thick am I?"

"Cut yourself a bit of slack Sarah," Jamie hushed. "So you took on face value what he was telling you – so what? So you

47

dared to trust someone? There's nothing wrong with that."

She smiled appreciatively.

"And another thing..." he went on. "Why feel like a fool... it's only me, Amy and Beth that know about it – and we're your friends. We're not going to judge you. We're here to help you."

Sarah let out another sigh as though relieved of some of her tension.

"Thanks so much Jamie," she gave him a hug. "I'd almost forgotten how helpful you are with this man stuff."

"It's my specialist subject," he grinned.

She smiled, despite herself.

"Right!" she stood up and began to pace the living room floor. "I need a plan of action. I am not going to waste one single second crying over that twat."

"Uh oh," Jamie grimaced. "Why does this sound worrying? You're not going to do anything dangerous to him are you?"

"Ha! No," Sarah waved a hand flippantly. "I'm thinking about that break-up test we invented the other night. I'm thinking we need to take it seriously."

"O-kay..."

"Where's that list we drew up?"

"Um... I dunno... Amy had it..."

"Right, let's phone her. I want that list. I'm gonna start over."

Jamie raised an eyebrow. *Sarah was like a woman possessed. Probably still in shock,* he mused.

In denial. Not wanting to feel the pain so trying to clutch at straws.

Best to let her get on with it.

"Amy?!" Sarah spoke urgently into her mobile. "Yes... yes I know you're at the hairdressers but I just need to ask you a quick question. ... What? Oh, Jamie told me that's where you are... yes, yes I'm at your place with Jamie... Look never mind all that – I just need to ask you something... That list... the

48

one on the napkin... Where did you put it? ... In your bin??
Why? ... Right well okay, but can I go and get it back?... No,
I'm serious... Yes I'm okay – well no, I'm not actually, but I'll
tell you all about that the next time I see you... Yes it's about
Stephen... I'll speak to you soon."

Sarah flicked her phone shut, marched purposefully into
Amy's bedroom, rooted through the bin and resurrected the
three crumpled napkins.

Chapter Eleven
JAMIE

Jamie noticed when he came downstairs that the note on the flowers had been taken out of the small envelope.

So she's read my apology.

He noticed that she'd left the note on the table.

Not scrunched up then. But not tucked away in her "Box of things I cherish" either.

He sighed.

Why do I have to such an utter prat at times? Why couldn't I have just bitten my tongue? Said nothing? Had a bit of self-control?

Now he would have to tip-toe around her and make his amends, and feel really uncomfortable for the next while until the awkwardness began to settle. He would have to cook her dinner, be really nice to her and ply her with pleasantries, until the rawness of it passed.

Why did I have to be such an utter prat? And her being so good and letting me stay in her place too while I did this work in London.

Swamped with guilt and remorse, he trudged his way into the kitchen and switched on the kettle.

She must have headed out to work already.

He sat on the sofa and nursed his mug of coffee.

No point in sitting around feeling sorry for myself, he thought.

I need a plan of action.

Something to stop him sitting around feeling sorry for himself. Something to switch this situation from pity to purpose.

He would go into town. He would buy ingredients. He would cook dinner for her on Saturday. He would buy some wine. He would ply her with some nice food and drink before they headed over to Sarah's for the night.

He might even buy some new clothes – a trendy shirt, Calvin Klein underwear, delicious aftershave, a seductive CD.

Empowered by his P.O.A. – Plan of action, he jumped into the shower whistling, and set about enjoying his Saturday seduction strategy.

First stop: HMV for a swoony cd.

Dinner was progressing successfully by the time Amy arrived home from the hairdressers on Saturday. The pots were bubbling, steam was curling up along the windows and a warm, inviting aroma hung in the air.

"Hi," she said, when she arrived in the door.

It was that awkward "hi." The awkward "hi" not long after a fight. A "hi" that says, "I'm being civil, because you're a friend, but really, I'm still a bit annoyed at you for your behaviour."

He said "hi" back. But his "hi" meant, "Hey look, I'm really sorry, I do feel really bad about it honestly."

"Good day?" he probed, gently.

She nodded. "Yeah...yeah, not bad."

She looked in the direction of all the pots and pans and steam and noise and smell, with an enquiring raise of the eyebrow.

"Oh," he said, "I thought I'd cook us some dinner..." he began, "...as a bit of an apology... you know..." he broke off awkwardly.

Her face softened. "Oh look its okay," she relented, as though suddenly a switch had flicked, as though suddenly she thought he was being a bit over the top with his apologies. "It's okay, honestly, it's forgotten."

"Cool, thanks," he grinned. "Well then, get your skates on, we're having dinner soon."

It was as though the ice was broken. As though a great big hammer had come along and whacked into smithereens the massive block of ice that had been wedged in between them.

"Oh Jamie, I might take a while," she whined. "I have loads to do; wash my hair, have a shower, pluck my eyebrows... you know... It'll take a good hour and a half at least... Can't you put it on to simmer or something? Have a beer while you're waiting?"

"Oh right," he pondered. "Okay... well you take your time; I'll just turn this off for a bit." He reminded himself he was still on parole. He needed to still be on his best behaviour. He needed to tip-toe for a little while longer.

"Cool, thanks," she smiled a smile that made everything worthwhile.

"And we're to be at Sarah's for eight, yeah?" he called after her as she was making her exit to the bathroom.

There was a pause then, and she returned, popping her head around the doorway.

"Oh... um... didn't Sarah tell you? I can't make it tonight... I have to go visit my mum..."

"Oh," his face dropped. Sarah was obviously too upset about the Stephen news to mention it. "Oh, that's a shame," he braved her with a smile. "Okay, well we'll just have dinner before you go then."

She grinned. "Yeah, thanks."

An hour later, he had drunk two bottles of beer on an empty stomach whilst watching a repeat of Top Gear. The beer had fizzed to his head and was leaving him feeling pleasantly relaxed. Suddenly the world seemed to have a nicer glow to it. He consoled himself that work was going well, that the set-up of their London office was off to a good start. That the bosses seemed pretty impressed with his work so far. That he could return to the Brighton office knowing that he'd done a good job. He reflected that he hoped the project would go on as long as possible. He could get so used to living with Amy. He could get used to ogling her all day.

Sure enough, she emerged from her bedroom to confirm his thoughts. A short black skirt, black tights that clung to her shapely slim legs, and a tight white shirt that curved around her breasts.

"You look nice," his eyes widened. He tried not to gulp, or drool, or sit with his mouth half-open, which was quite a feat in itself.

"Aw thanks," she purred. She went to the fridge and poured herself a glass of wine. A trail of delicious perfume wafted behind her.

She poured the wine and sipped back a long mouthful straight away. Then she topped up her glass again. Strangely she seemed…. Nervous? Nervous about visiting her mum? Surely not?

Her heels click-clacked along the wooden floor as she moved around the kitchen, going from pot to pan and sniffing the food.

"This looks gorgeous," she called over.

"Thanks," he quipped. "I'll heat it up again now in a minute."

Then she bit her lip and said, "Um… if I don't eat a lot, I'm sorry in advance… I don't have a big appetite at the moment… but anything I don't eat, I'll re-heat and have tomorrow night."

All of a sudden, he saw his seduction routine slipping through his very fingers. His CK underwear, his sultry tunes, his romantic candlelit dinner, was now disappearing into a reheated microwave meal in front of the TV on a plastic tray.

"Oh, okay," he answered, trying to hide his disappointment. "Are you okay?" he asked her.

She had sat down on the armchair and had leaned over the coffee table to pick up the remote. Her white shirt was tight, and as she leaned over, he caught a glimpse of her cleavage.

Gulp.

"Yeah, why?" she replied distractedly. She looked nervous, fidgety, as though there was something on her mind. She flicked through the channels, turning off his beloved Top Gear and turning on some silly documentary about women's makeovers and making them look ten years younger.

"I dunno," he said, "You just seem a bit... worried... or something... "

There, see? I am such an understanding man of the modern day.

She shrugged her shoulders. "No, it's okay. I'm just... you know..." she began, and then she just trailed off and said abruptly, "I'm fine."

Jamie kept quiet then. He decided it was none of his business. He decided that it was her house, her Saturday night and who was he to be so nosey?

Except that he did wonder to himself, "Why is she getting so dressed up just to go and see her mum?

She went to the bathroom. He got up to sort out the dinner. And when he did get up, her phone hummed. A gentle purring sound. A text coming through. He looked at the screen.

"One message received: Gav."

Jamie noticed a hammering feeling in his chest. He noticed that his fingertips felt cold. He felt a slight nauseous feeling in his stomach.

I bet she's not seeing her mum tonight at all, I bet she's actually going to see Gav.

She returned to the kitchen.

"Your phone beeped," he told her, in an off-hand manner.

"Oh?" she replied, all interested. She picked up the phone,

read the message, and smiled to herself.

"Your mum?" he asked, testing her.

"Yeah," she lied.

They sat through dinner. The Channel Four news was on in the background. Wars and people being killed and soldiers dead and politicians waffling on.

"Thanks very much," she said, after she'd eaten a morsel. "I better head on. Leave the dishes, I'll do them later."

She started to rush out the door but unfortunately his obnoxious attitude had returned already.

"Do you need a lift?" he asked her.

"Oh, no no no," she waved a hand, "I'll get the train, honestly."

"Don't be daft – I'll give you a lift," he said.

"No", she said flatly. "You've been drinking."

"Oh yeah." He'd nearly forgotten.

"See ya later," she called quickly, as though escaping.

"Yeah, bye," he whispered softly, to the closed door.

He pulled out his mobile. He decided he had made a big enough prat of himself already. He decided that he was just as bad as Beth and Sarah and Amy put together. He decided he was well and truly barking up the wrong tree. He decided he needed to listen to his own advice.

He decided to flick through his contacts list and invite someone to visit.

He decided to call Stacey.

Chapter Twelve
<u>SARAH</u>

Sarah tucked the napkins carefully into the inside pocket of her handbag.

Plan: Break-up test meeting

She would buy bottles of wine, and packets of crisps, and tea-light candles. She would pamper herself and look nice. She might even convince them all to hit a night club afterwards. She would close the door on Stephen for once and for all...

Wait at pedestrian crossing.

Spot smug loved-up couple at other side of road holding hands and having a quick kiss on the lips whilst waiting for the lights to shift colour.

Urgh. Get a room.

Horrible sight in my head of Stephen and Kat's bodies writhing together. Lying in bed with each other discussing wedding plans and having more babies. Gentle whispering. Bodies moving slowly and silently together.

Blink away image.

The green man bleeped, bleeped, bleeped and Sarah strode across the road, past the sickly sweet couple, resisting the urge to throw them a dirty look.

Tescos. Wine section. Wine, wine and more wine. In fact, she couldn't wait to get her lips around the edge of the glass and gulp it back, like a life-saving medicine. Perhaps she could swim in a pool of it, drinking all the pain away, or better still, if it could be attached to her like a drip, feeding her veins intravenously, washing away the sight of Stephen and Kat's bodies writhing together.

Utter. Fecking. Using. Bastard.

She took a deep breath, grabbed a trolley, and whizzed it around the aisles like a soldier steering an army vehicle.

Out of my way.

Angry woman in the vicinity.

She fired objects into the trolley: wine, beer, crisps, chocolate, ice-cream, even a pack of cigarettes for good measure.

Never again.

Never again am I going to put up with this crap.

Never again am I going to live in a bubble.

Never again am I going to pretend everything is moving along smoothly.

Never again am I going to keep silent, not ask questions, try to please.

From hereon, Sarah is going to be Sarah. Sarah is going to be honest about how she feels.

And if people don't like it, tough! Move on swiftly!

At the roly-poly belt, the items beeped happily.

Bottle of wine. *Beep!*

Chocolate. *Beep!*

Cigarettes. *Beep!*

End of using bastards. *Beep! Beep! Beep!*

"Welcome!" Sarah pulled the door open energetically as Jamie appeared on the doorstep.

"Er... hi..." Jamie replied, somewhat bemused at Sarah's over-enthusiasm.

"Come in! Come in!" she grinned, apparently already tipsy, as she led him through into her dimly-lit lounge. Candles, nice music, bowls of crisps, glasses of wine, beer for Jamie, comfy cushions…

"Oh Sarah…" Jamie began, "this is amazing! Thank you so much! You've gone to so much effort!"

"I have enjoyed it!" Sarah shrugged her shoulders effortlessly. And she had. It enabled her to take her mind off things. It enabled her to take her mind off Stephen and Kat's writhing bodies.

"So.. no Amy?" Sarah confirmed.

Jamie shook his head crossly. "Nope."

At that point, Beth emerged from the bathroom.

"Oh hey Beth, you're here already!" Jamie went across the room to give her a peck on the cheek.

"Hey," she smiled. "You okay?"

She had obviously picked up on his prickly vibes, which were flying effortlessly around the room.

"Yeah," he sighed, sitting down and gratefully opening the can of beer that Sarah had set out for him. "Just pissed off at Amy."

Beth raised her eyebrows. "Why? For visiting her mum?"

Jamie sat back and crossed one leg over his knee. "She's not visiting her mum, she's at Gav's."

Beth took a sharp intake of breath and Sarah's eyes darted from Jamie's to Beth's and back to Jamie's again.

"Oh dear. Poor Amy," Sarah mused.

Jamie sipped his beer. "You think? Not 'poor Amy', more like 'playing with fire Amy'. "

Beth looked uncomfortable, as though she didn't know what to say.

Sarah took a deep breath. "Well, I suppose she'll have to keep going back for more until she gets sick of the pain."

"Or until he stops inviting her over," Beth offered.

Jamie grunted. "Well that's not going to happen. He'll keep taking what he can get won't he?"

Beth stared into her wine glass, as though contemplating. She sighed, as though totally tired of all this chat. All this realistic Jamie man-advice. It was too real. Too depressing.

Give me a good old fairy-tale any day.

"Any word from Karl yet?" Jamie asked her, as though reading her thoughts.

Beth shook her head. "Nope."

Jamie rolled his eyes.

"He's probably just busy," Beth began. "He'll probably be in touch to arrange something next week. I don't want to put pressure on him..." she trailed off, trying to ignore the glare that was coming from Jamie's direction.

"*You* don't want to put pressure on *him?*" he asked, almost spluttering on his beer. "*You* don't want to put pressure on *him?* What about what *you* want? You've said about what *he* wants... What about what *you* want?"

Beth shrugged her shoulders, felt her heart hammering in her chest and resisted the urge to cry.

God, Jamie was in foul form tonight.

"Right!" Sarah clicked her fingers, as though sensing the mood. "Break-up test rules!"

Sarah read through the crumpled napkins. "Yes to as many invites as possible.... Open mind about other fellas... Dates with other guys..."

She reeled them off, as though the font of all knowledge, as though holding a key to the end of all pain and suffering, as though she was resolute everything would be okay.

Jamie let his fingers rotate a coaster round and round, as though bored of all this already, as though it was all a load of rubbish and just Sarah's last ditch attempts to try to avoid the pain of Stephen's rejection.

Beth, on the other hand, was contemplative, taking it all in, the cogs in her brain turning and turning.

Now, maybe if I went out on other dates... Karl would sniff the competition and come running...

Chapter Thirteen
SARAH

Operation: The Break-up Test
Pamper self once / week. Check √
New clothes (Retail therapy ALWAYS works!) Check √
YES to as many invites as poss. Check √
Open mind about other fellas. Check √
Dates with other guys – just for the laugh. Check √
If a bloke says he's not interested, just accept it and move on. Check √
Let the guy ask you out. Check √

"Chop off as much as you want!" Sarah exclaimed as she sat in the swirly chair, sipping strong coffee from a porcelain cup and saucer.

Amber the hairdresser eyed her carefully. "Are you sure?"

Sarah nodded her head abruptly before she could change her mind. "Yes! Whack it off!"

"They tell you not to do anything drastic to your hair for at least a month after you've split up with someone…" Beth had warned her, but Sarah had swatted that off.

"This is different."

"How?" Beth gave Sarah an amused smile.

"I wasn't officially 'going out' with Stephen, was I?" Sarah shrugged gently. "In fact, it seems I was very much a third wheel."

Beth gave Sarah a sympathetic look, but Sarah acted as though nothing was wrong. In fact, it worried Beth that Sarah was so upbeat about the whole thing. She was nearly worried that suddenly she would hit a brick wall; that this whole façade would one day very abruptly run its course.

"Anyway…" Sarah went on. "This is different. I am pampering myself. And I am going on a date. A girl should prepare herself for a date."

Amber had the good grace not to ask her five million questions. It took her three hairdressing salons, three different stylists and a range of cuts and colours, to find the perfect hairdresser – one that doesn't give her the third degree every time she visits.

You know the type;

"Going out tonight?"

"Any holidays planned this year?"

"Going out at the weekend?"

No, Amber was the BEST hairdresser in the world. Ever. ™

She sits you down in the chair, sticks an apron around you, asks you a few questions about how you'd like your hair cut, and then she proceeds to do it! Perfect arrangement, no?

She then lets Sarah sip her coffee in peace, read her magazine, stare at the other girls, and text people she needs to text, without the Spanish inquisition!

Sarah flicked through the magazine, soaking up the glamorous images – the clothes, the styles, the articles about sex, the articles about relationships – 'how to tell if he's falling in love', and the real-life stories – 'how I met the man of my dreams at a school reunion' – and for a moment, she was part of that world. She was one of those girls, with the stylish hair, and the glamorous outfit. She was one of those girls heading out on a Saturday night date, with not a booty call in sight.

Just for today, she, Sarah Jones, was a Dreamgirl.

Sarah drifted off into happy thoughts – of Jamie and Amy and Beth, all rooting for her. She imagined how delighted they would be when she reported back on her enthusiastic start – of how happy she will be when her and mister date will fall in love and walk hand in hand along the beach on their honeymoon, the sun warming their faces and a gentle breeze rustling through their hair.

She thought of all that, until her phone bleeped, snapping her out of her reverie.

'One Message: Stephen'

She would say that inwardly she took a deep breath, that her heart jumped, that her stomach churned, that all of those things happened, but actually, nothing like that happened.

Actually it was just a big nothingness of shock while her fingers trembled to open the text.

"Hey huney... I really miss you... we really need to talk... S x x"

That was when her heart started hammering. With anger.

The cheek of him!

Now, she knew at this point, that any sane, normal, rational individual would delete his number immediately, and block him to boot.

But Sarah, lacking in normality, was obviously getting some sort of sordid pleasure out of his texts.

Like Eve in the Garden of Eden who couldn't resist the juicy red apple on the tree, she was a sucker for seeing him crawl.

Block his number and not have the knowledge of how much he's pining after me? Please. What girl could actually resist?

(Note: A sane one)

The texts and messages dispersed themselves throughout her glorious day.

River Island – New, tight-fitting red v-neck top, great quality material.

Text: "Please ... would you consider talking to me just for half an hour – just so I can try to explain? ... S ...x x"

Delete.

Top Shop – Short black skirt with floaty, puffy thing going on and several layers.

Text: "Please Sarah ... at least let me explain... at least let me do that...S...x x"

Delete.

Café Nero – Exceptionally strong black coffee with a large focaccia style baguette laden with cheese and other tasty herb things going on.

Text: "Well, I'm here....if you change your mind and ever want to talk – I'm here...S...x x x"

Delete. Delete. Delete. Delete.

The walk home was vibrant, refreshing. The sun twinkled over the river. The arc of the bridge was silhouetted against the blue backdrop. Birds swooped in the sky.

Something had changed. In her.

She had turned a new leaf, started a new chapter, closed the door on a bad situation, made a fresh start.

Something had changed.

Her date was already sitting in the café when Sarah arrived. It was one of those late night coffee shops.

He jumped up the minute she arrived. First impressions were: Cute. Very cute.

"Hi," he grinned. "Good to meet you."

"Hi," she smiled back.

The café had mirrors lined the whole way along. She caught a reflection of her hair, straightened to perfection by misses no-conversation-hairdresser.

"Coffee?"

"Yes please. Americano."

He went up the counter and she took a seat. She saw him pull his wallet out of his back pocket and she noticed *'nice bum.'*

She was also feeling spoiled because he was buying her a cup of coffee. She noted how her self-esteem must be at sub-zero temperatures when she's happy just because a bloke's buying her a cup of coffee. This from a girl who had to ply herself with three bottles of wine before she could entertain mister ten o'clock man.

He returned with the coffee and he was very smiley.

And most importantly – he actually seemed normal.

He had a job (actor) and he lived in his own place (a flat), and he had a cat.

The conversation was light, refreshing, normal – films, music, books, exercise, hobbies, general chit-chat.

"Shall we head down to The Venue and watch a bit of music?" he asked.

"Sure."

She liked that people recognised him and came over to chat.

"This is my date, Sarah," he said. He introduced her as his DATE.

She hadn't been called that in a long while. She may have smuggled a guy into her bedroom, yes, but being introduced as "my DATE".…. not in a long while.

And then it was home time and he walked her to the taxi-rank and he said, "I'll call you – I'm not just saying that – I will call you!"

And the next thing, she was in the taxi, and the door was shutting and she was waving goodbye, and she was off home.

"Did you have a good night?" the taxi man winked.

"Yeah," she smiled.

"Let me guess… first date?" he grinned.

She should tell him to mind his own business. She should tell him that she's paying him to take her from A to B, not to give her the Spanish inquisition. But she was happy, so she smiled, "Yeah."

"Like him?"

"Yeah."

"Shame," the taxi man winked. "I was wondering if you'd want to go out for a drink with me one night?"

And that was how she lined up date number two.

Amount of self-pitying moments: None.

Amount of moments of feeling good about herself: Many.

Amount of times a little voice piped up in her head saying "I feel happy": One.

A single girl's Saturday: Pretty successful.

The break-up test working? : Definitely underway.

Chapter Fourteen
BETH

Beth's shoes were red and pointy. They were womanly shoes. High-heeled. Bright red. The pointiest she could find.

Beth's shoes were powerful. Vibrant. In control.

Her shoes knew where they were going. Her shoes were action. Her shoes had a plan.

Normal black flats wouldn't do. Or even fashionable trainers. It had to be red shoes.

Her red shoes were crossed and her legs were bare, laden with fake tan.

One red shoe rested on the rung of the bar stool, the other red shoe was facing towards her date.

Her date was called Peter. Peter was a guy from her office building. Peter worked on the first floor. Beth worked on the second floor. Beth and Peter discovered that her desk was directly on top of his.

Beth and Peter met in the staff canteen, next to the roasted potatoes and the boiled carrots.

Peter smiled, asked her name and asked if he could join her at her table. Beth knew that Peter had dated half the entire building, but for that brief moment, she didn't care. Peter was a welcome distraction from the void that was lack of texts from Karl.

"Do you want to go out for a drink one night?" he asked, following his script impeccably, and doing so with ease and confidence. His lack of awkwardness alarmed her slightly. Perhaps if he'd been nervous, it would have meant more. He would have meant that he'd have spent weeks rehearsing and practising, gearing himself up to the big ask. However, when the big ask happens all the time, with all the secretaries and all the female accountancy staff, then it's not so daunting.

"Yeah, that'd be nice," Beth replied, knowing that nothing would come of it; knowing that it was a fruitless attempt to get over Karl, but at least she was trying.

She had hoped, perhaps even on a subconscious level, that somehow Karl would pick up on her busy aura and sniff out the competition, like a cat running after a mouse.

Friday at seven pm and Beth was situated on a bar stool in the window of Juno's, chatting to Peter.

Her red shoes were doing all the talking for her. Her red shoes were saying, "See!? There's no sitting around at home in my bedroom slippers watching Corrie and waiting for your text mister! Life goes on!"

If there was any competition to be sniffed out, her red shoes would have a strong aroma of sex.

Except she had no desire to have sex with Peter. No desire at all. He would probably be the type to fold his clothes beforehand and step into the shower straight afterwards.

It got to eight forty-five and she was having a horrible sinking feeling that her evening was a total wash-out, when hey presto, mister hasn't-texted-for-five-days walked through the door.

His eyes did that nearly-about-to-pop-out-of-their-head look when he saw her. A look that said, "Oh! You're on my territory! I kind of expected you to be at home in your slippers watching Corrie!"

And she just did her smile. Her calm, composed smile that said, "Yes, I am on your territory – but tonight it is my territory too!"

He trundled off with his mates and they sat in a booth which happened to be facing her and the red shoes. The red shoes were teamed with a black skirt and a tight red top, and all she had to do was flick her hair a few times and look totally interested in Peter's accountancy chat.

She could almost smell Karl's curiosity. She could almost feel him sizing them up. She could almost see the cogs turning in his head. She could almost see him think, "Hang on a minute, last week I met up with her and we kissed, and we were supposed to meet up for a drink again, and now she's out with some suited-up bloke. What's going on?"

She was *nearly* worried that he would say to himself – "Oh well, she's seeing someone else so I'll not bother her."

But of course, she knew that was nonsense.

She knew his competitiveness would kick in and then it would be game on.

And of course, she was right!

The minute Peter left his stool to go the "gentleman's," Karl was over, like a shot.

"So, how've you been?" he asked, all smiles, perching himself on the stool which was still warm from Peter's buttocks.

"Yeah, I've been fine." ("*If you wanted to know how I've been so much, you could've phoned me.*")

"You look great."

"Thanks."

"So …. Erm…" he nodded his head towards an imaginary Peter standing next to him. "Hot date?"

She did this apologetic shrug-gy shoulder thing which implied, "Yeah, sorry if this is awkward, but, you know, I hadn't heard from you... so we're not really dating, so…"

He nodded his head, in a way which she interpreted to mean, "Yeah, I'm sorry, I'm a twat, I should've been more on the ball."

Then she did a little half-smile that said, "Ah don't worry – never mind eh – you missed the boat."

It was a glorious, glorious moment indeed. One of those moments that would be up there with say, getting a job you really love, or doing really well in an exam, or passing your driving test.

The look on his face was priceless too – a kind of disappointed look, coupled with a metaphorical kicking himself, together with an "I'm a twat" putting his head in his hands – kind of look.

"Well," she shrugged her shoulders helplessly.

Peter arrived back at that point, all brisk and sexless, and she could visibly see Karl sizing him up, as though they were fighters in a boxing ring. The gloves were on and the silly preparation dance had begun – moving the weight of their bodies from one foot to the other, as though in an adrenalin-induced warm up.

Karl's sniffing was more like a surprised snort – here he was, being ousted for some fella with a sexless demeanour and a snotty air. It was too much.

Karl nodded, abruptly, at Peter, who also gave a territorial nod back (*"Keep away, she's mine."*)

"Well," Karl retraced his steps like a wounded animal. "I'll be seeing you around?" he asked hopefully, as though his life depended on it.

"Sure," she shrugged.

Peter and Beth didn't sit on much longer after that. Her work was done. And anyway she wanted to get home, put the feet up, have a nice cup of tea, and catch up on Corrie.

She half-expected Karl to be texting straight away that night.

She expected that the moment she got in the door, her phone would bleep straightaway. But it didn't.

Bless. Maybe he feels a bit awkward. Maybe he's worried I'm sitting here with Peter. Maybe I should reassure him.

And before she knew it, her fingers had found their way to the keypad. The words were typed before she even had time to think about it. The 'send' button was pushed before she even knew what was happening. And then there it was, a text careering off towards him, totally without her control or planning.

"Hey Karl, was good to see you tonight. Hope you enjoyed your night. ... B x"

Chapter Fifteen
SARAH

Sarah's date with mister taxi man took place on the following night – a Sunday evening.

In fact, Sarah had woken up on the Sunday morning to a prompt text from said taxi man in her inbox.

"Was great to meet you. How about dinner tonight? I can get the night off work x x x"

Three kisses. Already. Very keen.

By the time she'd had breakfast, showered, gone for a walk, had a coffee in town, tidied her flat, planned her date night outfit, she'd hardly had a spare minute to think about Stephen all day.

She was to meet Martin the taxi man in the new Italian restaurant down by the river. At 7.10pm, she was fashionably late by a whole ten minutes.

"I'm here already," he texted, at 7pm precisely. "Got here early so we'd have a seat and wouldn't have to queue. I'm down at the back of the restaurant x x x"

She arrived in the restaurant and it was packed.

She practically *swept* down to his table. She was not nervous.

"Hi," she smiled, when he stood to greet her.

She felt nice. She had dressed in black – a figure hugging top and a black short skirt – but the combination made it look like a dress. She had sprayed on her favourite perfume. She had been waiting for the right opportunity to wear her favourite perfume, but smuggling Stephen into her bedroom at ten o'clock didn't really seem an appropriate occasion.

"You look great," Martin breathed.

He was wearing black also – black trousers and a black shirt. He had a large glass of wine in front of him, which was half-empty.

He made a nodding 'clicking' gesture to the waiter – he didn't *actually* click his fingers, but he did this nodding 'hurry up and serve me 'cos I'm important' type gesture, which he probably thought looked domineering and macho and authoritative, but she thought it seemed rude.

"Drink?" he nodded to her.

Again, authoritative. Not just to the waiter, but to her too. *Again, rude.*

"Am…. A glass of white wine please."

He did the whole – 'this is the best type of wine – blah blah blah' chat, but it was all like white noise to her. She thought it was interesting that a cheap bottle of Tesco wine in her bedroom with Stephen was far more appealing than the pick of the crop of the blah blah blah list of fine wines in the fancy restaurant with Martin.

She just nodded and said, "Yeah, that'll do."

She picked up the menu.

"I know what I'm having already," he told her. "I got here early so I had plenty of time to choose."

She supposed she should have found that flattering. That he was well-prepared. Keen. Enthusiastic.

But somehow it unnerved her. A sub-conscious sort of unnerving. That it felt a bit weird for some guy to go to all that effort. For little old her. When he knew nothing about her.

She picked what she wanted. He ordered from the waiter (same abrupt nodding type gesture going on).

She chided herself inwardly. *Right, you're not being very fair here. Stop picking on all his faults. Try to focus on his good points.*

She complimented him on his hair.

"Thanks," he grinned. "I told my staff today about our date

– and I asked them what way I should wear my hair – I wasn't sure whether I should have the quiff to the left or to the right."

Again, too much preparation for little old me. When he knew nothing about me.

Oh God, I have turned into a prize bitch. I have turned into someone on the receiving end of needy behaviour.

"And I'm not normally this weight" he advised, as though priming himself for an interview. "I put on half a stone recently but I'll lose it again."

I'll lose it again for you. If you'll have me. Please have me.

She kicked herself. Metaphorically. Very, very hard.

Don't be such a bitch. He is just nice and trying to be liked.

So she listened.

And listened.

And listened.

She listened for an hour and an half.

While he talked.

About his business.

About his child.

About the divorce.

About learning to love himself again.

About being ready for a new relationship.

About how much he had been looking forward to meeting her.

About how he had a really good feeling about her.

About all that.

Stephen danced in the back of her head like a gentle reminder.

"It's me you fancy, remember? Why are you putting yourself through this? You know you'd rather be tucked up at home with a good book rather than have to sit through all this. Why don't you just return my texts? I still want to keep seeing you."

She blinked away the image. It seemed wrong to think about Stephen when she was sitting across the table from her date.

But Martin was continuing on with his monologue, unaware of her internal battle. And the problem was, Martin's monologue was laced with "F" and "B" swear words. And he said the "F's" and "B's" loudly. She wouldn't have even minded about that. Except that there was a young family sitting at the table next to them. A mum and a dad. And three girls all under the age of ten. The dad looked tired and worn out, as though he was exhausted with supporting his family. As though this was their one little treat in the week (or the month?) and here they all were, sitting next to a guy with a quiff who was sloshing wine from his glass regularly and saying the "F" word a lot.

The mum had an embarrassed little downward look going on, as though she was mortified about her precious children's ears being exposed to such vulgarity.

But Martin was totally oblivious. Totally wrapped up in his own stream of thoughts. His own monologue of chat about himself and his own verbal diarrhoea.

After an hour and a half of listening and trying to add her two cents worth in, a little voice in her head said, *Please, please ask me one question about myself! Just one question!*

But he didn't. He talked on and on and on.

And eventually he asked if she'd like to go to another bar, and she said, "No, sorry, I've a really sore tummy. I'll have to go home. Sorry."

So they walked towards the taxi-rank, and he stopped her in the street, and he held her hands and said, "Please. If there's anything I can do. Any way I can get you to stay out later. Any way I can help your tummy feel better, please let me help. I'm here for you. I don't want this night to end."

She could feel the desperation hanging out of him. Like an invisible cobweb that was trying to curl its way around her and suck her in.

"No. Really. It's fine. I just need to go home and get into bed."

Her heckles were rising now. As though she was stuck in a trap and she needed to run to get away.

"Please."

"No."

"Please."

"No! I'm going!"

And she walked away very abruptly.

And sure enough, the minute she arrived home, a text flashed up on her screen.

Martin: "I hope ur tummy feels better soon x x x"

She didn't reply.

And first thing the following morning, another text appeared.

Martin: "How is ur tummy this morning? X x x"

YES to as many invites as poss. X

Open mind about other fellas. X

Dates with other guys – just for the laugh. X

Sarah noticed with horror that this dreadful date had done the opposite of propelling her away from thoughts about Stephen, and in fact was catapulting her closer towards thoughts about him, making her compare and contrast.

In an effort to not obsess about Stephen and be tempted to contact him, she forced herself to remember that everything was not perfect with Stephen. She forced herself to remember the bad times.

The Bad Times # 1

There was an exhibition. A photography exhibition. The photographer was a girl. A girl called H. That's what she was called. Not a nice, normal name, like Helen or Harriet or Helena. Just H. She had blonde hair and quirky clothes. She wore knee-high socks. Sarah would never have the nerve to wear knee-high socks. Knee-high socks implied sex in a saucy, unforbidden, school-girl type way. And Sarah would never have the nerve to make that sort of statement.

H was a friend of Stephen's. Whenever Stephen and H greeted each other, they gave each other a kiss on the mouth. Not a full-blown snog. But a kiss on the mouth. With their lips touching.

Sarah found it unnerving. Of course she did. But she pretended not to mind. Because she wanted to appear trendy and cool and 'with it', and if this is what people in the trendy Brighton nightclub scene did, then she'd go along with it.

H had a key to Stephen's front door. H lived up the road from Stephen's new flat, so H could pop in at any time, unlocking the door and letting herself in and saying, "Hi honey, it's just me."

Sometimes Stephen and Sarah would be cuddling together on the sofa when this would happen, and for some reason, they'd sit up, fix themselves, re-arrange their clothes and sit presentably, as though they were teenagers and their parents had just arrived home.

"Why does she have a key?" Sarah had asked once, trying to say it in a non-committal, non-demanding, non-intrusive way, as though she were just asking a conversational question, like commenting on the weather.

"Oh, you know, I might forget my key, or lose it, so she keeps a spare copy."

That was a reasonable excuse right enough, Sarah thought. If one had to stand up in a court of law and give that excuse, she believed that that excuse would go down very well, and the judge might even bang his little hammer on the table and confirm "case closed" to that excuse. However, Sarah couldn't help but wonder why it enabled H to let herself in at all hours. What if they had decided to have sex on the carpet in the middle of the hallway? Not that they did that anymore. They did it once, when Stephen had just moved in, and there was no furniture, and Sarah was just so relieved that he'd finally got a flat away from Kat, that she shagged him with gratitude. It wasn't very good, and she came away with carpet burns on her knees, and she couldn't help but be glad when he came and it was over. But all the same, it was a nice shag. It was a shag that said, "Now you're mine." It was a shag that said, "Thank God you don't live with her anymore."

But of course, she still couldn't really say, "Now you're mine," because he still didn't feel like "mine," especially with the quirky blonde photographer poking her spare key in the lock.

She wondered, in her own little sick and twisted way, if she had become the new "Kat." If now H and Stephen were running around behind *her* back. If, on the occasions that H turned the key in the lock and Sarah wasn't there, that Stephen would kiss her full on the lips, and bring his hand up in between her legs, past the knee high socks and up her skirt, so that her legs would melt themselves open and she would fall gently back against the wall, and they would shag there and then in the hallway, on the floor, under the glass panel doorway, H getting carpet burns on her knees above her knee-high socks, and wondering if Sarah would turn up at any moment, her silhouette becoming visible behind the glass panel.

That was in her sick and twisted moments.

But mostly, Sarah tried to get on with it, to tell herself that everything was okay now, that there was nothing wrong with the girl with the knee-high socks and the spare key and the kiss on the mouth.

At the exhibition, there was a row. Well, not a row as such, but a moment.

A memory of the look on Stephen's face. A memory of his words, "Why do you always do this? Why do you always push me away?"

The exhibition was busy. Lots of trendy Brighton types.

People with cool clothes and disinterested demeanours, drifting around looking at the photographs with a mildly interested yet not interested enough air. As though they had much more important things to be getting on with, like snorting a line of coke off the toilet seat.

The photos were daring. Sexual. Provocative. Lots of sweaty bodies and intense stares and women cavorting around on the floor, their breasts pointing upwards, their eyes begging at the camera.

Stephen was pinned to H's side, talking to their mutual friends, telling them all how proud he was.

And something inside Sarah's soul just *snapped*.

Maybe it was the cheap white wine in the small circular glasses that she had been knocking back.

Maybe it was the sight of H cavorting around the room in her short frilly skirt and her knee high socks.

Maybe it was jealousy at all her brave, sexual, provocative photographs, the weight of them groaning against the walls.

Maybe it was Sarah's own inadequacy. Her envelope sticking job. Her safe clothes. Her insecurity with Stephen.

Something snapped.

Like a fan belt in a car that suddenly broke apart and forced the car to stop dead in its tracks.

The same happened with Sarah's soul.

She made her way to the toilets.

She felt like she couldn't breathe.

She stood beside the tiny window in the shitty toilets and tried to gulp in the air.

She tried to push the window open further but it wouldn't budge.

She gulped back the cheap white wine from the tiny circular glass and she wondered just what was wrong with her.

She felt like squeezing herself out of the tiny gap in the window and running away.

But she didn't.

Instead, whatever mental twist was going on in her head, she just decided to go.

Just leave.

Just walk out.

Just disappear.

She didn't return to the exhibition. She didn't retrace her steps and pick up her coat.

She just left.

Walked out of the toilets, turned right instead of left, and walked out the front door.

The cool air hit her face.

It mixed with the sparkles of the cheap wine that still fizzed around her head. She walked with a strange sense of freedom. With a strange sense of not caring.

It wasn't until she was halfway home that it began to dawn on her that she had not picked up her coat. That the cool night air was pinching at her skin. She hugged her hands around herself and noticed an army of goose bumps lining themselves protectively along her arms. She thought of her coat lying unattended and alone at the exhibition. Her lovely red coat from Top Shop. The one with the red and white polka dots and the thick red belt. She had abandoned her coat.

So now, she was just a girl, walking away from an exhibition, with a curious mental twist going on in her head, and no coat to keep her warm.

Just a girl, walking away from an exhibition by a girl with blonde hair in knee high socks. A girl who was friendly enough to have keys to her boyfriend's flat.

Boyfriend.

Was he her boyfriend?

She wasn't even sure.

He was a boy, that was true.

And he was a friend.

But was he a boyfriend?

So she was walking away from the cheap white wine in the

small circular glasses, away from the provocative photos adorning the walls, away from the people mingling and the chat and the laugh and the growing sense of isolation and the uncaring attitude. She walked away from all that, and her breathing became more laboured and heavy.

Walking and walking and walking, until she heard a "Sarah?! Sarah?! What's wrong?"

And she turned abruptly, to find that it was Stephen, running towards her, with a panicked look on his face, her red polka dot coat draped over his arm and then the words,

"Why? Why do you keep doing this?"

The memory surprised her, like being in a car and the driver slamming on the brake and her head bolting forward and her seat belt pulling her back.

And, if her life was one big jigsaw puzzle, this would be one of those moments, when she'd been hunting for a particular piece for ages, and finally she would find it, slotted in between the myriad of other pieces, and she would jut her finger on it and say "Aha! There it is!" and she would triumphantly pick it up and slot it into place.

"Why? Why do you keep doing this?"

Chapter Sixteen
BETH

Karl did text back.

It took him a full twenty-four hours, but nonetheless, there was still a response.

Of course, during those twenty-four hours, Beth couldn't help but wonder what he was up to.

She couldn't help but wonder what pressing, ultra-important stuff he was up to that prevented him from sticking his beady little finger on the keypad and writing her a short message.

She couldn't help but wonder if, after she left Junos to go home and watch Corrie, a short-skirted, big-boobed woman appeared who grabbed his attention. If she lured him into one of the booths, got drunk with him, and snogged him. If she took him home to shag him all night long. If he wandered out of her house this morning, dazed and confused, staggering home to fall into his own bed to sleep all day, and that was why he was only getting round to texting Beth now.

She couldn't help but wonder.

However, he texted.

"Yeah, it was a good night. Was good to see ya. We should go out for that drink. K"

She smiled to herself. Knowingly. Well, he was the one suggesting they go out. It wasn't her doing *all* the chasing.

Yeah, but you did text him first. He probably felt obligated to reply with something.

It was as though there was an angry, negative voice on her shoulder the whole time, parroting away at her. Like a vile, ugly man in her head, surrounded in beer cans shouting nasty comments at her, sprawled out on an old smelly armchair. No matter how much she pushed and prodded and tried to shove him out of her head, he'd stay there, laughing at her for even trying.

"Sure," she texted back. "When would suit you?"

She was careful not to put an 'x' at the end of the text. She didn't want to scare him off.

They arranged to meet that Saturday night. In a little club called "Rene's." It was cosy; all red lights, candles, romantic. She took that as a good sign.

That he was wanting to spend his Saturday night with little old me.

When she arrived, he was there already.

He was smiley, fresh-faced, glowing, as though he were happy to see her.

"Hi," she smiled shyly.

She was wearing her red dress, tight around the boobs, with a tie around the waist, and then drifting down into a floaty dream down to the knees. She also wore her red pointy shoes. She had decided that they were lucky.

"Wow," he smiled, looking her up and down. "You look great."

She glowed. Inwardly. Saturday night, being complimented by Karl, being dressed up. Heaven.

They sat at one of the circular bar tables and Karl went up to get them some drinks.

She wondered to herself if this counted as one of her dates from The Break-up test. If Sarah and Amy would say, "Good for you Beth! You're on track! This is working". Or if they would say, "Um.. Hello?? You're supposed to be doing this test to get over him – not get under him!"

She felt a twinge of guilt prick at her, conscience, but then she quickly shrugged it off. Karl was returning to the table. He was smiling. It was Saturday night. She was in her red dress.

What was there to feel guilty about? Life's too short, she told herself. There are people out there suffering from diseases. She was perfectly healthy. Why didn't she just enjoy herself?

That was her reasoning.

During the drink, Karl was chatty, smiley, full of news and tales and banter. And it was nice. Just casual. No fuss.

Then they went through into the next room, where the music was playing.

There were lots of tables for two. Lots of tea-light candles. A saxophone was playing. A girl with long hair sang soulful songs.

They sat.

The moment they sat, the candle blew itself out.

She was horrified.

Is this a sign from above? This is not meant to be!

"Do you have a lighter Karl? Our candle has blown out," she tried not to sound panicky. She told herself she was just being superstitious. She berated herself for being so negative.

He flicked his lighter and the candle came to life again, the flame dancing merrily in front of her.

The woman sang. Sad, soulful songs about break-ups, and unrequited love, and heartache.

And Beth really wanted her to shut up.

Stop! Stop please! Please make this torture stop!

She was conscious of Karl sitting beside her listening to the drivel too.

She felt as though the rest of the room had fallen away, and this woman was singing to her specifically.

She felt as though the words were for her. As though the singer was trying to tell Beth to stop kidding herself, that this was all phony and Karl wasn't that fussed on her, and she was leading herself down the path of complete torture.

Please stop singing! Please make this end! Please!

Thankfully, the singer stopped.

Everyone clapped.

Beth clapped her hands unenthusiastically. The only thing she was thankful about was that it was over.

The music changed then. Into something more fast-paced. And tables were moved out of the way, and people were up dancing. And by then, Karl was tipsy.

His hand was on her leg. He leaned over to kiss her.

It was okay that he was kissing her, because it was a dark bar, and they were in the corner, and no-one was taking any heed, and for a moment, there she was, drifting in heaven, because he was kissing her, and she was lost.

However, then his hands started to wander.

His hand was under her top. It was moving up towards her breasts, it was feeling the line of her breasts under her bra. He was getting aroused. He wanted her. Which was fine, but she was worried that people could see them. She was worried that people might have been looking over and saying, "Look at the state of those two – common as muck. You'd think they'd go and get a room."

So she said to him, "Do you want to come back to mine?"

He nodded, immediately, as though he'd been waiting for her to say it all night.

She thought to herself that sub-consciously she must have planned for him to come back to hers.

Because she had cleaned her room out.

She didn't mean that she had tidied it and folded all the clothes away and plumped the teddies up nice.

She meant that she had cleaned away things-that-she-would-not-want-Karl-to-see. Like her self-help books, and her visualisation board about being married, and her diary.

So she knew in advance that her bedroom was safe. It was a bit like shaving your legs 'just in case', or wearing your sexiest knickers 'just in case'. Although obviously she had done that too.

The minute they got in the front door, he was all over her, kissing her, pulling at her, wanting her right there on the sofa.

84

But the thing is, she didn't want it to be just about sex.

So she said, "Do you want a cup of tea?"

He groaned.

"Umm.. Yeah... okay, if you're having one."

She trooped off to the kitchen to make tea and toast, and she even put on the sky TV, so that he could watch football.

And while he was sitting there on the sofa, looking so cute, watching the footie, she made tea and toast, and for a tiny slice of time, thought, "aww... look at us, don't we look like a right little couple."

They sat and ate the toast and drank the tea, and then he wanted to eat her.

He turned the footie off, and he kissed her, and he manoeuvred her so that she was sitting astride him, and he lifted her top, and pulled down her bra, and he was kissing her nipple. Kissing her nipple and looking up at her. And it was total, complete heaven.

They decided to go up to her room. Her room devoid of any self-help books or visualisation boards, with durex carefully positioned in the bedside cabinet, and they started kissing.

Sitting on her bed, facing each other.

She took off his top, and there it was, his lovely hairy chest looking back at her.

He lifted her top, and there was her black bra staring back at him, and he groaned.

They were eating each other up, licking and sucking and groaning and looking up at each other, and it was pure, complete heaven.

She was lost.

Then it was all over.

And the next thing he was talking about going home.

She was thinking, *"Home?! Home! Why are you wanting to go home? It is heaven here! We are in heaven? Why are you wanting to go home!"*

But he was pulling on his top, and saying something about

how she would fall asleep straight away, and he'd be awake for hours yet, and anyway, she gets up at the crack of dawn, whereas he lies on for hours, and all this blah-blah-blah stuff that just sounded like a big blurry hazy fuzz.

Home?! But we have just made love! You can't go already! That would just make me feel... USED.

She wanted him to stay in bed, so that she could go off to sleep, his arm around her, her hand on his chest. She wanted to sleep soundly, waking up and leaning round to put her hand on that nice safe place again, that nice stretch of hair on his chest that was warm and comforting and felt like home.

But of course, she couldn't say all that. In-case it would make him run a mile. In-case he would say, "Whoops! Bunny boiler alert! Call out the search party, I need to get home!"

So there he was, putting on his shirt, without a second thought, giving her a grin as though it were no big deal, and there she was, smiling back, pretending that she didn't mind, when actually her heart felt hammered down into the size of a thimble.

She put on her dressing gown, so she could cover her nakedness and walk him downstairs to the front door.

She was aware that her hair was a mess, like a bird's nest.

She was aware that the make up on her face had disappeared and her face was flushed.

She suddenly felt unattractive, exposed, vulnerable.

Earlier she was lost. Now she was snapped back into a self-conscious agony.

Earlier she was in heaven. Now she was in hell.

"I'll let you get some sleep," he smiled. As though that were a good thing. As though she would want to return to her empty bed, still able to smell him on the pillowcase.

His smile was nice, genuine, warm.

But somehow, she felt like the biggest lump of shit on his shoe.

"Karl…?" Beth called, as he was retreating down the street away from her house.

She stood on her front doorstep, in her dressing gown, her hair still standing out like a bird's nest.

He turned, smiled, and cocked his head.

"Yeah?"

"C'mere."

Her heart was hammering in her chest. She knew she was about to make a prize tit of herself. She knew that words were going to flow out of her mouth like verbal diarrhoea and she knew she would regret it tomorrow.

But for now, she didn't care.

Perhaps it was the tiredness. Perhaps it was the drink. Perhaps it was the frustration.

They had got drunk. He had come back to hers. They had shagged for approximately the length of one album. He had pulled on his clothes. And now he was retreating down her street, tail between his legs. It just wasn't good enough.

She felt used.

She felt frustrated.

She felt fecked off.

And she no longer wanted to put up with it and pretend she didn't mind.

"What?" he asked, the smile still on his face.

"What are we doing here?" she asked.

He rolled his eyes.

He rolled his eyes.

Twenty minutes ago he was inside me, now he's rolling his eyes.

All her "games" went out the window. All the playing it cool, all the tip-toeing around him, all the not texting straight back, all the rubbish rules she'd been drip-fed from magazines for years.

"What's happening here?" she asked again.

He shrugged his shoulders. "I'll call you."

"When?"

She knew she was being needy and annoying. She knew she was being far from mysterious. She knew that in the book of cool, it was game over.

But quite frankly, she no longer cared.

If he liked her, he'd be trying his best to reassure her.

If he liked her, he'd want to lie and cuddle her all night.

If he liked her, he'd want to make sure he'd be seeing her again soon.

"I dunno…" he shifted his weight from one foot to the other, as though caught in the act, as though being put under unnecessary pressure. "I dunno… I'll call ya soon…"

Beth folded her arms and looked at him crossly, like a frustrated parent to a naughty child.

"This is nothing more than a fling, is it?"

He sighed. As though this was a waste of his time. As though an inconvenience. As though he should be at home, tucked up in bed, not having to listen to crap from this girl who'd just given him a good shag.

Well, I'm sorry. Perhaps you should have left money on the bedside table if you wanted a performance to your satisfaction.

He shrugged, impatiently.

"Look, I'm sorry….I thought you just wanted something casual… Let's just be mates… Let's not do this again if it's messing your head up…"

Beth stood on her front door step, in her dressing gown, her hair like a bird's nest, her make-up worn off, and she experienced a new low.

Something casual.

I just thought you wanted something casual.

Find me ONE girl who wants something casual!

What girl wants to waste her time flirting, being coy, playing it cool, acting shy, plucking, exfoliating, tanning, and preparing for casual sex?

What girl wants casual sex?

Girls don't do casual sex.

Girls do pretending they want casual sex.

Girls do cuddling afterwards.

Girls do lying with their heads on the hairs of his chest and feeling comforted.

Girls do compliments and soft kisses and having our hand held.

Girls do chatting about our day.

Girls don't do complete intimate intensity and then passing him over to the next girl so she can do complete intimate intensity with him too.

Eff. Off.

"I don't do relationships," he said, impatiently now, as though he was fed up with this, as though she had performed badly, as though this chat was an inconvenience.

What do you do?

Sleeping with as many girls as possible?

As many different styles, colours, varieties as possible?

Why have a main course when you can have multiple appetisers?

Like sitting in a sushi bar and lifting one plate after the other off the roly-poly belt?

"Fine," Beth practically spat. "Well then please don't contact me again."

I am no plate of sushi. I am a main course.

She closed the door, felt her heart hammering in her chest, stomped up the stairs, and felt a sudden need to strip her bed and put on fresh sheets.

She got into the shower and let the cool fresh sprays calm her down.

She dried herself and enveloped herself into her fresh new bed.

And that was the night she vowed to herself that never again would she be a plate of sushi on anyone's roly-poly belt.

Chapter Seventeen
JAMIE

Jamie was sitting at the train station. There was a coffee shop and he was waiting, perched on one of those uncomfortable silver steel chairs, listening to the sound of overhead announcements and people's voices scurrying by.

The train from Brighton was due in half an hour. He was early. He sipped his hot coffee and waited. An attractive woman in a red coat and red heels tottered past. She threw him a look – a slight smile? And it was so uncommon for any person in London to throw a stranger a smile, that he was slightly taken aback.

She was gorgeous. He almost wanted to hold his hands up in front of his chest like a puppy dog and make drooling gestures towards her, but then she was gone. Off in the direction of platform 14 and the spuds-u-like counter.

He reminded himself that he should not be eyeing up strangers in London's Waterloo station. He reminded himself that he was sitting there waiting for Stacey. Stacey the girl he was going to give things a go with. Stacey the girl who was besotted with him. Stacey the girl who jumped at the suggestion of going to London to visit him. Stacey the girl who gushed, "Oh Jamie! That would be so wonderful! Thank you soo much for inviting me! Oh! I am going to get to meet all your friends! How exciting!"

Jamie had been slightly taken aback by the strength of her enthusiasm. He almost expected her to tell him to feck off. That it'd been too long since he'd been in touch and she wanted nothing more to do with him. That she had better things to do that sit around waiting for him to get back to her.

But no, she hadn't said that. She had said, "That's so nice of Amy to allow me stay – are you sure she doesn't mind?"

"No, she's cool about it- honest."

And she had been cool about it. That was the thing about Amy. She was cool. She thought nothing of opening her house to complete strangers and letting them settle themselves among her furniture and feel at home.

And anyway, Amy had been in a stupidly good mood ever since the supposed night she'd visited her 'mum'. Of course Jamie knew she'd really been visiting Gav, and on account of Amy's fantastically good mood, clearly it had gone well.

It made Jamie sick with jealousy if he thought about it for too long, so he decided not to think about it. He decided to pick himself up and carry on. He decided to stop beating about the bush with Amy. He decided to stop kidding himself that one day she'd suddenly go off Gav and wake up and realise what a great guy Jamie was. He decided to move on with his life.

And what better way to move on than with Stacey. Sure wasn't she mad about him? Wasn't she ready to drop everything in a nano-second for him?

And besides, Sarah and Beth had put him up to it. The last break-up test meeting was a disaster. Sarah had gone to all the trouble of setting out drinks and nibbles and having nice music and lighting soft candles, and Jamie could see that she could not hide her disappointment that Amy had failed to attend the first meeting already.

This only seemed to add to Jamie's already angry mood. He'd arrived at the meeting, fresh from witnessing Amy's deliberate lying and his mood was foul. When he saw Sarah's disappointment, this just topped off his annoyance and he found his usual obnoxious behaviour returning forthwith.

"She's 'supposedly' at her mum's," Jamie crossed his arms,

his face set with annoyance, his eyes rolling to one side.

"And you don't think she is?" Sarah probed, opening a bag of kettle chips and spilling them into a bowl.

"Nope," he replied defiantly. "She's with Gav."

There was a sharp intake of breath then from Beth, who looked from one of them to the other.

"Really?" Sarah asked calmly.

"Yup," Jamie relayed the whole story to them angrily, knowing that he was being an out-and-out gossip, and realising he would have to expose his sneaky looking-at-her-mobile-phone behaviour, but he couldn't stop himself. He was so pent up, so *frustrated* that he felt he had to unload the whole incident to them.

"Well," Sarah answered calmly, now relaxed on the armchair, the little tealights twinkling around her, taking a sip from her large wine glass, "Maybe she's still blocked. Maybe she's full of fear."

She went on to say things like, "I suppose this is to be expected when we are trying to help each other, there will be waves of doubts, times when people come and go. It's resistance. It's fear. We're all doing very well to have actually turned up today."

Jamie nearly choked on his kettle chip. "And what self-help books have you been swallowing recently?"

Sarah laughed. "It's true though. Amy just needs to go back and have a bit more pain until she's totally fed up with him."

There was a silence then. Jamie didn't like the thought of Amy going through more pain. Jamie didn't like the thought of Amy having to suffer more for that fella. To be in his bed – to have him use her and then... just toss her away.

He realised that he had been staring into the bottom of his glass. He realised that he had been doing this and he wasn't sure how long for. Because when he looked up again, Beth and Sarah were watching him, with concerned expressions, and Sarah did this "Are you okay?" gesture, as though they were sitting in a self-help circle, and it made Jamie uneasy. He chirped up, "Sure I'm okay." But it was forced and obvious and he realised that Sarah had glimpsed something. And he didn't like that.

"So…" he quickly changed the subject. "How have you two been getting on? Tell me all your wonderful escapades…"

So they did. They chattered and chatted and Jamie let the wine sink down to his belly, creating a soft comforting glow. And every now and again, Sarah would magically disappear to the fridge and magically reappear with a fresh bottle of chilled white wine with condensation running down the side and she would top up his glass, as though it were a never-ending fountain.

And there, on the comfy sofa, with Beth and Sarah re-telling their stories and suddenly it became okay. Suddenly his head settled and things didn't feel so chaotic and suddenly it didn't really matter anymore. He wasn't alone. And it wasn't the end of the world. And everyone went through their up's and down's and sure isn't this what life was all about? And no, he didn't know what was around the corner and he didn't know what his happy ending would be, but maybe he needed to give up on Amy for a while. Maybe he needed to let her get Gav totally and utterly out of her system. Maybe he needed to just forget about her for a while.

"Just do one thing for me though, would you?" Jamie asked.

Sarah smiled and nodded.

"Take her out a bit. Amy. Even if it's just to the shops or for coffee. Even if it's not to come to these chats. Even if it's just to get out for a drink somewhere. Just so she has someone to talk to – confide in, you know?"

Sarah smiled and nodded again.

Jamie thought he saw something in her smile. A look that was more than just concern. A look that was something else. But he couldn't put his finger on it. So he just forgot about it, and swilled the rest of the wine from the bottom of his glass into his mouth and got up to use the loo.

In the toilet, he checked his phone. Just to see if she'd texted. Just to see if she was okay. But nothing. Probably down to her bra and knickers and being devoured by Gav right at this precise moment in time. He shuddered at the thought, flushed the toilet, and returned to the living room.

Right, he told himself. *Enough of this. I am as bad as Sarah, Amy and Beth put together. I am equally as obsessed as the three of them. Forget about her. It's a lost cause.*

And that's when Jamie decided it was definitely a good idea to invite Stacey to stay.

Amy had been in jovial form the day after meeting Gav. Obviously the 'date' had gone well. She had been chirpy and happy when he broached the subject of Stacey coming to stay.

"Sure!" she smiled. She was opening the windows and polishing the furniture and half-dancing to the music coming from the radio. She was wearing a vest-top and hot pants and her hair was pulled back in a bandana.

"It went well with your mum then?" Jamie mused.

"Yeah, went great!" Amy lied.

Jamie nodded.

"That's cool about Stacey coming to stay," Amy had said when he asked. "I'd like to meet her."

"Okay thanks," Jamie said, before hurrying off. He didn't want to hang around. He didn't want to concentrate on the sight of Amy in her hot pants and vest-top dancing to tunes because she was in a good mood about Gav.

And now, here he was, at the train station, waiting for Stacey, with ten minutes to go until she arrived, checking out beautiful strangers in red coats with red shoes and blonde hair.

This was the thing Jamie noticed about beautiful blonde strangers at train stations. Just say he gave Stacey the green light. Just say he said, "Okay then, let's shack up. Let's date for a while." He'd know that that would be that. That Stacey's hopes would be built up and she would expect them to enter into the stages of a meaningful relationship. And that would be that, and he would be destroyed. Never again would there be any possibility of a flirt with a stranger at the train station. Never again would there be a possibility of the blonde girl with the red shoes and the red coat suddenly returning his smile and instead of heading towards the spuds-u-like counter, she would sit down beside him. She would caress her red high-heeled shoe gently up his leg and she would make come to bed eyes to him. Except that instead of coming to bed, they would nip into the toilets and they would have fast and furious sex and it would be wonderful and liberating. And then off she would go on her trip and Jamie would walk around free, knowing that he could do that at any time and not feel guilty.

Except Jamie knew that even if he wasn't with Stacey, the chances of a glamorous blonde girl with pointy red heels wanting to shag him in the smelly public toilets of London's Waterloo station and then go on her merry way with her life, were about five million to one.

So he told himself to wise up and not be so stupid.

And anyway, when he turned to look at the spuds-u-like counter, he saw that glamorous blonde girl had fallen into the arms of some Greek god, who had just appeared out of platform 14, and probably the only reason why the blonde girl was smiling in the first place was because she was happy that she was about to have a shag-fest with mister Adonis.

Jamie's phone bleeped.

Stacey.

"I'll be there in ten. Can't wait to see you x o x o"

Already Jamie felt slightly breathy. Her over-enthusiasm was over-whelming.

The train pulled up and he could see her bound towards the barriers, a mass of thick red hair billowing behind her. Hair like Amy's, he noted, with interest.

She grinned as the barriers broke her free and she fell upon Jamie with a massive hug.

"Oh! It's sooo great to see you!" she grinned. Lots of people were looking at them. Jamie felt his cheeks flush red with embarrassment. People would think she had been away to the other side of the world for a year rather than down the road in Brighton for a week.

"Erm… shall we go for a drink?" Jamie asked, hoping the alcohol would calm her down. Hoping that a nice beer garden and a sunny day and a drink laced with copious amounts of alcohol would settle her, wrench some of that hyper enthusiasm out of her.

"Ooooh! Yes! That'd be lovely", she breathed.

They found a beer garden, and Jamie ordered pints and plates of chips, and they sat at the wooden picnic table under the sunshine.

"Oh this is so perfect!" Stacey grinned. "I am so happy to be here! I am so happy you asked me! I am so excited about meeting your friends!"

Jamie felt something tighten around his throat. A breathy feeling.

"I'm sooo flattered to be meeting your friends! It just feels… REAL… you know?"

She gave him a big toothy smile and squeezed his knee.

It was at this point that Jamie decided to get VERY DRUNK. He ordered shots and salt and lemon and Stacey giggled and said, "Isn't this a bit much for a Saturday afternoon?" but Jamie had shrugged his shoulders and grimaced at the bitter sweet taste of the lemon.

To passersby they might have seemed like a cool London couple, Stacey just arrived in from some exotic flight, her suitcase on her side, Jamie with his trendy sunglasses perched on his nose, pints and tequilas and lemon in front of them at only one o'clock in the afternoon.

But really Jamie just felt like a lost soul floundering in the dark, rather than some hip London lad sitting in the sun.

"I must look a state – I do apologise," Stacey nervously ran a hand through her hair.

"Eh?" Jamie eyed her quizzically, the make-up laden on her face, an immaculate outfit she had obviously prepared well in advance, a suntan that had either taken months to develop or was an expensive spray tan.

"My hair," she pointed apologetically. "I straightened my hair to perfection this morning . . . but all the travelling – it's probably put a kink in it."

Jamie nearly sniggered at the 'all the travelling' comment – as though she'd boarded a first class 747 to America instead of a train cabin from Brighton.

"Your hair looks fine," he shrugged.

And then he reproached himself at the use of the word 'fine'. He could see Stacey recoil a bit – as though 'fine' was mediocre, as though 'fine' was average, when actually she had prepared all week for this visit.

"You look great," he reassured. "You look really great."

She smiled then, a big grateful relieved smile, and for some reason, it made Jamie feel like the biggest bastard on the planet. If only she would just chill out! If only she wouldn't give a feck what he thought! If only she'd be herself! If only she'd arrive up in her jeans and a t-shirt with a baseball cap over her head and slogan across her breasts saying, "Take it or leave it you ungrateful bastard'. Maybe then he might relax more. Maybe then he'd know he'd fallen off the great judge & jury position and into the heap of "you'd only get me if you were very fecking lucky" category. In a sick sort of way, he'd think he'd enjoy that more.

They drank on. And on. And on.

Until they were plastered.

And somehow they made it home.

A taxi? A kebab and chip on the way?

A taxi-driver complaining about the smell in his cab?

Jamie telling him not to be so ungrateful – that he should be happy to get the fare 'in this current economic climate.'

Stacey apologising for Jamie. Jamie saying, "Don't apologise for me! I don't want to apologise!"

The taxi coming to an abrupt halt.

Jamie and Stacey having to walk the rest of the way home.

With Stacey wheeling her suitcase. Her straightened hair now drastically frizzy.

Standing on Amy's doorstep. About to meet Amy for the first time.

Jamie ringing the doorbell because he couldn't find his keys.

Amy opening the door with a sleepy expression, one closed eye, and wearing only hot pants and a vest top.

Jamie saying, "Way!hey!hey! What about a threesome?!"

Amy throwing him a disgusted look.

Stacey giggling nervously.

And then they fell into bed.

There was a romp. Definitely a romp. He definitely remembered he and Stacey had summoned enough drunken co-ordination to do that.

And then nothing. Black-out. Sleep. And now this.

His head pounding.

Inability to move.

His throat felt as though someone had tipped a truck-load of sand down it.

He leaned his head slightly to the left.

It hurt.

Stacey was lying with her head on the pillow facing him.

As though she had been lying like that all night watching him.

"Good morning honey," she smiled.

Chapter Eighteen
<u>BETH</u>

Beth found a cheap artist's studio to hire. Even though it was slap-bang in the middle of Richmond, one of the most prestigious spots in London, it was dirt-cheap. This might have had something to do with the fact that it was one tiny room in a high-rise block of studios. In fact "room" was an understatement – it was more like a broom cupboard, with a cardboard partition for a wall – but no matter, it was an art studio, and it was hers. And more importantly, it had a gorgeous view of Richmond. When she stood at the window and looked out, she could see the river rippling by. She could see people strolling past on the walkway. She could see trees and greenery piled up behind it. She could see the clouds curl themselves in the background and she could see the flat blue sky beyond.

This comforted her somewhat. It comforted her that she could tuck herself away in a studio and look out at all this nature. It comforted her that she had found it, and the rent was cheap. The handshake with the landlady was quick, she signed her name on a piece of paper, and that was that.

She loved that she had been able to book ten days off work. She was glad that she had holiday to take, and she knew she needed the time. Time to lick her wounds. It had been over two weeks and Karl had not texted to see how she was. She felt chucked away, like an apple core, gobbled up in several bites and tossed onto the ground to decompose.

So this time apart was what she needed. She planned on

seeing nobody. She did not want company or idle conversation. She did not want needless chit-chat about clothes or hair or shopping or anything else. She just wanted to be left alone.

Her studio had become her haven. A sanctuary to tuck herself away. A space, she hoped, where if she just enclosed herself for long enough, she could emerge, refreshed. Like being in hibernation, or a time capsule, where all of a sudden, the pain would pass, and then she would come out again, and get on with life.

She had forgotten about her love of drawing. It had been neglected over the years, and suddenly it emerged, wanting to be played with again.

Drawings of kittens, and puppies, and ponies. Drawings of vulnerable, innocent, beautiful creatures. Drawings that reminded her that despite all the pain and hurt and resentment in her world, there was still innocence, and purity, and beauty.

She tacked the photos of the young animals to her easel and then she drew them, with a fine, slim pencil. A pencil that she sharpened from time to time, the shards falling into her bin, a soft little mound rising after time. She played classical music on a tiny little stereo that she had carried in with her, and she made herself cups of coffee from the tiny kettle she had set up in the corner. And she engrossed herself. The soft strokes of the pencil lulling her. The easy repetitive motion, the rhythm of it, making her forget. Allowing her to put the pain aside. Allowing her to think about something else, anything else, than Karl.

Allowing her to forget that last night, the intense look in his eyes as he looked up at her, his mouth around her nipple, and that intense look. It stuck with her, fresh in her head. Closely followed by his quickness to say, "Let's just be mates". That one quick comment, which she had conveniently chosen to forget, now came flooding back. That one quick comment like a sharp pair of scissors slicing through an umbilical cord. That one quick comment that did all the damage. That one comment that said the beginning of the end. Because no matter how long she wanted to sit in the land of denial; to pretend that he didn't say that, or even, didn't mean it; to pretend that their attempts to be 'friends' would actually materialise into something more meaningful, it was over.

Over because it had never started in the first place, and over in her head.

But while she was drawing, she didn't have to think about that just yet.

That was the beautiful thing about being in the land of denial, she thought. It gave her mind and body time to adjust. Time to let the information sink in. Time to cope with the sharpness of the words, "let's just be mates." The "let's just be mates" comment came too quickly after the intense look in the eyes whilst the mouth was on the nipple part, and the two just didn't compute. What should have been the beginning was dramatically the end.

But then should it have been the beginning? Perhaps her expectations had been too high? For he had never promised her anything, had he?

He had never at any point whipped out a contract, dipped his pen in his own blood and signed it with a steadfast assurance that this was it – he would treat her like a princess from now to infinity.

No.

In fact, what had happened was that their eyes met over a crowded room. His lopsided grin had given her all the clichéd reactions all the books had promised her she'd have – the flutterby in her tummy, the raised heartbeat, the widening eyes.

The excitement.

Of course, it helped immensely that he was standing on a podium, a microphone in front of his mouth, and spotlights shining down behind him.

It helped that he was a singer in a band. An unheard-of band, granted, but that was beside the point. He was still singing – and singing to *her*. In fact, she would go a cliché further and say that he seemed to have singled her out, found her among the crowd, and directed his lines completely towards her.

Or was that just a trick of the light?

She had the *brass neck* to approach him afterwards. Sidling up next to him at the bar, perching on a stool, smiling at him and complimenting him and having him smile back.

She approached him.

He didn't chat about gigs, or his music, or his singing, or anything about himself. Instead, he made her feel as though she was the most important person in the room. As though she, Secretary Beth, was more interesting that any band, any gig, any singer, or any other gifted talented person who happened to be in the vicinity. He made her feel special. And wanted. And fancied.

And all by a flick of the eye and a genuine smile.

She was hooked.

So hooked that she approached him again, via the little number that was emblazoned across his business card – "Slippery Demons" – the card read, along with a website address, a facebook page and a mobile number.

He reciprocated. Of course he did.

If it's offered on a plate…

If there's a line of sushi plates on a roly-poly belt and they're free then…

He was used to it. There was one after the other. One gig after the other. One attractive, horny female wanting sex with a singer. Sex that they presumed would be exciting and passionate, if the mouth wrapping around the microphone and the way he gyrated around his phallic pole was anything to go by.

It was. Exciting that is. And then it was over. And then he was thinking about the next one. For there were too many. Blonde. Brunette. Red. Tall. Small. Big-boobed. Curvy. Shy. Confident. Why stop at one when the menu was vast?

Variety, the spice of life.

Why eat bread and butter every day when you could try a chilli burger, or a plate of chunky chips, or even a finger lickin' spare rib?

Besides, the last bread and butter had given him too much torture. Monitored his every move. Made him text her fifty million times a day. Gave him dagger stares if he so much as looked sideways at another woman. Expected him to spend his Friday and Saturday nights curled up with her on the sofa when he would rather have been out gallivanting, meeting new people, casting his charismatic smile around for lots of girls to enjoy.

Plus there was the fact that relationships were a pile of pretend rubbish. People keeping secrets from each other. The amount of affairs he'd heard about. Misses right sneaking a cheeky fag when mister wrong wasn't looking. Mister wrong eyeing up the pages of boobs in FHM when misses right was downstairs bathing the weins. It was all a load of pretense in his eyes. So why bother?

Beth took a break from her artist's stool. She put her pencil down and rotated her wrists. She flicked on the kettle and went to the window. She watched the river trickling by. She watched the birds swoop in the sky. She saw the people stroll alongside the river. Couples.

Couples, couples everywhere.

She was amazed at these couples. Their supposed indifference to how EASY it was for them. They were just strolling along hand-in-hand, as though this god-given gift was just plopped in their path and they didn't have to DO anything for it – didn't have to work at it – manipulate anything – coerce anything – just turn up and say, "Cheers

God! Nice gift! Thanks very much!" and then they went off in their happy little way, smugly walking along the riverside.

Just then there was a knock on the door.

"Hallooooo?" A voice came. A woman's voice. Chirpy sounding. Vibrant.

Beth's heart sank. She did not want to be interrupted. This was her nest. Her hibernation zone. She did not want to be sociable.

"Hi?" she replied tentatively.

"...um... can I come in? ... I just wanted to introduce myself!"

Beth rolled her eyes behind the doorway. "...Um, sure, two secs..."

She switched the kettle off and made her way to the door, flicking open the lock and pulling the door open.

Behind the door was a woman with blonde frizzy hair that looked rebellious and out of control. Big wiry curls bouncing out behind her. She had a fresh face – no make-up and traces of a few lines around her eyes.

"Hi! I'm Mary!" she beamed. "Or mad Mary as they like to call me here!"

"Hi" Beth smiled politely.

There was a brief pause then. This was the part where Beth was supposed to invite her in, to show her the studio, to talk about their common love of art, to ask questions about how long they've enjoyed art for, to talk about their dreams and hopes and aspirations, to talk about whether they had partners or children or cats.

But Beth was quiet.

"So...?" Mary persisted. "You're new here...?"

Beth nodded her head and gave another polite smile.

"Great! That's just great!" Mary went on, a little nervously now. "Well, we just like to welcome people to the building, introduce ourselves – you know – it's like a little family here – all these artists under one roof!"

Beth softened. She felt immediately guilty. Here was a woman, probably in her forties, with mad rebellious hair, nervous by Beth's lack of social graces.

"Thanks very much," Beth smiled warmly. "That's very nice of you."

Mary took this unspoken olive branch and ran with it, like all she needed was one small opening, one crack in the hard exterior.

"So... can I show you where my studio is? Just in case you ever need to borrow a cup of sugar or anything?" she grinned again. That same vibrant smile, as though life was just one big happy adventure. And Beth wondered how she ever got to that. How did this woman get to be so happy?

"Um... sure..." Beth found herself saying, even though she was being forced out of her nest far more quickly than she had planned.

"Great!"

Mary led her down the corridor, past the ladies toilets, with the bright pink paint on the walls and the glittery tiny mirrors decorated above the toilet. She took her down the windy staircase ("Don't attempt these stairs in high heels when you're drunk!" she exclaimed. "Been there, done that, amazed I'm alive to tell the tale!") and finally to the destination – her studio. It was as Beth expected. Light and airy, with a bright orange paint all over her walls and then huge yellow sunflowers painted on top of the orange.

"I presume you painted this studio yourself?" Beth asked, not able to keep the awe and surprise from her voice.

"Yes!" Mary grinned. "Well, myself and my partner Todd – he's a painter too – he lives on the top floor – tucked away most of the time – but he can be helpful when he puts his mind to it," she grinned. And then she added with a wink, "or if I bribe him with sex!"

Beth felt herself wince inwardly. Firstly at Mary's outlandish honesty and secondly at the mention of sex. Beth didn't want to think about other people having sex, especially as she was being deprived of it.

"Well, it was nice to meet you," Beth said hurriedly, ready to make her excuses and leave.

"Oh! Hold on!" Mary practically pounced on her like a cat on a mouse. "Let me just introduce you first to two of my most favourite artists. Jake and Roseanne. Please."

Beth's heart sank again. She did not want to meet Jake and Roseanne. She needed another loved-up couple in her life like she needed a hole in the head. She felt anger rising in her. Anger that made her want to scream "Would you all ever just FECK OFF??" Anger that made her make a mental note that she was going to have two separate signs for her door; one that said, "I'm busy. Go away" and one that said, "I'm here. Pop In."

She felt pretty sure that sign number one would be up for the foreseeable future.

She reminded herself that this was *her* time off. *Her* holiday. *Her* precious ten days off work. This was *her* time to heal. And here she was surrounded by people who were trying to invade her space with bright sunflowers and loved-up couples.

Roxanne was curvy. And bubbly. With a big loud laugh and a warm smile. And she could talk. Talk for England. In fact, Beth couldn't help but like her. There was something warm and comforting about her. Perhaps it was the fact that as long as Roxanne chatted, Beth didn't have to say anything. She could just nod her head in all the appropriate places and not have to make much effort.

"So that was Roxanne," mad Mary whispered, as they walked away. "She was married," Mary whispered. "But her husband died. A year ago. Very sad. But she's picking herself up. We're all trying to help her."

Beth's mouth dropped open. "But I thought... Roxanne and Jake..."

Mary laughed. "No! Where did you get that notion? No,

they're not an item, don't be silly."

Beth followed Mary along the corridor. Her head swam. Roxanne. Husband died. One year ago.

And then the thought came to her, "Other people are suffering too."

"So!" Mary announced. "This is Jake". She kicked open a door and called, "Coooo-ieeee! It's me!"

They sidled inside to see a guy halfway up a ladder, balancing with one foot on and one foot off, wearing headphones on his ears and singing a happy song.

Just as his voice was climbing an octave higher, Mary shouted, **"HALLLLLOOOOOOO!"**

"Woooah!" Jake startled, tore the headphones off his head and grabbed on to his ladder.

"Bloody hell Mary! How many times have I told you not to do that?"

"Whoops! Sorry!" Mary apologised. "But I have someone I want to introduce you to."

Jake looked over at Beth and climbed down the ladder. He outstretched a paint-stained hand.

"Hi", he smiled. "I'm sorry about the swearing". He glanced over at Mary. "But some people don't seem to understand the notion of manners."

"Sorry!" Mary rolled her eyes playfully, followed by "Get over yourself."

There was a bit of banter between the two of them – as though they were brother and sister and this sparring was all very normal.

Beth noticed that Jake was attractive in a quiet, unobtrusive way. He had dark hair and was average height. He had a genuine smile and appeared to be a good listener. And then after that, Beth placed a mental "NO" under his name. She had had enough of men, thank you very much. And right at this moment in time, she just wanted to retreat to her nest.

"So…" Mary told her, "We go out for coffees from time to

time. There's a lovely little café down the road from here – all nice comfy sofas and gorgeous cupcakes. We usually head down on a Friday at above five – and then head on for drinks after. Come along on Friday if you fancy it?" Mary's face was expectant, as though she thought Beth would jump at the offer.

"Yeah, it's a good laugh," Jake chipped in. "Come along. Pleeeeaaaase. I need some new company. Mary's doing my head in."

Mary slapped him and Beth smiled politely.

"I'll see," Beth replied.

Beth didn't want to commit to stepping out to *any* public place. Just say Karl was there. Just say Karl had some stunning girl on his arm. Just say it turned out that Karl *could* be committed to a relationship – just not to a relationship with *her*. Beth didn't think she could take any more pain or rejection.

"I'll see?" Mary grimaced, nudging Jake. "I think we've been politely blown out mate."

Jake made a pouting gesture with his lips – lips that Beth couldn't help but notice were quite full.

"Oh alright then, I'll go," Beth conceded. "But just for a little while."

Chapter Nineteen
<u>AMY</u>

Saturday night at Gav's was no different than the other times. There was a glass of water by the bedside for her – no great expense made for this date. No three-course meal in a restaurant, no bunch of flowers, no box of chocolates. Just a glass of water, by the bedside, and Gav's undeniable ability to unfasten her bra strap in record time. She wondered if he set himself goals.

How long will it take this time? One hour? Half an hour? Twenty minutes?

She banished the thought from her head. *Where did that bitchy idea come from?* she thought.

Instead she told herself to think positive thoughts.

Listen to the way he's talking about coming home in a month's time, she thought. *That is surely a sign to tell me that he's looking forward to being home with me – to spending more time with me.*

"It'll be so great to be home," he said. "To not live out of a suitcase. To have a whole house to roam around in. To slouch on my sofa. To see my friends."

She smiled. She was looking forward to having him home too. To getting little texts from him each week, inviting her over each weekend. To spend more time with him. To get to know him better.

He had used the magnetic effect to peel her top off and swiftly unfasten her bra. Her breasts sprang out to attention, longing to be played with.

Like the last time, they were halfway up the stairs when he

caught a glimpse up her skirt and stopped her, right there, on the stairs, and that is where they played for a while. And then, like the last time, the finale was on the bed, with his purple cock pointing at her, and then it was over.

This time she volunteered to walk herself home. She had control this way. If it was her idea to walk herself home, then she couldn't be annoyed if he didn't offer. And so he stood at the doorway, and waved her off, and the whole way home, she repeated to herself, "This is my CHOICE, this is my CHOICE, this is my CHOICE." Like a mantra, so that she couldn't let the negative voices creep in. The voices that were screaming, "Uh oh! Glass of water, shag halfway up the stairs, having to walk yourself home. Another night of being USED."

She couldn't bear those negative voices. She wanted to put her hands over her ears and sing, "La la la la la I'm not listening," so she ignored those voices, and she went home.

The house was empty. Jamie was over at Sarah's place. Amy curled herself up on the sofa for a while. She thought a glass of wine would help her to sleep. She told herself positive thoughts. She flicked through her myriad of "How to" books. "How to keep him keen," "How to understand men," "How to love the man you love without hating him." Books to that effect. And they all said the same thing, "Don't text him. Don't hound him. Give him space. Let him pull away to have space and watch as he bounces back." All that type of thing. She read all of that and she tried to ignore the big empty void swelling in her chest already.

The big empty void as she undressed for bed, still smelling the scent of Gav on her. The big empty void as she got into her big empty bed alone, hugging herself to keep her warm, and thinking about the sight of him, his naked body about to enter her, and the intense look on his face. She wondered to herself if she even enjoyed the sex with him anymore? Had she not been too tense to actually come? Had her body not reacted in a way that her subconscious was telling it to?

110

I can't relax. I can't relax with this man.

Those little words, issued from the subconscious and travelling down to her pelvic wall, so that it stood, firm, like a barricade. With a "do not enter" sign on the wall. She might have thought she wanted to shag him, but her body said differently. She didn't come, and he did. And she walked home alone.

Of course, if she had confessed to her mum what was happening, her mum would have "read her the riot act," as she would say.

Out would come all the clichés she had listened to for years:

"Start as you mean to go on."

"Don't do as I did, do as I say."

"Don't get married – once the honeymoon is over, you'll be lifted off the shelf and stuck in front of the kitchen sink."

"Treat 'em mean, keep 'em keen."

"I'm only trying to save you from the mistakes I made."

…and on… and on… and on…

Give me a good romantic comedy any day.

The clichés were repeated over and over, but the day of the big red door and the orange and special biscuits was never discussed again.

Dad had just 'gone away' and that was that. No further contact. No birthday card, no Christmas card, no postcard. She wondered if he'd moved as far away as America? Or even Australia? She'd certainly never spotted him hanging around the streets of Dungiven. Nor had she spotted them on their trips to Derry.

She thought she might have seen him strolling up Shipquay Street, or browsing The Richmond Centre, or even in Foyleside.

But no.

Perhaps he had moved to Belfast, settling into one of those

nice apartments looking over the River Lagan.

She even wondered if she'd recognise him if she saw him again. His face had become blurred, like an old black and white photo that was curling at the edges.

In her early teens, there was a time that she eyed up every male stranger as potentially her father. Day trips to Giants Causeway were less about the beautiful scenery and more about trying to catch sight of him that was long lost.

Whilst the other girls were crossing the Carrick-a-Rede rope bridge and squealing with excitement, there was a sort of dullness on Amy's face; a lack of interest, a void.

And then, after a while, she gave up.

She gave up wondering.

She gave up asking.

And she became as closed about it as her mum.

A closed chapter.

It was easier that way. More final. Less painful.

It seemed that as far as her mum was concerned, dad might as well have gone off with the angels.

For whilst he was with 'the angels', she was with Paddy, then Micky, then Seamus.

Tom. Dick. Harry.

Some were nicer than others.

Some brought chocolates and sweets and rustled her hair and tried to be liked.

Others, meanwhile, were too engrossed in her mum, sitting across the table from her, enchanted by her long red nails, her perfectly painted face, her immaculate clothes.

Her mum; with the job and the independence and the control and the "you can't treat me like crap 'cos I won't stand for it" air.

But of course, Amy knew it was a front.

Amy caught her once looking through the old wedding photos, with a trembling hand and a tear running down her perfectly made-up face.

Amy knew to slip away, to pretend she hadn't seen that.

For all mum's independence, there was the day she drove Amy to the airport for university.

Eighteen years old and leaving little old Northern Ireland to fly to London. London with its chaotic tube station map that made her brain fuzz.

Amy with only one suitcase on the roly poly belt.

On the way to the airport, Amy's mum talked incessantly.

A nervous chatter.

"Make sure to call me anytime. Even if it's three o'clock in the morning."

"Okay."

"And never, ever, walk home from a party. Always get a taxi."

"Okay."

"And no dodgy taxis either. Proper ones with the sign on top."

"Yes mum."

The incessant chat was making that churning feeling in her stomach whirl even further.

London.

Tube stations.

Hectic.

Chaotic.

A world away from Dungiven.

What was she doing?

They drove along the Glenshane pass, the sun casting a warm glow over the fields and scenery, the Sperrin mountains standing proud. Amy feeling small and insignificant.

At Belfast City Airport, the churning stomach whizzed further.

There was the coffee shop. Mum's nervous chit-chat with the sales assistant.

"Grand day. Weather's held out rightly, hasn't it?"

"Oh aye, grand. Let's see how long it lasts."

There were the soup-bowls for coffee cups. There was the two of them sitting opposite each other, talking about everything but goodbye. There was the people-watching.

"Look at yer one," mum nodded her head towards a girl with a mid-riff top and a short skirt.

"Sure did you ever see the like of it in the six counties? Don't you be gallivanting round London like that, d'you hear me?"

There was the check-in desk, the one-way ticket, the barriers, mum's heavy sigh.

"Well, I suppose this is it then," she said, acting stoical and brave.

"I suppose it is," Amy replied, giving her a little smile.

"Ah sure, you'll be home for Christmas in no time," mum said, giving her a firm hug.

The sun shone brightly through the large windows that were lined from one end to the other, floor to ceiling. Planes waited patiently outside.

"Off you go," mum nodded, assertively. "And take care of yourself."

"I will," Amy whispered softly, giving her hand a tight squeeze and passing herself over to the woman in the security uniform who was waiting to pat her arms and legs.

Amy turned back to give her mum one last wave.

And there she was, looking so lost and lonely, dwarfed in that big green coat.

It was only later, much later, that she'd found out that her mum had cried the whole way home, having to pull the car over on the motorway to wipe her tear-stained face.

And that was the day Amy's mum promised herself to move to London too. There was no way she was going to let another one slip through her fingers.

The following Saturday night there was little sleep for Amy. Not least because her head was tormented by thoughts of Gav, but more because the doorbell rang consistently at silly o'clock in the morning. Jamie. And Stacey. Standing on her doorstep. Plastered.

Jamie slurred something about a threesome and Stacey was all bright-eyed and gushing about "It's so great to meet you," and Amy had grunted and gone back to bed.

She had hoped it was a mirage. A dream. That she would fall into a pleasant sleep and wake up the next morning refreshed.

But no.

The banging started.

Jamie's bedpost rocking back and forth. In a repetitive, mechanical motion.

And Stacey's moans, "Oh Jamie, Oh Jamie, Oh Jamie, Oooooohhhh…"

Amy grabbed her pillow and crushed it into her ears.

Selfish bastards! she thought. *Selfish fecking bastards!*

The pillow did nothing to decrease the sounds and in fact, Stacey's moans mounted in the level of her volume.

"Oh! Jamie! Oh! Jamie! Oh!"

Bloody hell! Amy muttered, tossing back her duvet and thrusting her feet into her slippers. She stormed out of her bedroom and into the living-room, not caring if they heard her slam a door or two. Even though she knew fine well that they would be totally oblivious to a bit of door slamming at the moment.

She sat on her sofa angrily, staring out of the window at the view across the town. Her insides were boiling. Lack of sleep, Jamie's selfishness, Gav making her walk home alone, Gav not texting her all week, pure and utter frustration. She picked up a pillow and fired it across the room, as though it was the pillow's fault. As though chucking a bit of material stuffed with foam would really make things better.

She checked her phone *just in case* Gav was nice enough to send her a 'Hey you, how's things going? x' text, but of course, nothing. She threw her phone across the carpet too, hoping that she didn't break that in the process.

"Right," she thought, "Tomorrow I am telling that Jamie that he can feck off back home and take his shagging partner with him."

"Good morning," Jamie said tentatively, when he opened the living room door and saw Amy sitting on the sofa, staring out the window, cradling a mug of coffee.

She turned her head, looked at him, said nothing, and sipped her coffee.

There was an awkward silence.

"Shit," Jamie said quietly. "I've really messed up this time, haven't I?"

"Yup." She was too tired, too worn out, too exhausted, to be aggressive.

Jamie ran a hand through his hair as though trying to rack his brains.

"Is it because I made that joke about the threesome?"

Amy sighed.

"It's about that. It's about the bed-post banging keeping me awake all night. It's about the fact that you're not even into her and yet you've invited her up here. It's about how all men are bastards. It's about how I'm tired."

Jamie looked at his hands, ashamed, unable to meet her gaze.

"I'm sorry," he said finally. "I'm sorry for keeping you awake. I'm sorry for inviting you up here. I'm sorry for being a man... And about Stacey... " he whispered in case she heard him, ".. you're right, I'm not into her.. and I know... it's selfish of me... but I was feeling... I dunno.. like I needed the company.. and she seemed to want to go along with it... and it's just a bit of fun... and well, sometimes in life it's okay to have a bit of fun... every fling doesn't have to lead to marriage and two point four children you know."

Amy rolled her eyes.

"Anyway, look – you're tired," Jamie advised. "How about I make you a nice hot milk and some biscuits and you go back to bed. Stacey and I will go out and give you peace and quiet and then we'll come home and cook us all a nice big dinner – and then she'll be on her way back home. How does that sound? Please... Aimes...?"

Amy said nothing.

"Look, I know I've annoyed you," he continued, "but I only have a few days left and then that's my project over in London. Please just let me stay these few more days and then that's me out of your hair for good. I promise."

Amy looked over at him, pleading with her, and her face softened. Here was Jamie, an old friend, asking for help, and who was she to take her bad mood out on him? Just because she was tired and frustrated and upset, was that really Jamie's fault? Could she really go through life pushing all her friends away at the first sign of any trouble?"

"Okay."

He brought her the hot milk and the biscuits, and the warmth comforted her stomach. She looked at her phone and there was a reply from Gav. "Hey u. Hope you're good too. See you soon x"

Her head hit the pillow, and she slept.

It was five o'clock in the afternoon when Amy woke up. Decadently late. A whole day in bed. Jamie and Stacey had obviously been tip-toeing around on egg-shells all day because there hadn't been a peep out of either of them.

After Amy had showered and dressed and looked at Gav's text five times ("Hey u. Hope you're good too. See you soon x"), she felt gloriously alive.

"Mornin'," she smiled, as she appeared in the doorway of the living room, looking over to the joining kitchen area and seeing Jamie and Stacey standing over the hob. Steam rising and pots bubbling and a lovely comforting smell of cooking hanging in the air.

"Good morning indeed!" Jamie said, over-cheerily, over-compensating for the bed-banging behaviour.

"Good morning!" Stacey smiled, wide-eyed and over enthusiastic. She came across the room quickly, extending a proffered hand to Amy. "It's *so* nice to finally meet you properly," she gushed, the 'properly' word said with a blush attached, obviously referring to her landing-on-the-doorstep-drunk episode.

"Nice to meet you too," Amy said politely.

"And thank you *so* much for letting me stay," Stacey gushed on, "It's very good of you."

"No problem," Amy said between teeth, knowing that Stacey's cries of "Oh Jamie!" would haunt her forever.

"So, what's going on here then?" Amy asked, pointing to the pots and pans and desperately trying to change the conversation.

"Well…" Jamie began, "Stacey kindly bought some *goose* and is cooking us a fantastic meal!"

"Goose!" Amy exclaimed. "Very pricey!"

Stacey shrugged her shoulders with a smile. "It's the least I can do – for you letting me stay."

Amy's heart caved. She suddenly felt like the biggest bitch in the world. Here was a girl, in love with a guy, just trying to impress him and his friends.

"Looks like there's enough to feed an army!" Amy exclaimed.

Stacey laughed. "Yes, there is rather a lot."

"Shall we invite Beth and Sarah over?" Amy asked, suddenly feeling gregarious and sociable. The marathon sleep had helped, along with Gav's text ("Hey u. Hope you're good too. See you soon x").

"That'd be cool!" Jamie smiled.

The girls were invited, and both had agreed, and before she knew it, Amy was alone in the kitchen with Stacey while Jamie was getting dressed.

Stacey had already changed, into a silk dress with a high neck and a pretty ribbon tied around the waist. It flowed down to below her knees.

"Your dress is beautiful," Amy admired.

"Thanks," Stacey grinned. "It's a Karen Millen," she said, practically in a whisper, as though it were naughty and over-indulgent. "I just wanted to treat myself, you know – for this weekend."

Amy did know. She knew how much Stacey was hoping to impress Jamie.

"It cost a fortune, and I'll probably be living on baked beans for the rest of the month – but hey!"

Amy wanted to say, "Hey nothing! Hey you shouldn't have! Hey you shouldn't waste your precious money on him! Hey you should treat yourself to a decent food shop from M&S every week rather than spend your money on goose and a dress for him!" But she kept her mouth shut. At least she managed that. And besides, she *did* understand. Hadn't she made the same colossal mistakes with Gav? In fact, Stacey would be a number one recruit for The Break-up Test, qualifying rightly, but Amy kept her opinions to herself.

"It just feels so *special*, you know?" Stacey asked. "It's just so nice to be meeting his friends – it makes it all seem so *REAL.*"

Amy nodded, despite herself. She would be over the moon if Gav introduced her to his mates.

Stacey had gotten further past the hurdles than her, if she thought about it like that.

"And it's so nice to meet YOU," Stacey went on, "He's said so much about YOU."

"Oh, I can't think what," Amy replied, flustered. "The amount of rows we have."

"Rows?! What? No.. no, he says about how great you are..."

119

Amy didn't know what to say, she wanted to say that Stacey could do better. That she shouldn't be stretching her credit card to capacity for his benefit, that she deserved more, that she seemed like a nice, giving, loving person.

But Amy didn't say all that. Instead she said, "Oh, that's nice, thanks...um… is there anything I can help with?"

"Oh no, no, it's fine," Stacey said, "You just sit down and chill out, I'll have this all ready in no time."

Beth and Sarah arrived in a noisy clamour; Sarah in good form and regaling the others of her tales. Stacey looked relaxed and happy, as though she'd taken a shine to all the girls already.

Amy went to the kitchen to get more wine, and Jamie followed her in.

"Thanks Amy,"

"What for?" she asked.

"Oh you know… letting me stay on... letting Stacey stay... inviting the girls over… just basically for being … wonderful."

The expression on his face was funny – different, Amy thought. The way he said 'wonderful' – it wasn't just any 'wonderful' – it wasn't just a throw-away 'wonderful' – it was a *loaded* wonderful. There was something else in his eyes.

Amy blinked it away. No, she was being silly. Jamie was just being friendly. And Stacey was sitting in the next room in her expensive Karen Millen dress to impress him. There was nothing wonderful about his 'wonderful' comment.

Even though Amy could not help herself thinking, "Is this Jamie one *that* great in bed? What *exactly* does he do to merit the 'Oh Jamie Oh Jamie Oh Jamie' comments?"

And just when she was wiping the surfaces, telling herself not to be so ridiculous, he brushed past her. It was accidental. The layer of the front of his jeans brushing lightly through the thin material of her skin. The front of his denim brushing lightly against the lightness material lining her bottom. And she felt something. A fizzle. A moment. There was definitely a moment.

"Oh, sorry," he said lightly, as her face turned to find his directly behind hers.

"Sorry," she repeated, her eyes lowering.

And when they returned to the table, Amy's face was still glowering red with heat, and even among the noise and the chatter and the carry-on, Sarah spotted it.

Sarah caught her eye, and glanced from Amy to Jamie, and back again.

Chapter Twenty
<u>SARAH</u>

The texts from Stephen were still coming thick and fast.

"Hey hunny... please... let's talk...x"

Delete.

"I'm here if you change your mind...x"

Delete.

"You know you want to...x"

Delete. Delete. Delete.

In the end, Sarah decided to block his number. Her head was too scrambled, and she believed the only way she'd ever move forward, was to delete his number for good.

She would have liked to think it was her own emotional maturity and business-like attitude that gave her the notion to do this, but actually it was her old friend Jill.

Sarah had phoned Jill and told her briefly about the bumping-into-Stephen day, and since then, Jill had continued to keep phoning Sarah to check that she was okay.

They met up in a bar in town, one of those ones with the beer garden and the large umbrellas, and a chance for Sarah to hide behind her dark sunglasses in a cloud of look-how-much-my-self-esteem-has-dwindled-away-to-nothing.

"So how are you feeling about everything now?" Jill asked, when they were on their third glass of white wine and they had outdone all the small talk of weather, summer clothes, children's clothes, work, Jill's husband, and weather again.

Sarah put her head in her hands and answered, "I just feel like such a fool..."

"Why?" Jill asked simply. "Because you fell in love and you chose to believe what he told you?"

Sarah took a deep breath. "Yeah, I guess."

Jill shrugged her shoulders. "Been there, done that."

There was a silence then. A moment of shock while Sarah processed this information. Sparkly, shiny Jill. With the perfect image and the twinkling engagement ring. Perfect Jill had been the other woman.

"What? When?" Sarah began.

"It was a long time ago now. I was young. I was naïve. It was a lesson."

"And what happened?" Sarah asked, intrigued. "And more importantly, how did you get over it?"

And that was the evening Jill told Sarah her story. Of how she was the other woman. Of how she spent weeks and months of sneaking around, coming and going, believing his lies, wanting to believe his lies, hoping that they weren't lies, hoping that secretly he did love her, hoping that secretly it wasn't just all about sex. Moments of intense pain and intense pleasure, highs and lows, ups and downs, a veritable emotional roller-coaster of adrenalin filled frenzy.

"You make it sound like a good thing!" Sarah replied, almost huffily.

"In many ways it was," Jill shrugged simply. "And that's what I had to see. That secretly I loved it all. That buzz. That excitement. That's why I kept going back for more. That's what I had to see – that I am responsible for my own actions – I chose to play the game."

"How did it all stop?"

"I had to come to see that it was my choice. The warning signs were there all along and I chose to ignore them. Her name had been mentioned and I chose to block it out. The only way I could get over the experience was to take my own responsibility for it."

Bad Times #2

Sarah and Stephen were cooking in the kitchen of Stephen's new flat. Correction, Sarah was cooking and Stephen was loitering around, poking his nose in the direction of the saucepans, sniffing, saying, "mmm..." and grabbing a feel of Sarah's boobs while he did so.

She giggled and swatted his hands away.

"You can have some when it's ready," she flirted.

"Mmm...can't wait," he grinned at her.

They ate, side by side on the sofa, with their plates perched on their laps and the TV chattering away in the background.

It was one of those moments, Sarah thought, that were perfect. One of those moments when she wished time would stand still, like a pause button on her sky player, and she could sit like that forever, savouring the moment.

But then the doorbell rang, and Stephen jumped up, setting his dinner plate on the floor, and traipsing down the hallway.

Sarah heard voices. Children's voices, and a woman's voice. Kat and the kids.

They came bounding down the corridor and suddenly Kat's face was there, like a territorial spy, sniffing out the enemy.

In those few short seconds, her eyes had taken in Sarah, the dinner on her lap, Stephen's dinner, the pots and pans, the comforting aroma of domesticity. She even wandered over to the hob and took in the sight of the contents of said pots and pans. And, if Sarah was not mistaken, there was even a curl of her lip, as though disgusted.

Kat turned on her heel and disappeared down the hallway again, calling Stephen behind her, and leaving Stephen's daughter sitting on the sofa next to Sarah. The daughter looked up at Sarah with curious eyes. She seemed impressed with her clothes, her make-up, her hair.

"Do you like my doll?" she asked.

She held up her rag doll, the leg of which was hanging off

and the eye of which had disappeared.

"She's beautiful," Sarah smiled.

"Like you," the daughter said, in earnest.

Sarah felt a tear threaten to sting at the corner of her eye.

"Are you daddy's friend?"

Sarah nodded. "Yes."

Voices were raised at the end of the hallway. Stephen and Kat must have been standing on the doorstep, arguing.

Sarah thought she could hear the words, "cooking" and "dinner" and "what about me," but that was all she could hear. She was also trying to entertain her new best friend, Stephen's daughter.

"What's your name?"

"Sarah"

"Well, that is what I am going to call my doll – Sarah," the daughter smiled, a big toothy smile, and Sarah could feel a lump rising in her throat.

All of a sudden, Kat appeared in the doorway, large and threatening and obtrusive.

"Come on. We're going home," she announced, sternly.

"Aw! I'm playing with Sarah! Look! My doll is called Sarah!"

"We. Are. Going. Home." Kat spat.

The little girl withered away, quietly trailing behind Kat and giving Sarah a small, quiet smile on her way out.

The memory made Sarah feel sick. Literally nauseatingly sick.

I knew fine well what was going on.

How could I have pretended that it was all so innocent?

How could I have stuck cotton wool in my ears and blind-folds over my eyes?

She had imagined that Kat and Stephen's 'argument' had gone like this;

Kat: *Why are you cooking for her and not me? You never used to cook for me. How come you're cooking for her all of a sudden?*

Stephen: Oh come on Kat... Look, I'm sorry, but you're going to have to accept it — Sarah is my girlfriend now — that is why I am living here — so that I can spend time with her.

When in actual fact, the conversation probably actually went like this;

Kat: Why are you cooking for her and not me? You never used to cook for me. How come you're cooking for her all of a sudden?
Stephen: Oh come on Kat... She's just a mate — we're just hanging out together — and anyway, she is the one cooking for me — she just likes cooking. God Kat! Am I not allowed to have female friends now?

Bad Times #3

Sarah was sitting in Stephen's back garden. She was in a scantily clad bikini and he was in shorts. They lay on sun loungers. The heat was beating down, making Sarah feel relaxed and horny. That, and the fact that Stephen was gently massaging oil on her body, making soft, circular movements up her legs, dangerously close to her groin area, over her stomach, tantalisingly near her breasts. Her insides were pulsating. Her nerve endings were practically shouting out, "Shag me now!"

Except this time, a noise at the door went again, and this time H appeared, letting herself in with her front door key, shouting "Halllooooo!" as she careered down the hallway, and finally found them both outside on the sun loungers.

Stephen seemed flustered, as though he'd been caught in the act. Sarah realised this in hindsight, but at the time, she had put it down to sexual frustration.

So H appeared, in her short skirt, her pink knee-high socks and her tanned legs. She may as well have had her hair in pigtails and a lollipop in her mouth to finish the look.

Stephen jumped up and said, "Oh! Hello! Come in! Can I get you a drink?"

H had smiled, confidently, lay down on Stephen's sun-lounger, and said, "Oh yeah! A drink would be lovely thanks!" and she'd adjusted herself on the sun lounger, peeling off her top until it was just her bra underneath.

"This is one glorious day!" she beamed, wriggling about as though to soak up the rays. She even lifted up a leg, peeled off a sock, and let Stephen catch a glimpse of her panties beneath her skirt.

"Right, well, I'll get the drinks," Stephen gulped.

Sarah decided that the only way to cope with all this head-melting, fecked-up situation, was to get drunk, very drunk. And drink they did. All afternoon and into the evening, until somehow they ended up in a pub across the way, playing pool and H sliding her bum up in the air so that all the punters could get a view up her skirt.

The memories were coming back thick and fast as Sarah and Jill drank on and discussed it. Sarah felt that there must be a neon sign above her head which read;

"I am a Fool"

"Fool is me"

"How thick am I?"

The only comfort she was receiving was from Jill, who tried to console her that at least she had woken up to the reality of the situation, and she would be more careful in future.

Sarah hoped so because the more she looked back on the Stephen episode; the more repelled she was by the blinkers she had on.

<u>Opportunities to End It #1</u>

The very first night Sarah met Stephen. When they had met at a party, and Stephen had drunkenly confided in her, "Kat and me... We live together, we sleep in a bed together... but we don't sleep together."

The party was in London. Stephen had disappeared from Brighton for the night to go clubbing with his mates Andy and Rick. After the club they ended up back at Rick's place in Richmond, having picked up a few of Rick's work mates along the way, Sarah being one of them.

"Well aren't you looking very hot indeed," Stephen had said, as they'd found themselves sitting side by side on the comfy sofa.

The music was playing, the lights were low, other people were too wrapped up in their own little conversations to notice Stephen and Sarah's flirting. It was just the two of them. In their own little happy flirty bubble.

"Well thank you sir," Sarah giggled.

It was Saturday night, she was tipsy to the point of being drunk, she had a week off work where she planned to do little else but sleep, eat and chill out. She was happy.

"Not looking too bad yer'self," she grinned, flirtatiously.

"'Yerself'? Is that an Irish accent I hear?"

Sarah bit her lip and nodded.

"Mmm... I love an Irish accent. Talk more and talk slowly."

She giggled, then relaxed, then lounged back into the sofa next to him, talking slowly and talking crap.

"Hi, my name is Sarah and I'm from Belfast. What's the craic with ye?"

He turned his head immediately to face her, so that his eyes were up close next to hers. The inhibitions had flown out the window long ago, probably along with the fourth drink in All Bar One.

There was no interview panel that night. No long mahogany

table with three Sarahs wearing intelligent looking glasses and holding hefty assessment folders. No questions like;

"And where is this chin-wag going to lead us mister flirt-bag?"

Into the sack, that's where.

"And what happens after the sack?"

I pull my clothes on and disappear and you won't hear from me again for ages.

"And what would be the point of all that exactly?"

Because it's fun. And exciting. And there's nothing more exhilarating than the sight of a fresh pair of breasts. There's nothing more deeply satisfying than the feel of your hair tickling down my body as you kiss your way down towards my...

"Yowsers!"

Indeed.

"Well then now what?"

And that was how they disappeared off to her place, not needing to say much, for their eyes did all the talking. There was the taxi, and her hand on his shirted chest as he kissed her, her insides melting like ice-cream disappearing on a hot summer's day.

There were the stairs, and the door closing behind them, and him kissing her the minute they stepped foot inside her bedroom door.

It was one of the suited girls on the interview panel that tried to pipe up something about Kat and the living together but it was her insides pulsing and the disappearance of the inhibitions that had flown out the window long ago that made her melt, and sink onto her bed, and to hell with it...

Amount of magnetic force Sarah had towards Stephen that night = 10

Amount of magnetic force Sarah should have had towards Stephen that night = 0

His Lack of emotional availability making him even more of a challenge = 10

It was Jill who pointed this out to her.

"If he had said, 'Yeah, I live on my own, with my cat and two goldfish, and all I need now is a woman to finish off the picture and be the mother of my children so that we can live together in perfect harmony for the rest of our lives,' you would have run a mile in the other direction."

"Really?" Sarah was surprised. "But that is what I want. I want to get married and settle down."

"Ah…" Jill said. "You *think* you want that, but you don't really. Really the thought of a committed relationship scares the feck out of you – otherwise you'd be in one."

If a bloke was really keen to settle down with you pronto, the following thoughts would be going through your head:

1. He's really keen on me. What's wrong with him? Why hasn't he been snapped up sooner?
2. He wants to settle down. Shit. That means responsibility. And commitment. And having to be accountable to someone.
3. Fear. What if I get hurt? What if I marry him and he ends up having an affair?
4. Boredom. What if I am to be consigned to a life of slippers in front of the TV and no sex?
5. What if there'll be no more drama, excitement, fun, challenge?
6. If someone says, "Here, take me," it's a bit like being given a free lunch, or a sale item – there's no value in it. Whereas if it's a challenge, and something you had to work for, you respect it more, and appreciate it more.
7. Fear. What if I'm stuck with this one guy for the rest of my life? And what if I wake up one morning and suddenly the sex is crap, or I've gone off him – and then I'm stuck with him?

Reasons why he's more appealing when he doesn't want to settle down with you:

1.Your subconscious thinks, "Ha! A challenge! Cool! How can I play a game with him and get him to change his mind?"

2.What do you mean, you don't want me? I am fabulous! What's wrong with you? How can I convince you of my loveliness?

3.Quickly followed by: am I not fabulous? Oh no, maybe I'm not! What do I need to change about myself? How can I become lovely?

4.Self-will – akin to throwing dolls out of the pram. Why isn't everything going my way?

5.Ego. This cannot be possible. Why would he want anyone else when I am on the scene? Houston – we have a problem!

Chapter Twenty-One
<u>JAMIE</u>

Beth and Sarah left just after 2am. Amy went to bed straightaway. Stacey grabbed Jamie by the tail of his shirt and said, "Come on big boy, take me to bed," as though she was some kind of femme fatale.

"Erm Stace... by the way...we can't ... you know... have sex tonight..."

"Why not?" Stacey asked, her eyes widening with that puppy dog expression that she always used.

"We just can't... make the noise... " Jamie squirmed. "Amy heard us having sex last night."

Stacey's hand shot up to her dropped-open mouth. "No way! Oh God! Oh God how embarrassing! Oh no! I didn't realise! I'm mortified!"

Jamie nodded.

"And is that what it is?" Stacey went on. "Is that what it is with us – just sex?"

Jamie looked at her, confused. *Was she really wanting to start a conversation like this at two o'clock in the morning? Two o'clock in the morning after copious drinks, a huge feed, very little sleep the night before and her due to head home in the morning?*

"Sorry?" Jamie asked, stalling for time.

"Is it just sex, or is it making love?" she asked, pointedly. No embarrassment from this one, just direct inquisition.

"Oh come on Stacey. It's late. You're tired..." Jamie trailed off.

"No," she persisted, her arms folded now. "I want to know

Jamie… what is this? What is *this?" She gestured her hands around her as though surveying the room. "What are we doing?"*

Jamie sighed, ran his fingers through his hair and said, "We are sitting in Amy's living room at two o'clock on a Sunday morning, drunk, talking crap – that is what we are doing."

Jamie knew he was being facetious. In fact, he didn't know who he was more annoyed at – Stacey, or himself. *Why had he done this? Why had he invited Stacey here? Was it not just some last-ditch attempt to make Amy jealous? Was it some need to feel wanted and fancied when Amy was obviously so oblivious to him? Was it not just for the sake of it? In which case, didn't that, quite rightly, make him an utter cad? A cad or just a guy wanting a bit of company? Wanting a bit of company with a woman who was readily available to give it to him? Readily available to him yet interrogating him now at silly o'clock in the morning.*

"Come on hun," he whispered softly, hoping that the 'hun' word would appease her, which indeed it seemed to. She seemed to visibly relax her shoulders at the sound of that word. "Let's just go to bed. We'll talk about it tomorrow."

"Okay," Stacey took his hand and let him lead her to bed.

The following morning, Stacey was due to get the twelve mid-day train from Waterloo to Gatwick and then on to Brighton. But there was a problem.

"I've lost my keys!" she exclaimed, as she rummaged through her hold-all, searching frantically.

"What?" Jamie asked. "But how?"

He watched her flap up and down the bedroom.

"Wait a minute – think back – you must have had them to lock the door on your way out?"

"No," Stacey shook her head. "No. My flatmate Jenny let me out. I distinctly remember her waving me off – so she must've locked the door behind me."

"Okay. Okay," Jamie said, his hands performing a little

dance in front of him. "So, your keys are safe somewhere? They must be in your house?"

"Yes," Stacey nodded. "They must be."

"Right!" Jamie grinned. "So, just phone Jenny and she can let you in?"

"Erm… one problem…" Stacey looked anxious, perplexed, and if Jamie wasn't imagining it, even a bit guilty looking. "… she's not home until tomorrow…I'll have to stay here another night."

Jamie blew out a low whistle and sat on the bed.

"Shit," he found himself saying, accidentally, before he looked up to see the face of thunder that had now lined itself across Stacey's face.

"Well, I'm sorry that that's so awful for you!" she blurted out, as though there had been a torrent of doubt bubbling under her skin for days and now it found a means to escape. "I am sorry that I am such a *burden!*"

She said *burden* as though she were a child, having a tantrum, as though she just needed to accompany it with a kick against the door and sticking her thumb in her mouth.

"I'm sorry babe," Jamie replied. *Babe? Where did that come from? He never called her babe?* "I'm sorry, I don't mean it like that. I just mean that I feel bad having to ask Amy… I feel bad imposing on her…"

Why did he feel like he was permanently on defence with this girl? As though he were in goalpost trying to fend off every football that came his way?

She softened too. "You're right. I'm sorry. I'm just panicking… and I think I must be pmt'ed… I'm just feeling a bit emotional today… and my tummy feels all bloated… so I must be pmt'ed… and … oh god…"

And then it came. The waterworks. Followed by an "Oh my god Jamie… I am so sorry… Imagine crying in front of you… please just give me a hug…" She went to him with outstretched arms, and he awkwardly put his arms around her.

134

"There, there," he hushed, gently patting her back and not knowing what else to do. "Don't worry about your keys. We'll phone Jenny and get it all sorted".

Stacey buried her head into his chest, tears leaking over his shirt. "Thank you", she snivelled, blowing her nose and giving him an embarrassed look. "Oh dear.. what a way to act in front of your boyfriend eh?"

Jamie gulped. *Boyfriend? Boyfriend? At what point had they discussed him being a boyfriend?*

Suddenly he felt the walls closing in on him. He felt his breathing quicken. He felt like he needed the window opened and a big gulp of air.

"I have an idea!" Stacey piped up.

Jamie brightened at her sudden liveliness. *Great! Ideas! Plans! Fun!*

"Let's go to Tesco and do a great big shop and make a nice big meal for Amy tonight again – as a thank you for her letting me stay another night?"

Jamie's heart sank immediately.

A Sunday afternoon. Trekking around Tesco with a trolley. Screaming kids everywhere. Analysing labels on food containers. Shoved into shopping aisles like sardines into a tin.

Gone was his idyllic Sunday. Lying on a sofa playing with his PSP. Amy on tap. Parading around the apartment in her hot pants. He even fantasised that added to the hot pants was a low fitting vest top exposing a little bit of cleavage. That magically she would be skating around on roller boots, carrying a tray with a bottle of Budweiser on. Leaning over to serve him the Budweiser whilst showing a little bit more of her cleavage whilst doing so, and making suggestive gestures with the bottle in her mouth. In his fantasy, Gav would have been killed off in a blood & guts style violent movie-scene-type-way. Amy would have grieved for about – ooh – five minutes – and during these five vulnerable minutes, Jamie would have loaned a very sympathetic and very sexual shoulder. Amy – so much in gratitude for his kindliness – would've shagged him as a thank you. And then in shagging him, would've decided that he was so utterly fantastic in bed that there just would never be any need to shag anyone else ever again amen – and she would be readily available for him any time he wanted.

"Don't forget your Tesco club-card," Stacey said, breaking him out of his reverie.

"What? ... Oh. er... right..."

Stacey looked at him sternly. "Were you listening to *one* word I said?"

"Of course I was babe," Jamie piped up quickly. *Babe? Why did this keep tripping off his tongue so casually?*

"Then what did I say?" she asked in an accusatory manner. She might as well have been pointing her finger and standing with her other hand on her hip.

"Um..."

"No," Stacey said sternly, like a teacher to a child. "I thought not."

Jamie sighed, wishing he could press a button to teleport himself into his perfect fantasy life, and said, "Come on then. Tesco here we come."

They trudged around Tesco. There were families galore. Shopping trolleys. Push-chairs. Random toddlers appearing out of nowhere waiting to be trampled on. Screaming children. Babies crying. It was hell.

"Oooooh! ... Look at that baby!" Stacey cooed. "How adorable!" She looked over at Jamie, expecting him to agree with her. His face was blank. "Look at the little bib! Look at it! It says 'Daddy's girl'! How cute!"

There was a pause then. As though Jamie was expected to say something. As though there was a missing script that he should have been handed on the way in.

"Don't you think?" Stacey probed.

"Er... not really... Not my thing..." Jamie grunted. He was tired now. Tired and fed up. More than anything, he just wanted to be left alone. Gloriously, deliciously, alone.

"Time's ticking on," Stacey announced, "You'll have to think about children one day."

Jamie tightened his hands around the handle of the trolley and made an abrupt turn into the next aisle.

All of a sudden, he heard the prison doors slam shut, the bolt sliding over, and the key turning in the lock. His typical Sunday of playing PSP, lounging around with his flatmate, eating pizza, drinking beer, had been snatched away from him from beneath his very feet. She might as well have been saying, "Here's your slippers and pipe, hang up your coat, your monthly pay packet is now mine, we'll be needing it for all our babies."

Was this girl for real? And how had it come to this? Traipsing around Tesco on a Sunday with some girl lecturing me about how I need to have babies? There is something very, very wrong. Yer man upstairs is playing some horrific cosmic joke. A joke I am very tired of. This is enough. As of tonight, I am going to have to sit her down and give her a severe talking to. This 'thing'... this 'boyfriend thing' ... is over. So well and truly over.

Chapter Twenty-Two
SARAH

They say that in times of relationship break-ups, work suddenly becomes an obsession. And so it was with Sarah.

For some reason, obsessing about work enabled her to flick a switch in her head from "constant thoughts about Stephen" to "constant thoughts about work." It was the lesser of two evils. It made her feel in control. It prevented painful, agonising thoughts of "what's wrong with me?" and "why doesn't he want me?" creeping in. The minute those thoughts crept in, she flicked the switch and thought about work, and that blocked everything else out.

Of course she knew it was a temporary situation. Of course she knew that one day she would have to sit down and think about what went wrong with Stephen, but later maybe, when things weren't so raw and painful, and she could be all grown up and mature about it, instead of wanting to poke things in his eyes and shove sharp objects up his backside. Yes, later. Later she'd be able to be all mature and spiritual about it and tell herself comforting emotionally mature things like, "there are just people for people" and "perhaps he has his own issues with commitment and intimacy." That would all come in time hopefully, but right at the moment, she was happy to bury her head in the sand of work and try to build her bludgeoning self-esteem by climbing the career ladder.

First things first, she knew she could not spend another day stuffing envelopes if she was to keep her sanity intact. The boredom and monotony of envelope sticking was making her mind drift back towards Stephen, and that was a no-go area. She sat down with her friend Jill one night and the two of them worked on re-doing Sarah's CV, highlighting with great exaggeration the marketing skills she had.

"Chief envelope-stuffer" became "organised mail merge documents and wide marketing campaign."

"Answering the phone" became "superb communication skills."

"Typing letters" became "RSA stage III in audio & copy typing."

By the end of the three hours, several cups of coffee and a mound of chocolate energy supplies, Sarah had an impressive CV worthy of any recruitment agency.

Next stop, she arranged a week off work and a packed schedule of traipsing round numerous recruitment agencies to offer her CV, do typing tests, have mini interviews and convince them of her expertise and enthusiasm. She dressed smartly in a suit and smart heels, treating each recruitment agent as though they were prospective employers. She gave herself little breaks in coffee shops, filling up on caffeine and snacks to bolster her energy and enthusiasm. And by the end of the week, she had signed up with an impressive eight agents, promising herself to make regular calls to chase up and make them aware of her interest.

Occasionally, thoughts of Stephen did creep into her head. When she'd be walking down the high street and would suddenly have a momentary panic that Stephen and Kat would appear, horror movie like, with Kat in a huge meringue wedding dress which would suddenly lift up and swallow Sarah in one go. That panic came and went, with Sarah repeating to herself, "Things are going to get better. Things are going to get better. Things are going to get better."

And they did!

An agent phoned her back about a marketing job in a company called Beauty Select!

Honestly, it sounded too good to be true. Marketing assistant for a bright pink shop that sold a range of girlie products – feathery things, accessories, hen night fancy dress, vibrators, false nails, handbags, cute accessories for the house, fairylights, *everything*.

Sarah was given an interview.

She wore a smart outfit that managed to have a creative 'flair' to it as well – to show her professionalism as well as her creativity. She wore a dark purple suit, with purple heels, a purple bag with sequins, and her hair held back with a purple feathery clip.

"Perfect," Jill quipped, as she perused her, giving her a final pep talk before she headed off.

"Be professional yet friendly. Give a good friendly smile and eye contact – oh, a good firm handshake. Try to answer her questions as best as you can – but try to stay relaxed too – all she's wanting to do is to get an impression of your personality. She already likes the look of your CV."

Sarah nodded. Armed with her knowledge and having dressed smartly, she stepped out into the big bad world, ready to take it by storm.

The marketing manager interviewing her was Tasha. She was gorgeous. Glossy hair. Sparkling eyes. Neat little bump. Sarah guessed her to be about six months pregnant but didn't dare to speculate in-case she was horribly wrong. She just had this 'air' about her. A softness, a pleasantness, a genuine friendliness. The pair of them clicked, over the subject of chocolate.

It was Sarah who'd spotted the bag of Cadburys moments, a new selection of chocolate circles that had come out only a few weeks previously.

"Oh! Do you like those too? They are my favourite!"

Tasha's eyes widened. "Aren't they the best?! I must admit, I have been eating nearly two packs a day! They are fast becoming my regular eleven o'clock coffee snack!"

Sarah laughed. "They're fantastic!" she grinned. "And this

shop is fantastic! It's so cute!"

Tasha beamed. "Do you like it? It's so cute and girlie. It's like another little world to me. I just love creating this atmosphere where women can step into another world for half an hour and it's girlie and cute and fun and it takes them out of their problems for a while."

Sarah nodded. "It's a fantastic idea. You really do get a sense of being propelled into something fun and happy and girlie."

Tasha beamed again, glad to see that her efforts had paid off, that the aura she had tried to create did in fact work.

The pair of them chatted for nearly an hour. About the structure of the shop, about how that it was the head office, about how there were sister branches throughout the UK opening up, about the exciting new venture that Tasha had created. Sarah did not realise an hour had passed. It was only when there was a knock on the door and a girl popped her head around the door and said, "Tasha? Your next appointment is waiting?" that Sarah realised. They had gone over time. Which was surely a good sign?

"Oh!" Tasha exclaimed, looking at her watch. "Tell her I'm sorry, I'll be with her soon."

Tasha smiled at Sarah, "Well, it's been really great to meet you – and I feel really inspired with all the marketing ideas. I'll be in touch with the agency and I'll let you know about the job as soon as possible." She stretched out a hand to shake hers, which Sarah did, firmly.

"Thank you, and do keep me posted. It's a fantastic job and I would be very keen, should you be interested."

It was putting her vulnerability on the line but she didn't care, she had a good feeling about it.

She stepped outside the shop, knowing, *just knowing,* that she would get the job. She wouldn't have confided that to anyone of course, but she just had a feeling, a very strong feeling, that the job was hers. She also knew that she'd love to work with Tasha. There was something about her demeanour, her attitude, her pleasant personality, that appealed to Sarah. The two of them clicked. They fired ideas off each other in a way that was magical.

I'd love to work with her, I'd love to work with her, I'd love to work with her.

Sure enough, the telephone call came the next morning at 9.30am. Sarah excused herself from her envelope stuffing and found a quiet space in the corridor to take the call.

"Hey Sarah," the recruitment agent smiled. "You got the job!"

Sarah's hand shot up to her mouth. "Oh my God! That's fantastic! I'm so pleased!" she grinned.

They talked about money and start dates and P45's and other work related things, and then that was it! Time for Sarah to go in and hand in her resignation! Time for her to sit in a pink cloud bubble for the rest of the day.

A good job! A job I'll love! A place I'll love! Getting more to do! A challenge! Moving up the career ladder! More money! Happy days!

On her lunch break she phoned Jamie and Amy and Beth and Jill to tell them the happy news.

After work, she treated herself to a little shopping spree where she bought some work related clothes. Clothes that were creative and colourful yet smart and professional at the same time. And then she met Jill for celebratory cocktails. And by the time she had put her head on the pillow that night, she realised that she hadn't given Stephen a second thought all day. Or even a first thought either.

Tasha was a joy to work with. Encouraging, motivating, professional. She gave Sarah good training and guidance, yet allowed her to be an independent thinker too. She was pleasant and kind to her, allowing her to take regular breaks and feel relaxed in the job, yet offering good advice and management to help Sarah feel motivated and directed.

Tasha was a woman of character. She treated people with respect. She seemed to go into her day wondering who she could help. From her staff, to people she spoke to on the phone, to people who came in with deliveries, to her husband. She was girlie and glamorous and dressed well and was presentable, yet she wasn't arrogant. She just seemed to like looking and feeling nice.

Sarah never heard her speak a bad word about anybody. She tried to see the positive in everyone. She also never said a bad word about her husband, which might have sounded like common sense, and yet Sarah was surprised at how many women seemed disgruntled with their husbands and spent copious hours complaining about his inability to put the dishes away or throw his socks in the laundry basket. Tasha was not like this however. And when customers or suppliers seemed angry or pent up on the phone, they would be put through to Tasha, who seemed to notice their distress, be immediately helpful and accommodating to them, and by the time the conversation was over, the person would be putty in her hands.

When her husband Tom appeared in the shop, Tasha had a knack of looking like she had dropped all things work related and switched her attention to her man. She had an ability to make him feel manly and respected and fancied and the most important person in the room. Conversely, she would often receive a bunch of flowers delivered for her to the shop, or a surprise night out to dinner where he would just arrive impromptu at closing time and say, "I have a table booked".

This made Sarah marvel.

Tasha and Tom became Sarah's secret new role model couple. They showed her, without having to say anything directly to her, that it was possible, quite possible, to have a healthy and happy relationship. They gave her hope.

Tom was gorgeous. The pair of them were gorgeous. They

had been dating since they were seventeen. He looked like something that had stepped out of a catalogue. He had female friends. Friends he went to lunch with. And yet, Tasha felt secure with him. Sarah marvelled at that. Sarah wondered, cynically, if Tom ever invited girls to his back garden, got horny with them, and then pretended they were just friends.

"Don't you ever worry?" Sarah found herself asking, when she'd been working there for a while, and she and Tasha had settled into a comfortable groove with each other, and they'd gone out for a relaxing dinner after work.

"I mean, I know you're gorgeous an' all, but don't you ever worry that other women might try to come on to him?"

"No," Tasha smiled simply. "No, I honestly don't. Tom's not that type of fella. He's friendly, yeah, but he's not flirty. Also, I know he loves me for my whole package. It's not just about looks and sex – it's about personality and chemistry and common interests and our whole lives together – we're like best friends as well as lovers – I know he loves our life too much to throw it all away on a one night stand."

"Anyway," Tasha went on, "Tom probably wouldn't know how to go about chatting anyone up! And do you know what? Even if he did, even if we split up, as horrible as it would be – I would be okay. My world wouldn't fall apart. I'd have my friends and family to help me."

Interesting. So Tasha and Tom became role models for Sarah. And Sarah started to see that maybe, possibly, it might be possible to have a healthy, happy relationship.

Chapter Twenty-Three
<u>JAMIE</u>

Stacey left in a flurry the following morning. Phoning work to tell them she'd be late. Phoning Jenny to double-check she'd be there to let her in. Giving Jamie a spiel of questions:

"When will I see you again?"

"You're home soon, aren't you?"

"One week to go? Well hurry back – you'll be home on the Friday night then, yeah? You'll head straight home on Friday after work? I could cook us a nice dinner and get a bottle of wine?"

But the thing was, Jamie was hoping he could hang out with Amy that weekend – have one last weekend together before he'd be gone. One last weekend before it might be another number of years until he saw her again.

But he decided not to get into that discussion with Stacey right now. Especially as he was planning a way to let her down gently. A way to break things off in a nice way, if that was possible.

And it was when he was in the hallway, popping in briefly from the kitchen to ask Stacey if she wanted some toast with her coffee, that he caught a glimpse of her in the bedroom, doing something that even he was surprised to see her doing.

Stacey was transferring a bunch of keys from the bottom of her suitcase into her handbag. Her house keys. The keys that she had 'lost' just the day before.

She looked up in shock when he entered the room, clearly not expecting him to return from his coffee making duties so

145

quickly.

"Your keys!" Jamie exclaimed suddenly, triumphantly even, as though she had honestly literally just found them.

Her face contorted into an awkward shape – travelling through the different emotions – firstly horror, that she had been found out, then flaming red with embarrassment, followed quickly by feigned shock. As though she had only just found them too. As though it wasn't a desperate folly that they'd been tucked in the bottom of her suitcase all along.

"Yeah!" she said, her eyes widening. "Goodness me! They were here all along! How stupid am I? Oh dear! I feel so silly!"

Jamie didn't know what to say. He felt rooted to the spot. First the horror that she would lie to him, that she would be so desperate to spend a bit more time with him that she would go to those lengths – the lengths of lying about lost keys – and secondly, the shock. The shock that someone would be that obsessed with little old him that they would go to those lengths – it didn't make sense. He was just him. Him who drank too much and lay around eating pizza. Him who eyed up every girl in a short skirt and a low top. Him who didn't have an ounce of gentlemanliness, never read any classics, never even really bothered watching the news, had no inclination to have children, and thought that the only good things about weddings were getting drunk and eyeing up the bridesmaids. He was no Mr Darcy.

But that was the thing. He knew Stacey's obsession was nothing about him and everything about her. And that was why he pretended not to notice the keys incident and just said, "Well, that's great – at least you found them."

The drive to the train station was in silence. There was a brief hug before she headed towards the platform. But there was little said. In fact, Jamie realised that they both knew, this was the
beginning of the end.

Jamie and Amy did decide on a Saturday hang-out day.

"One last day before I don't see you for another ten years," Jamie had said, wording it as though it were dramatic, eventful. The end.

Amy rolled her eyes playfully.

"Okay, great – a fun day out and then I finally get rid of you."

Jamie gave her a pretend pout. "Have I been that bad?"

Amy nodded. "Yes – and worse." She rhymed off a list of faults: "Smelly socks on the bathroom floor. Crap choice in TV programs. Talk crap. Drink too much. And bring unsuitable guests. You remind me of why I love being single and having a place to myself."

Jamie feigned being wounded.

"Okay," he grinned. "Let's have a good day out and I'll make it up to you."

They started off in Covent Garden, strolling around the cobbled streets, wandering into different shops, Amy picking up items of clothing and Jamie saying, "You'd suit that." Amy disappearing off into the changing room to try the items on, Jamie sitting on the plush sofas outside, trying to catch a glimpse of her half-naked body behind the curtain. The sales assistant coming over and saying, "Does your girlfriend need a hand with different sizes?"

Jamie smiling and just saying, "No thanks, we're fine." Not bothering to go into an explanation with the sales assistant girl. Not bothering to feel he should say, "Oh.. no.. you see.. you don't understand... she is not my girlfriend.. she is a girl I had a crush on the whole way through uni.. and then we didn't see each other for years.. YEARS! Can you imagine? And now we see each other again and I fancy her just as much as ever .. and I'm pretty sure there's chemistry. except.. well... she's mad abut some twat... some bloke... and I was kinda seeing this girl... except it didn't really work out... so now we're just hanging out here today as mates ... before I head home tomorrow... and it'll probably be years before I see her again..."

Jamie was thinking all that but of course he didn't say it to the sales assistant. Of course he just said, "Oh no… it's okay... We're fine thanks."

He was interested at his use of the royal "we" but then forgot about that when Amy emerged from the changing room twirling around in a fabulous outfit. A short skirt with ruffles that tickled either side of her lovely slender toned legs, a top that was tied under the boobs and floated down to her waist, a top that dipped slightly in between her cleavage showing only the slightest hint of curved lines.

"Gorgeous," Jamie declared. Matter of factly. "Buy it."

As an after-thought, he realised that Gav would probably get the full benefit of the gorgeous outfit and on second thoughts he should have swayed her from buying it, but it was too late, her credit card was slapped on the counter and the girl with the long sparkly nails was whizzing it through the machine.

Off they strolled, stopping occasionally to watch the street performers, the man sprayed in gold and standing as still as a statue until a young child threw a coin at his feet and watched him jump to life. A young man drawing pictures on the ground with charcoal that made the ground look as though there was a hole in it with pipework underneath. Three clowns tottering around on stilts. The sun was out, music was being played, and Jamie and Amy were strolling around without a care in the world. The only thing to make it complete now would be if Jamie was to drape his arm around her shoulder and walk about, with everyone thinking, "Oooh… look at him with that hot girl…" and him knowing that they would go home and fall into bed and have slow delicious sex.

That would be what would make it complete.

But instead they went for dinner. A fancy spot that was large and sprawling with huge plants and big artistic paintings on the wall. There was a huge chandelier hanging from the ceiling and massive wine glasses on the tables.

"Ooooh! This is lovely!" Amy cooed, as the waiter showed them their seats.

"Very posh indeed," Jamie agreed.

"What'll I have…" Amy thought aloud as she perused the menu. "I'm starving."

That was the thing about Amy that Jamie loved. She loved her food. She loved her food and she relished eating it. She didn't, like Stacey, pick at food and complain constantly, "I shouldn't eat so much. I should be careful." She didn't grab her (non-existent) belly and poke at it accusatorially. She didn't say things like, "Look at that! Stretch marks! The onset of stretch marks!" She wouldn't then get annoyed if Jamie examined her stomach to look for the aforementioned stretch marks. He realised, too late, that he was supposed to say, "Stretch marks? What stretch marks? Don't be silly! Of course you have no stretch marks! You have a delectable figure to die for young lady!" He didn't know he was supposed to say all that. He often wished someone could have given him the imaginary script he was supposed to know, on the way in, just so he could be prepared.

"Steak and chips," Amy smiled to the waiter. "Thank you very much."

The waiter smiled back and disappeared, and the two of them settled into chit-chat. Chat about nothing really – music, films, what's on the TV that night, chat about the painting on the wall and the fact that the woman's breast looked a bit lop-sided. Chat about nothing in particular – and that was what was so gloriously refreshing. There was no intensity. No "where are we going?" No "what do you see us doing in five years time?" No "what are your plans for marriage and mortgage and babies?" It was just simple talk. She didn't even pry about Stacey. She didn't even say, "Well! That was a colossal mistake if ever there was one, wasn't it?"

149

She didn't say anything like that. But it was Jamie who couldn't help himself prying a bit. It was Jamie who said, "So... any more thoughts about the Break-up test? You didn't bother going on any other dates did you?"

Amy screwed up her face. "Nah, I couldn't really be bothered." She played with her coaster for a bit. "I mean... just say I went on a date with some guy..."

Jamie nodded, a twinge of jealousy stabbing his heart.

"...and then say I went on a date with another one...and another...and another..."

Jamie nodded again, more waves of jealousy stabbing him.

"...and then say I was out on a date and bumped into dates 1, 2, 3, and 4! It would be awful!"

Jamie chuckled and his heart swelled with pride.

"So...what now then?" Jamie found himself asking, the words tripping over his lips before he could stop himself. "What about Gav? He's due home soon isn't he?"

Amy nodded.

"And then...? All systems go?"

He knew he was treading on very thin ice. Especially after the last time when he let his big mouth do all the talking and Amy had stormed out of the coffee shop.

"Who knows?" Amy shrugged. She didn't indicate as to whether he'd texted, as to whether he'd been in touch, as to whether there were any plans of reconciliation. She just said, "Who knows?"

And then the waiter appeared out of nowhere and made clunky noises as he set their plates down, and asked them if they wanted any more wine.

So they opted for another bottle.

"After all," Amy grinned, "it is a celebration."

"Is it?" Jamie raised his eyebrows.

"Yes. I'm finally getting rid of you."

He hit her playfully across the arm. "Charming! Thank you so much! Well, this is on me. So you may as well drink up."

"Woo! Hoo!" Amy cheered, raising a glass and clinking it with his.

They headed on to a smaller bar after that. One with cosy booths and comfortable seats.

They sat, they drank, they chatted, and when Amy went to the ladies, Jamie checked his phone. Four texts from Stacey.

"Hey. Been thinking about you today. Is everything okay? x o x"

Followed by:

"It's just that...it seemed really awkward in the car...really quiet. I hope everything's okay x o x"

Followed by:

"Oh dear. Okay. Obviously everything is not okay. Can we talk? x o x"

And then:

"Right. You must be really pissed off. Well feck you anyway!"

Jamie drew in a sharp breath. He felt like screaming: "Would you ever feck off?"

He felt tormented. Hassled. Aggravated. Stalked. He just wished she'd just get on with her own life.

"Everything okay?" Amy asked as she returned from the ladies and saw his annoyed face.

"Yeah," Jamie lied. And then corrected himself, "No. Not really," he began. And then he told her.

Maybe it was the drink. Or the fact that they'd had a nice day. Or the fact that he was relaxed with her. Or the fact that he was going home the next day, or maybe he was just plain drunk. But he told her. He told her about the keys. About how Stacey had them all along. About the texts. About the 'well feck you anyway' comment. He told her about all of that. He didn't tell her that it was Amy he wanted. That he'd been hoping that Stacey would take Amy out of his mind. That in fact it made him want Amy all the more. He didn't tell her that. He just said that he'd have to break it off with Stacey, even though he wasn't sure how it had ever started in the first place.

And somehow, somewhere, in the middle to end of that conversation, somewhere, somehow, Jamie's hand had accidentally brushed against Amy's breast. Somehow there was a frisson of something.

"Oh! I'm sorry!" he said, breathily, his lips tantalising close to hers, her face looking up at him, as though she expected him to lean his lips down, and close them over hers, and feel the warmth of her lips on his.

"It's okay," she whispered, with what he could have sworn was a croak in her voice. Her leg was resting next to his, there was chemistry and electricity running up and down via their legs and around their lips and he wanted to grab her and take her. He wanted to say, "Amy! Do you remember that time in Uni? Do you remember the night we snuck under the duvet? Do you remember how good your skin felt next to mine? Do you?"

He wanted to say all that, but that was the moment, the crucial moment, when some plonker with a too-tight t-shirt straining across his bloated beer belly, with a food stain tripping down the front of his chest, pulled up the stool opposite them and said,

"Anyone using this seat mate?"

And the moment was smashed.

Chapter Twenty-Four
<u>SARAH</u>

Sarah got the impression that Tasha was training her up to be deputy manager. It was an unspoken thing, but there were times when Tasha said things like "I'll need to show you this for when I go on maternity leave" and "you'll need to know this when I'm gone" and "do you think you'll be able to manage this part when I'm away?"

Sarah was experiencing a feeling about work that she had never experienced before – a buzz. She had never thought it possible to have a buzz at work. She thought work consisted entirely of clock-watching and skiving techniques. She did not think the term 'buzz' applied, but it did.

The first buzz happened when the photographer of "Interior Weekly" came to visit.

Tasha had phoned Sarah on her mobile at 8am. "Sarah, I'm so incredibly sorry but I cannot make it in until later today. I'm as sick as a dog this morning. I thought the morning sickness would have passed by now but apparently not. Would you mind dealing with the photographer?"

"Of course not Tasha! You just take it easy!"

"I'll try to come in later…"

"You'll do no such thing. Rest yourself. I'll be fine here. And anyway, Tina's here too so we'll be fine on our own."

Sarah heard a relieved sigh down the other end of the phone.

"Oh! Thank God! You're such an angel!"

She gave her some instructions on how she wanted the

photo-shoot done, and then it was time for Sarah to re-apply her lipstick "just incasey." She didn't want to get stuck in a shot without her lippy on.

The photographer walked through the door at 10.30am on the dot, wearing a crisp blue shirt, a wide smile and a confident air.

"Hi," he grinned, offering his hand. "You must be Sarah."

"Yes, that's right," Sarah smiled, feeling her face flush despite herself.

"So, where do you want me?" he asked, exuding extreme sexual innuendo from the offset.

"Ahem…" Sarah cleared her throat nervously. "Well… let's begin with this collection in the window…" she stated, leading him towards the pink display of lights, umbrellas, crockery and cuddly toys.

"Your wish is my command," he grinned.

Sarah smiled, nervously, despite herself.

"Coffee?"

"Yes please. Just milk. I'm sweet enough."

He winked, which Sarah did not like. Every single sentence he had said so far had some sort of innuendo or flirtation attached. As the steam rose from the kettle, she had firm words with herself.

Keep this professional. Don't get sucked in. Watch for the sleazy ones.

And for the next hour, she directed, led and co-ordinated. She waltzed around the shop pointing to the displays she wanted photographed. She was confident, in control and buzzing.

"Yes, that display there," she'd say, pointing to the collection of different coloured wellington boots.

"And that one…" Reams of pink cards and wrapping paper.

"And what about this one?" he asked, an eyebrow raised. He had found the vibrators, boxed up in neat packages.

"Yes, why not?" she replied confidently.

154

"And... er... have you tested these products for their efficiency?" he grinned.

"Ah, now, that'd be telling," she laughed him off, as though totally unaffected by him.

Tina stood behind the till counter, throwing a few sidelong glances. Glances which Sarah could've sworn were full of contempt.

"Well, great meeting you," photographer guy said. "Here's my number – give me a call." He thrust a business card into her hand.

She wasn't sure if he meant "give me a call about the pictures" or "give me a call about going out one night," so she just replied, "Thank you. I look forward to seeing the pictures in the magazine."

And off he went.

Tina rolled her eyes as the shop door rang shut.

"Are you okay?" Sarah asked, a concerned expression on her face.

Tina nodded. Then shook her head. Then quickly fought away a tear that tried to roll down her cheek.

"That guy?" Sarah asked. "Something happened?"

Tina nodded reluctantly. "Using bastard," she practically spat.

Sarah sighed. "Okay. Let's have a cup of tea and a chat. It's quiet in the shop anyway. You take ten minutes and have a breather."

And later, after Tina had told Sarah about the photographer – aka – a guy who might as well have been Stephen number two – Sarah had great pleasure in taking his business card, ripping it up, and throwing it in the bin.

However, Sarah did not give up on the men situation entirely. She had not forgotten Jamie's advice about being open-minded and going on other dates.

The first male customer to ask her out was a guy called Adam. He had come into the shop to buy a birthday present for his sister, when he plucked up the courage and asked her out. He texted her that evening and continued to text her on almost an hourly basis. In fact, that was probably the single most attractive quality that she found in him – the fact that he was so keen.

"Hey Sarah. It's Adam. Just checking in. Thanks for your number x o x o"

Just checking in? Holy feck!

What was she? A hospital? An hotel?

And the 'x o x o' was a bit much – no?

Immediately she told herself off for being so ungrateful and she replied to him.

Sure enough, he texted straight back again. Like a game of table tennis, where the ball pings back automatically. She found it quite entertaining in a way, as though it were a fascinating trick that had never happened before.

But actually, mainly, she found it quite stifling, claustrophobic, uncomfortable.

His texts were endless.

"What type of music do you like? X o x o"

"Who do you live with? X o x o"

"Why are you single? X o x o"

It felt … intrusive.

She scolded herself.

Come on now Sarah. Here is a fella who is nice. Here is a fella who wants to contact you lots. Here is a fella who seems to want a relationship rather than a quick romp. Give the fella a chance.

So she did. She decided to go on *one* date with him – just to give him the benefit of the doubt.

They met in a hotel bar. The idea was that they would have a drink or two and then go downstairs to the restaurant and have dinner.

Adam arrived but instead of the chatty confidence Sarah had

expected, there was a painful shyness. And it really was painful. Awkward silences. Moments where he'd shift in his seat uncomfortably and then just come out with some random attempt at a conversation starter. Like, "So what's your happiest moment to date?"

It was unnerving, weird, awful.

Sarah, not wanting to appear rude, and feeling like she should sit it out for the entire evening rather than run away down the street which is what she wanted to do, said, "Another drink?"

She wondered, optimistically, if a drink would help, if it would lessen his inhibitions, if it would take away the random question generator.

At the bar, she felt his eyes boring a hole into her back the entire time. He was staring at her. As she walked back from the bar, he kept his eyes firmly planted on her, as though trying to drink her in. It was the single most off-putting thing she'd ever experienced in her entire life.

Oh God, I'm such a bitch, she mused. *What is he doing wrong exactly but fancying me? He is a nice fella. He wants a relationship. He is nervous to be out with me. Just what exactly is wrong with me? Here is a fella who is nice and I am unnerved by him? I must be single-handedly, right royally, messed up.*

She took a deep breath and tried to start again with the evening.

But at dinner, he reached across the table and took her hands. "I am so happy to meet you Sarah," he said. "I know it is early days but I have a feeling that you are very special and this is the start of something very wonderful."

Sarah experienced a tightening sensation around her throat, as though someone had their hands gripped on either side of her, and were making light gripping movements.

He was tipsy, granted, so perhaps it was the drink talking, but all the same, they were only three hours into their date- was that really long enough for him to assessing her as "something very wonderful?"

Or was she just filling a void in his life? Akin to a starved dieter in a chocolate shop?

However, it was the piece de resistance that finished her off and made her want to run home with her tail between her legs.

Back in the bar area, after their meal was finished, and Sarah had agreed to 'one last drink' to finish off the night, Adam had bumped into an old work friend at the bar. He was quite drunk by this stage and he had grabbed his mate and said, "Come and meet my new girlfriend" and had led him the short distance to where Sarah was positioned on the sofa, trying not to show the metaphorical noose that was hanging around her throat.

"This is Sarah," Adam beamed, as though she were a trophy, as though he'd just lapped round twenty-six miles at record pace and had her to show for it.

"Hi," Sarah smiled politely, wishing the ground would swallow her up.

Adam's old work friend disappeared, an amused expression on his face. Adam sat beside Sarah, taking her hand in his. The drink had certainly inebriated him. There were no more painful silences. Instead he was saying things like, "Sarah?"

"Yes."

"Now that we're going out, I would have to say that...with your work and everything...I know you really love it...but I wouldn't be happy with you working on a Saturday. I would like you to see about getting Saturdays off. Saturday would be our day together."

All of a sudden, it was as though Sarah saw a neon "Exit" sign above Adam's head, with the picture of a little stick man running as fast as his legs could carry him.

Sarah prised her hand away from his grasp, feigned 'sore head' excuses, and made a sharp exit towards the taxi-stand.

She left abruptly, away from the confused look on his face,

and stood under a shelter in the pouring rain, with the table tennis of thoughts careering around her head:

What's wrong with me? Here is a man who really wants to be with me! Am I really messed up beyond all compare? Am I only attracted to distant men? Why do I find nice men claustrophobic?

Even with all that careering around her head, she took a deep breath, and in a firm voice that she felt like screaming out loud to the world, she told herself,

"I DON'T CARE ANYMORE!"
"IF IT'S GONNA HAPPEN, IT'LL HAPPEN!"
"IN THE MEANTIME, I'D RATHER BE SINGLE!"

Chapter Twenty-Five
<u>BETH</u>

A week passed and Saturday night approached. Beth had spent the entire week cooped up in her studio with "I'm busy, go away" on her door. She did soften the message with a :o) smiley sign and three kisses x x x, but nonetheless, her message was serious. She needed, nay *craved* time on her own.

Every so often, she'd hear the pitter-patter of feet along the corridor, she'd hear the voices "I wonder if Beth's up for going for coffee" and then she'd hear the brief pause as they must have been reading the sign, and then she'd hear the voices retreat away again. And she would breathe a sigh of relief and return to the soft strokes on her easel, the gentle rhythmic motion of her pencil, and she would forget.

But of course, she didn't really forget. Of course, the whole time she was thinking; discussions whirring around in her head in a confused yet effortless manner. *If only things had been different. If only I'd have gone with the flow. If only I'd have not minded that he only wanted a casual fling.*

Beth thought about all those times she had spent staring at her phone, willing it to bleep with a message. Or the times that when she *did* get a text, relief and optimism flooded her as she believed everything was going to be okay. She believed everything was moving along at the slow pace it was meant to move.

And then when they *did* meet and he disappeared straight after sex, her optimism faded slightly when she realised that the reality of the set-up was nothing more than a casual sex scenario.

She had forced herself to form the words she had refused to believe; "This is nothing more than a fling, is it?"

He mumbled a reply about "Let's just be mates" and "I don't do relationships." She searched his face for reassurance and found none. Confused thoughts swirled in her head. "What could possibly be wrong with me? Why doesn't he want me? If I was really attractive and cool and interesting, he wouldn't be able to resist me – so what is wrong with me? She wondered that if she was a Kate Moss lookalikey, would he suddenly reconsider his stance on relationships and be happy to shag her from now to kingdom come? Yes, she thought, and that pained her.

She braved her thoughts to Sarah and Jamie at the Break-up test meeting. She was tempted to act stoical and brave, like she had gotten over the loss already, and it was no big deal, but they could see through her, like a newly washed thin pane of glass.

"So, still missing him then?" Sarah asked, tentatively.

Beth nodded, slowly.

They were seated in their usual fashion, in Sarah's living room, on her comfy sofas, surrounded with bowls of nibbles, glasses of wine, scented candles and soft music in the background.

"Just forget about him – he's not worth it," Jamie said abruptly.

Sarah gave him a ghastly stare. "That's very insensitive Jamie," she scolded.

"What?"

"Beth is going through a grieving process – she does not need abrupt words from you – she is trying to deal with this in her own time – It's not going to help if you sit and make abrupt comments like that."

Jamie seemed to sink into his chair further, truly reprimanded.

"Anyway," Sarah continued, "I think you're transferring your anger about your own situation onto Beth."

"What's that supposed to mean?"

"We'll talk about that another time," Sarah said. Then she redirected her gaze to Beth. "You take as much time as you need Beth – you'll have good days and bad days. You talk about it as long as you want."

So Beth did. Beth voiced all her confusion and guilt and "what if's" and "why's" and all the thoughts that had been running around and around in her head all week.

Sarah sat and listened, nodding her head in all the right places, not interrupting, not trying to tell her she shouldn't feel like that, not scolding her, not disagreeing with her, just listening. And passing the box of tissues to her when she saw a tear escape from the corner of her eye.

It was a great release. Beth felt emptied out. Of all the turmoil she had been processing in her head all week.

"I'm glad you got all that out," Sarah smiled. "And the point is, that is how *you* feel and that's important. Now I could sit here and tell you from my observations you did nothing wrong. You could say "What if" until you're blue in the face, but the point is, you *were* fed up watching your phone. You *did* find it too difficult to just be a casual sex partner. You *did* need to talk … so... from my humble opinion – I think it was totally okay to say all those things. Also, I get the impression that you feel you manoeuvred the situation somewhat – that it was all your fault – that you chased him … but he reciprocated at every turn – so it's not your fault."

Beth took a deep breath. "So what you're telling me I couldn't have done anything differently?"

"Yes. Yes that is what I'm saying."

Beth took a deep breath of relief. "Okay… but why does that not feel like enough? It feels like I need to learn something from this. It feels like something good has to come of it – otherwise I am just going to keep on and on making the same mistakes."

Sarah nodded. Beth noticed that Jamie looked interested despite his quietness. He looked snug and half-asleep on his favourite armchair, but he was listening all the same.

"I know what you mean," Sarah agreed. "And believe me, this helps me talking to you – because I identify so much with you." She took a sip of her wine. "I suppose I have told myself that I will be more careful from now on. I have not sworn off men forever – although that was a tempting thought at one stage – but I have told myself that I will watch for the red flags from now on."

"Red flags?"

"Yes, you know – a red flag would be – he's married – or, he has a drug problem, or – he's living with an ex and saying they don't sleep together."

Beth nodded, "Or he doesn't text for five days."

"Yes, that's it."

"Or he leaves straight after sex."

"Or he breathes," Jamie joked.

"Yeah, pretty much," Sarah laughed.

"But you know – I think that's been the thing," Sarah went on. "I think when a girl isn't content with her life and not that happy with her lot, I think she's desperate to have a relationship in the hope that it makes her feel complete. And when she's desperate like that, she doesn't spot the red flags. She has the blinkers on. She wants him to be perfect, so she only sees what she wants to see."

"Yes, I suppose you're right," Beth agreed. "I suppose it's about finding a way of being happy with your own life and not needing a relationship to fix you."

"Then you can be more choosy and learn to spot the red flags."

"That's exactly what I've learned from this," Beth nodded, as though that was her raison d'être. As though that made all the pain worthwhile. As though she could walk valiantly on now, preventing herself from any further pain. She found herself curling up on the sofa. Sarah and Jamie continued with idle chit-chat and Beth suddenly felt tired. Tired or relieved, she wasn't sure which. But whatever emotion it was, for some reason, she fell asleep. Sarah placed a cosy duvet around her and propped a pillow under her head.

Saturday night arrived and Beth had dressed herself immaculately. Just in-casey. Just incase she bumped into Karl. Just in case he had a Kate Moss lookalikey on his arm. Just in case it turned out he CAN do relationships, just not with her.

She had her hair done, and went for a tanning session, and exhausted her muscles in the gym, in the hope that some serotonin induced chemicals could race her way. She had rubbed on some bronzer and dusted herself with shimmery glitter, and she had put on her favourite black dress. Little shoe-string straps, a tie under the boobs, a good thick bit of padding around the boobs, and then material floating down to her knees. She knew they were only going for coffee, but they might have ended up going for drinks as well.

"Wow" You look great!" they all exclaimed when she joined them. She smiled shyly and soon she was positioned among them, sipping her coffee and nervously awaiting the arrival of Karl and Kate Moss Lookalikey. Even though the chances of him going to a coffee shop on a Saturday night and picking the same coffee shop in the whole of London, were a million to one.

Part of her *wanted* to bump into him. To show bravado. To show him; *look at me. Look at what you missed out on. Now that I'm looking fantastic and surrounded by friends. Arty friends, no less, from my arty studio, where I'm busy doing my own thing.*

But there was no sign of him.

And the next thing, Mary was inviting them all back to her apartment, and then they were in a taxi, and they were pulling up outside a big red door, and they were tucked indoors. And that was it, her first public outing out of the way, over and done with.

Mary's apartment was *amazing*. Leopardskin print on the bed. A big bit of material draping from the ceiling down to the bed, making it look like a tent. A water-bed. A small fountain in the corner of the room. A gorgeous kitchen with spotlights and marble worktops and a shiny floor. And the lounge next to it which was dark and cosy with bean bags and low sofas. Heaven.

"Wow!!!! This is sooooo cool!" Beth exclaimed. "How on earth can artists afford this?" The question was out of her mouth before she could help herself. It was a nosey question and totally inappropriate, but May seemed un-phased.

She shrugged her shoulders. "Well, I worked in business for years and earned a lot of money that way, until I became frustrated and realised I needed to be creative. And then I came into a bit of inheritance... and I suppose that's it really."

"No wonder you're so happy," Beth mused aloud.

Mary laughed. "You think? Oh, I've had my hardships too – I just concentrate on what I'm grateful for, everyday – and that seems to help."

Beth nodded. Something that she needed to do too.

"So Beth," Roxanne said, as they all settled on the sofas and Mary brought them glasses of wine and bowls of nibbles.

"I have an exhibition coming up soon...I would be happy to hang one or two of your drawings if you want?"

"Want?" Beth's eyes widened. "I would LOVE that! Are you sure? I mean, are they good enough?"

Roxanne laughed. "Of course they are. You have real talent there. I would be happy to hang them for you."

Beth beamed. It was the first time in a long while she had felt genuinely... alive. Up to now, she felt like she was just dragging herself through one day after the next, trudging on. But this, this was exciting. This was great.

The night went on, and there was chat and laughter and a few games (charades, twister), and then, before she knew it, Roxanne had gone home and Mary and her partner Paddy had disappeared somewhere (she thought the toilet, but obviously to bed).

So that was that, the night was over, and she had had fun, and she hadn't thought about Karl all night and then it was just her and Jake, on the sofa, talking.

"So, come on then," Jake said, "What are you hiding?"

Beth looked startled. "Excuse me?"

"You, you're hiding something. Something in *here* that you're not telling anyone about."

At the word *here,* he brushed his fingertips over the base of her neck – the smooth area of skin just above her chest. The softness of his fingertips made a butterfly effect tingle inside her. Chemistry? Or perhaps she was just ticklish.

"What makes you ask that?" she asked, avoiding his question.

"Oh come on," he said gently. "There is some serious thinking going on inside that head of yours. Either that or you're just a very intense artist."

Beth raised her eyebrows. "You think?"

"I don't know," he said, "I'm just trying to get you to talk."

They laughed then. A nervous laugh. A mixture of drink and embarrassment and relief at the ice being broken, and the awkwardness of the two of them being left in the one place together, alone.

"I got dumped," she blurted out.

He stopped laughing abruptly and his face fell. "No way."

She nodded.

"I know it's a silly thing to be upset over," she said, "I mean, it happens the world over – right? I mean, every day someone is being dumped or dumping someone and it's not really any big deal – but it's a big deal to me ..." She knew she was rambling now. She knew it was a mixture of the drink and the nervousness and the awkwardness of the situation, but she rattled on, "It's a big deal to me because... I don't know, I just feel *trampled* – I just feel like shit – and it just crushes your self-esteem and..."

He grabbed her hand.

"Come here," he said.

He pulled her gently so that she had to stand up and follow him.

"Where are we going?"

"I want to show you something."

She followed him, perplexed, and realised that he was leading her to the bathroom.

"Look," he said.

They had stopped in front of the sink. They faced the wall which was lined from one end to the other with a mirror.

"Look."

"What?" she asked, confused.

"This." He stood behind her, put his arms around her with his hands cupping each side of her face.

"Look at you," he replied. "You're gorgeous."

She gasped in surprise. His revelation. His validation. The confidence of his statement. His lack of embarrassment.

"You Beth –whatever-your-surname-is – you Beth – the artist – are gorgeous."

They stood there like that for a moment, until Beth felt a tear threaten to poke out from the corner of her eye. *Please no, do not cry, not here, not now, it would be too corny, please don't cry.* But it was too late, the tear had plopped out and plumped its way down her face.

He took her arms and gently manoeuvred her around until she was facing him. He ran his finger along her cheek catching her tear. Then he placed his fingertip, the one wet with her salty tears, and put it to his lips and kissed it, as though kissing her better.

And then he leaned his face towards hers, and his lips, his

167

full lips, found their way onto hers, and kissed her.

The kiss, Beth thought, was amazing. Soft and gentle and tender, yet passionate. Their mouths were on each others, pressing, devouring, as though they'd wanted this from the first moment they met.

The weight of his body gently pressed against her and she leaned back against the wall.

"Oh Beth," he said, between kisses. "Oh Beth."

And then suddenly, she broke off. Suddenly, for no reason apparent whatsoever, she stopped him.

"I'm sorry," she shook her head. "I can't do this. I'm sorry. I have to go."

And before she knew it, she had grabbed her coat and her bag, and ran away.

Chapter Twenty-Six
<u>JAMIE</u>

Jamie positioned himself on the train, elbowing his way into one of those seats with a table, so that he could get a nice view out the window. He set his baguette, pack of crisps, cardboard cup of coffee and FHM mag on the table. A woman came and sat opposite him. She had unruly hair and large, stubby fingers, which were grasped around a novel entitled "Jenny gets hitched!" There was a picture of a bouquet on the front of the cover, as though just tossed from the bride's hands. The 'getting hitched' reader had no ring on her wedding finger, and Jamie wondered about her: *In a relationship and hoping the guy would 'tie the knot' or single & looking?*

Because of the way she kept giving him a few sidelong coy glances, Jamie got his answer: *single and looking.*

Jamie buried his head into his FHM mag. The last thing he needed was another woman on the scene, thank you very much.

The train picked up speed, whizzing past trees and fields and greenery. It was hard to imagine after the hustle and bustle and build-up of offices and houses, they were greeted with such greenery in such a short distance out of London.

The train propelled itself valiantly towards Brighton, as though wanting to catapult Jamie as far away from his London chapter as soon as possible. As though wanting to close that experience and start afresh with something new.

London. And its hustle and bustle. Its excitement. Its energy. Its vibrancy. The fast pace.

Yes, he knew Richmond wasn't exactly London. It was softer, calmer, more serene. But even that commute into Central London every day, with the noisiness, the vibe, the atmosphere, the busy people with busy places to go, the cattle market as he bustled his way through the barricades at the tube station, that was excitement.

Or was it exciting? Did the excitement emanate from London, or from Amy?

Was it the daily sight of Amy in her hot pants and vest top, prancing around her apartment, oblivious to his ogling eyes? Was that the real excitement? Added to that was the fact that she was totally, frustratingly unavailable? That she only had eyes for Gav? Not even just 'eyes' for him, but blinkers infact. Blinkers that blocked out anyone else from entering her vision. As though she were in a dark tunnel, and Gav was the light at the end of it, and she could see nothing else around her.

Despite the fact that he and Amy had had a great time together. Despite the fact that they *looked* like a couple when they were strolling around Covent Garden together. Despite the fact that they could *easily* have passed for girlfriend and boyfriend – without the hand-holding and tongue down each other's throat business that is.

And then there was that *moment*. That definite *moment*. The near-kiss. The frisson of chemistry. That moment where – if they'd had just one second more, their lips would have touched, and they would have snogged the face off each other – and they would have moaned between gasps – "God! Why didn't we do this ages ago?!" – and they would have jumped into a taxi and rushed back to Amy's and ripped each other's clothes off – and the rest, as they say, would have been history.

But no. That big galumph of a bloke had to come along and ruin the moment.

That big galumph of a bloke had to alter the course of Jamie's destiny.

That big galumph of a bloke had to ruin everything.

Because shortly after that, they'd called a taxi, and went home, and Amy conked out on the sofa, and there was no way that any chemistry was going to filter through her snores.

So Jamie carried her to bed, took her shoes off, pulled the duvet over her, kissed her on the forehead, and switched off the light on his way out.

And then the next thing, it was morning, and he was due to go home, and the only atmosphere that hung in the air was a tiredness, a blurriness, a hangover, and a complete disappearance of any chemistry whatsoever.

Amy had gone to the train station to see him off. There was no movie scene moment. No black and white image of him hanging out a train window while she ran behind the moving train. There was no script of her declaring her sudden affections – "Jamie! I've loved you all along! Please stay!" There was none of that. There was just a coffee in one of those train-side cafes. The ones with the cardboard cups and the uncomfortable steel chairs. There wasn't even any final declarations. No "It's been so great to get in touch with you again – Let's not leave it so long this time." None of that. There was just a:

"Thanks so much for letting me stay" (from Jamie), and a:

"You're welcome, any time" (from Amy).

Jamie wanted to pick up on the "anytime" comment and run with it.

He wanted to flirt a bit and say something like "Anytime? Oh aye?" but he decided it wasn't appropriate, and instead he just said, "Right, I'll be off then." And that was that.

And Jamie wished that sometimes real life could be like a black and white movie – it would be nicer – but it's just not.

So he took his cardboard cup of coffee, his baguette, his pack of crisps, and he settled on the train getting ready to flick through his FHM mag.

The woman opposite him was rather distracting with her

sidelong glances, but other than that, he tried to lose himself in his magazine, with his occasional glances out the window at passing trees and fields, and his decision to put his London chapter behind him and move on.

He tried to tell himself that it had been a complete waste of time pining over Amy. That she was clearly out of his league and not one bit interested in him. He tried to tell himself that surely he was as bad as Beth, Amy and Sarah put together. Wasn't he as equally obsessed and pathetic as them? Didn't he just want what he couldn't have? Was he not a prime candidate for The Break-up test if ever there was one?

Look at Stacey – he thought – a perfectly nice girl who was clearly mad about him and yet he couldn't summon the excitement for her.

Clearly he was a commitment-phobe. Clearly the first sign of responsibility or commitment had him running a mile.

Clearly he would rather pine over some unreciprocated love – some woman who would never return his affections – rather than have to face the responsibility of actually having to date someone.

Clearly the responsibility of having to trail around Tescos, listening to screaming kids and analysing labels on food containers was too much for him.

Perhaps if Amy had turned to him and said, "Okay big boy, let's get together," perhaps he would run a mile too?

He wondered.

He thought about Stacey – about all the effort she went to – cooking the goose, about how she was so keen to spend more time with him that she pretended to forget her keys. He thought about how quiet he was with her on that morning he took her to the station.

He knew for a fact that if he called her up there and then and invited her over, she'd jump at the chance. He knew for a fact that he could have a meal cooked for him that very night, followed by a weekend tucked up in bed having a shag-fest, followed by Sunday afternoons in the pub – several pints and a roast dinner. He knew he could have all of that, at the drop of a hat, if he wanted.

And then there was another part of him that thought – 'hold on, I fancy a lad's night for a change'. He'd been surrounded by women and their hormones for long enough recently. He could catch up with some of his male buddies. They could head down The Laines. They could have a few pints, end up in some club down beside the beach. He could eye up some girl, he could flirt, he could have fun, he could try to get his life back to normal.

He focused on his FHM mag. He tried to ignore the woman opposite him giving him the sidelong glances. He wondered if he should get up and go to the loo, in the hope that some other fella would take his seat. And the other fella would strike up a conversation with her, and the other fella wouldn't be such a big waste of space commitment-phobe like him. The fella would chat away to her and ask her out and take an interest in her and find out that actually she was a fantastic cook and extremely passionate in bed. A sort of Nigella Lawson type.

Jamie prayed that for the train girl, in the hope that the universe would pick up on his altruistic gesture and nod in his direction, rewarding him with karma points.

Jamie's hand hovered over his mobile phone. Who to call? Stacey or the lads?

He diverted his attention back to his mag. His eyes feasted on the images. Girls with big boobs, tiny bums, fingers lifted to their mouths in suggestive poses.

Why was it that all he could think of was Amy? That Amy's face seemed to magically juxtapose itself on top of their bodies?

His phone rang.

Amy.

He picked it up, and rather than say hello, he quipped

warmly, "Missing me already?"

He noticed that train girl's shoulders seemed to sag disappointedly.

"Yeah, obviously," Amy joked sarcastically. "Glad to have a bit of peace and quiet more like."

See? All in my head.

"You forgot your CD's," she went on. "Do you want me to post them to you?"

The thought sickened him. That he would never be returning, even to collect a few CD's. That he was on a fast-track to Brighton, with a one-way ticket and no return.

"Am...yeah..." he mumbled. "That'd be great...if you don't mind..."

He wanted to say, "No, it's okay. I'll hop off at the next stop and I'll return. I'll reposition the two of us into exactly the same set-up as we were in last night and we'll pick up from where we left off."

He wanted to say all that, but instead he croaked, "I'll send you money for the postage."

"Don't be daft," she said. "You over-stayed your welcome long enough – a few postage stamps will hardly break the bank."

It was a joke, to be fair, but it stabbed.

Overstayed your welcome.

Harsh.

It was like a finger jabbing at him.

See? It was all in your head. Get Over It. Totally Out Of Your League.

And suddenly, he lost his appetite.

Not just for the crisps.

But for the FHM mag.

He put the images back in his bag, and instead resorted to staring out the window at the passing fields.

Chapter Twenty-Seven
<u>AMY</u>

Amy returned home to her apartment, closing the door behind her and letting out a low, tired sigh.

A sigh of contentment, perhaps?

For wasn't this what she had craved for weeks? The place to herself?

She took a ceremonious walk around her flat, as though she were a prison officer on inspection duty.

There was the kitchen sink, with the remnants of that morning's tea-bags, which Jamie had kindly crushed into the plug-hole for her, like mouse droppings.

There was the coffee table, with the empty cereal bowl sitting next to his half-drunk mug of tea, which he had slurped back fast, accompanied with a "Come on Aimes! I'm gonna be late!"

She had stood at the door, tidily awaiting him, her coat neatly tied at the waist and her pointy shoes clicking neatly together.

"I'm ready," she'd said calmly.

"Oh buggery balls," he'd replied, grabbing his trainers and jutting his feet into them. "Why do I always have to leave everything 'til the last minute? Why didn't I pack yesterday?"

"Because we were too busy getting drunk," Amy yawned. "Remember?"

Jamie grimaced. "Remember? Um... some bits..."

He seemed to stare into mid-air for a second, as though reminiscing, and then the thought that he had to catch a train and be at a meeting on time, stabbed his head and he quickly grabbed his coat and said, "C'mon then! Let's go!"

And they were off, the apartment door slamming behind them, and a great big silence descending on the flat, like a sheet.

She inspected the bathroom; toothpaste marks lined along the insides of the sink. At least the smelly socks, usually draped along the bath, had disappeared. So too had the pile of clothes, which had rarely been acquainted with a hanger, and the absence of which now left a nice, clean, empty space on the floor.

Amy breathed. A sigh of relief?

She opened some windows. She took a long sip of ice-cold water. She put on her marigolds. She allowed the fresh air to whip through the corners of her hungover head. She did not even put on music – usually she preferred to do her polishing to the sounds of Madonna or Kylie, but today the girls remained mute. She worked in total peace.

It didn't take her long. Amy and her marigolds were a team. They had a habit of whizzing through housework like it was a really good dose of therapy. Every inch tidied creating more order and niceness in her head. She thought of the calm she was embracing now. Never again would she have to listen to Stacey's moans of "Oh Jamie, Oh Jamie, Oh Jamie, Oh…."

Never again would she be woken at silly o'clock in the morning to a banging front door, a drunken Jamie on the step and the slurs, "Whadda boutta threesome…?"

With Jamie, there was always noise. Whether it was the radio he'd have chattering on in the background, or his iPod linked to the pc that he constantly played with ("You gotta hear this song Aimes.. tuuune!"), or else he'd have the TV on, with Top Gear, or Formula One, or football, or anything else that involved tyres screeching or crowds cheering. Just general *racket*.

And he was always whistling, or singing to himself, or just

generally talking *rubbish*. Thinking aloud, humming, chatting to himself, whatever was in his head usually tripped out of his mouth.

Amy was the opposite.

Amy was internal. Introverted.

Amy thought before she spoke.

She didn't say anything unless it was useful.

She was a thinker.

Jamie was a talker.

He was constantly asking her questions, wanting to play little games with her.

"Amy..?" he'd ask. "What are your top five songs of all time?"

She screwed up her nose as though thinking about it.

"I mean..." he went on, "If you were stuck on a desert island for ever and ever and you could only get to listen to five songs ever again in your life – what would they be?"

Amy drew in a long breath at the time. "Ooooh... that's a toughie.." she'd said. Hands in her marigolds and elbows up to hot water in dishes. "Let's see... well.. it'd have to be something classical."

"Beautiful choice."

They chattered on like this for quite a while, and then it was some time later, when they were sitting in the park, on the freshly cut grass, with the birds chirping nearby, that he'd asked,

"And what would your top five songs for your funeral be?"

"Jamie!" she exclaimed, hitting him playfully.

"What?"

"I don't want to think about that!"

"Why not?" he'd asked. "Would you not be really pissed off if they played really shit songs at your big day and you had no say in the matter?"

She looked down her nose at him, as though he were a puppy, or a kid brother, or someone she had to humour. "I

177

think that'd be the least thing on my mind."

Jamie shrugged. "I'm just sayin'"

She laughed. And hit him playfully. And then he hit her playfully back. And they'd had a little arm wrestle.

"Ooooh! Look at you two love birds!"

They'd looked up, to see Sarah standing there, with a know-it-all smile on her face.

This isn't how it looks, Amy was tempted to say.

"You two are outrageous flirts," Sarah had plopped down beside them, helping herself to a strawberry from the plastic tub.

No, not me, I couldn't flirt to save my life.

That was then, Amy thought, *and this is now. And the flat is clean and everything is back to normal.*

She caught a glimpse of her CD rack, a number of Jamie's CDs flung in between her neatly arranged pile.

She picked up her mobile and flicked through her contacts, calling him.

"Missing me already?" he'd asked.

She rolled her eyes. "Yeah right. Enjoying the peace and quiet more like."

She told him she'd post the CD's to him, and he'd said, "Cheers hun," and hung up.

And that was that.

Silence.

Deafening silence.

Amy imagined that he'd be heading to Stacey's later that night, regaling *her* with top five questions and general chitter chatter. Doing things to Stacey's body that made her moan, "Oh Jamie, oh Jamie, oh Jamie, oh…"

Amy had never moaned like that to Gav. Amy hadn't even come with Gav. She was obviously far too tense around him. But Stacey, Stacey sounded very relaxed around Jamie. Unless of course she was faking it, which was always a possibility.

Amy thought about yesterday and how she and Jamie had

strolled around Covent Garden. Looking at street performers and strolling into shops. Eating dinner in the restaurant and drinking beers in the pub.

She thought about that moment in the kitchen, that night, when he'd brushed past her. About how her breath had caught at the back of her throat. She thought about the way he had played with a tea-towel, twisting it in is hands and flicking it playfully against the work-top. She thought, with interest, about the way the muscles on his upper arms had danced with this gesture. It fascinated her, how this simple playing with a tea-towel stuck in her head.

She thought about the way he had said to her, "Thank you… for just being so….*wonderful.*" She had wondered, at the time, if there was a certain meaning behind that *wonderful.* If there was more to it. And then she chided herself for being silly.

How outrageous, she told herself. Here was a bloke, shagging a girl the night before, having her moan, "Oh Jamie oh Jamie oh Jamie oh…" and here was she, thinking there was something loaded in one simple word *wonderful.*

She told herself off. *Imagine being so UP MYSELF to think he has notions on me!*

But somehow, somewhere, a smaller voice was more certain.

A smaller voice was saying, *No, there was definitely something in that 'wonderful'.*

The smaller voice also lulled, *In fact, have I not been so DOWN on MYSELF for so long that it's about time I tried to be a bit more UP MYSELF?*

And in that split second, while Amy stacked the CD's in a neat pile, pulling out a padded envelope and slotting them inside, it suddenly occurred to her,

Was there something under my nose all along?

It was like a light switching on.

As though she'd been stumbling around in an attic room for ages, tripping over old cardboard boxes, her breath being clouded by sawdust and old cobwebs, and then she'd suddenly found a pulley-switch, and she'd grabbed it, and tugged on it, and a light filled the small attic space.

Am I having notions on myself, or does Jamie fancy me?

Has he been flirting with me all along?

Amy brushed the idea aside, as though swatting a fly off her shoulder.

Don't be so ridiculous!

Followed by;

Typical of me to think this now, now that he's on a train careering home. Now that he's distant. Now that he's winging his way into the arms of another woman. Now that he's unavailable.

Amy continued cleaning. Until the apartment was spotless. Until the fresh, clean, Richmond air blew through the flat.

She had a shower, washed her hair, and let the dust and grime disappear down the plug-hole.

She sat on her sofa, hair styled, make-up on, all dressed up.

With no place to go.

She was restless, irritable and discontent.

She knew Beth and Sarah would be busy.

Beth was cooped up in her studio creating a masterpiece.

Sarah was probably working late.

And then there was one.

Of course her phone lay silent.

Like a brick.

Not a peep from Gav. It was just another week and then he'd be home. She didn't even need to check the dates in her diary anymore. It was welded on her head, like an identity stamp on a farmyard animal.

One week to go.

One week and then he'd be home.

For Good.

The thought was too exciting for her to even contain herself. And yet…

Yet there was a nagging feeling…

A horrible, yucky, nagging feeling lurking at the back of her mind..

That maybe things wouldn't be any different at all.

That just because he'd be living in the same town, nay, several streets away, would that really change anything? Would her phone suddenly bleep to life?

She doubted it.

She thought back to that first night she met Gav. It was a night she liked to think about from time to time. A memory that made her smile and gave her a happy flutter tummy. She had been at work, tidying up reports, printing off paper, slurping down coffee, watching her clock, hoping to get away at least before half-six.

Everyone had skedaddled already. Off for Thursday night pints and eagerly watching the weekend roll in.

She'd heard steps creaking up and the stairway and it made her uneasy. *Who was hanging around at this time of the night?*

"Hey.... Sorry to interrupt..." he'd smiled, watching her surrounded by piles of paper and looking up from her dark rimmed spectacles. If only she'd stuck her hair up in a bun and worn a short skirt and heels for maximum effect.

"...I'm from the production company and we just need a key to get into the back stage office.."

Now Amy knew that "they" tell you that mister right never comes knocking on your door. That you'd never meet him over the garden peas in the frozen section of Tesco. That you need to get yourself *out there*. But tonight how wrong they were.

He, Gav, stood there at the doorway, with his polite smile and his quiet questioning, asking for a key.

In her greater fantasies, she would imagine that he took her there and then, scooped her up in the middle of her piles of paperwork, tore off her dark-rimmed spectacles and lifted her onto the desk... But of course that was just fantasy, and all that didn't happen.

Not for another twenty-four hours anyway.

"Oh right. Yes. Of course," she replied, flustered, taking off her glasses and stepping over her piles of paper and walking in his direction. "I'll find Ginny and ask her to help you."

Ginny was the theatre manager, while she, Amy, was the mere finance person, stuck well and truly behind the scenes.

He had a beard, and a shaved head. She had never gone for bearded men before. All that stubble rubbing against one's cheek must be atrocious for the complexion. But it was his eyes.

All in the eyes.

They were dark and deep, and they looked as though they fancied the pants off her. As if they were amused by her, entertained, aroused.

"Will you show me where she is?" he asked (in a boyish – please help me so I can follow you around and look at your bum – type way). "I'm a bit lost in here."

She nodded, suddenly with a humongous self-awareness of every movement she was making, the nod of her head, the sound of her voice, the strides of her legs as his eyes bore holes into her backside.

"This is a nice theatre," he said, for conversation.

"Yes. Yes it's very cosy."

"How long have you worked here?" he asked, along with, "Where do you live?"

A conversation ensued. Words bandied about, with Amy not focusing on anything exactly, apart from the self-conscious awareness that he was staring at every single inch of her.

"Well, this is it," she announced, as she'd located him near Ginny's domain.

"Thanks," he smiled. Eyes to her eyes, down to her lips, back to her eyes again.

Oh. Please. You must use that trick with every woman.

"Thanks Amy," he looked at the badge that was situated ever so strategically just above her right breast. "You've been a great help."

"You're welcome," she croaked, rooted to the spot. Not wanting to leave in case that would be the end of their encounter. She would disappear back to the mountain of sums and figures while he would live in the dark room next to the stage fiddling with knobs and buttons and all sorts.

"It was nice to meet you," he prolonged his gaze.

"You too."

"Stay for a drink after the show...?"

Her eye contact dropped to the floor. She had planned to go home, wash her hair, put the bin out, cook a decent meal, fall into bed and have an early night.

"Sure," she found herself saying.

He nodded, as though that was the correct answer, and off he went, in search of Ginny and the keys and the quiet cubby hole next to the stage.

She watched the show, sidling in through the back door of the upstairs section, making sure her phone was switched off, watching the actors prance their way around the stage, full of drama and tension and shouting voices.

She did not concentrate on one single word. Instead she thought of Gav and her staying on for a drink. Everyone leaving. Ginny telling her to 'lock that side door on your way out'. Gav putting on a few soft stage lights. Gav and Amy making love, on the stage. But of course, that wouldn't happen.

Not straight away anyway.

He bought her a drink and they chatted, and it was all gobble-de-gook for she was far too nervous to pay much attention to the detail. And anyway, when two people fancy each other, do they really give two hoots about what their favourite film is? Or how well they think that actress delivered the scene?

No.

More likely than not, they're watching the line of your mouth as your face breaks into a smile. They're imagining your mouth on theirs. They're imagining the pleasure.

"Do you want to meet on Sunday? Go for a walk around the park? Go for lunch?" he suggested.

Her heart fell. The antics on the stage wouldn't be happening after all.

"Yeah, sure…" she said. She had visions of a cold fresh wind whipping through her and having to wrap herself up in gloves and scarves and multiple layers of jumpers and coats and tights.

And the antics on the stage fell even further away.

"Great," he smiled. "Meet you at mid-day?"

She had nodded, he had left, and she had locked up the stage door on the right, punching a few security numbers into an alarm system. And that was that.

He had gone, walking down the street and away from her, probably thinking to himself,

I wonder does she do this with all the stage hand fellas?

No! No I don't! her answer would have been.

And then perhaps his next thought would've been,

Well, she seems keen enough. Let's strike while the iron's hot. Let's take the opportunity while it's arisen, as it were.

Like a young lad finding a gate lying open and deciding he may as well burgle the house.

Well why not? It'd be rude not to.

Perhaps if Amy was anyone else, say she'd been a Ruby who was up for a quick romp also, then the fusion would've been electric. Two souls, wanting the same thing, at the same time. Electric.

Except that the conflict for Amy was that she spelled one thing and wanted another. She spelled S.E.X. and yet she meant. R.E.L.A.T.I.O.N.S.H.I.P. and that's where the trouble lay.

Perhaps Gav swooped from one theatre to the other, preying on the girls that spelled sex, thinking he was doing a good service to all women all over, totally unaware of a splattering of broken hearts left behind.

The negative voices were full blown now and hammering at her.

Just fooling yourself.

What makes you think anything's going to be any different?

You think he hasn't been shagging half the country since he's last seen you?

Horrible, horrible, DOWN HERSELF thoughts that she wished she could block out, like sticking pillows to her ears and singing, "La! La! La! La! La! LA!"

Amy decided that some retail therapy to defeat the boredom monster was in order.

Clothes, books, DVD's, magazines, anything to keep her occupied. She wondered if she should even take up knitting. Who knows, she could even try to get into the Guinness Book of Records for knitting the longest scarf ever. Or something.

The boredom monster hit her big-time then as she found herself texting Gav.

A super-needy, super-emotional, boredom text.

"Hiya. Just thinkin' of You. When are you Home? Be good to see you. Aimes x x x"

She wished, for a brief moment, that her phone would reject the text. Like taking a sip of something rotten and spitting it out immediately.

That some turn of miraculous events would make a warning message pop up on her screen.

Something along the lines of:

"Sending failed."

Or:

"Insufficient credit."

Or:

"Are you really sure you want to send this Amy?"

Or:

"Are you out of your mind missus??? Where's your dignity???"

But no, dutifully her phone sent the message. Like a really good paper boy, cycling past Gav's garden and dropping the message effortlessly onto his lawn.

"Message sent"

Damn her phone and its unlimited text messages!

She suddenly felt raw and exposed and vulnerable. She knew she was doing everything the "how to" books told her not to do.

"Do not chase him."

"Do not text him first"

"Do not sleep with him too soon."

"Do not make a tit of yourself."

She had long since broken all the how to's.

She needed some serious distraction.

She grabbed her keys, her coat and her bag and she disappeared to her haven- that which was the shops.

She retuned home later with several tops, several pairs of shoes, several delicious new books to devour, several DVD's to watch, and a severe dent to her credit card.

And later, when she was curled up on the sofa, gliding effortlessly into Chapter 5 of the new novel she'd bought that day, her phone bleated, like a lamb.

Gav.

"Hey. I'm home on Sat. Wanna pop round at 8? X"

Suddenly, she had *lots* to do. A week full of plucking, tanning, exercise, hair conditioning and bikini-line waxing.

The only problem, she inwardly cursed herself for, was that she'd be missing Beth's first exhibition.

Chapter Twenty-Eight
<u>SARAH</u>

"Hot chocolate for mid-afternoon break?" A voice appeared from the shop door.

"Danny!" Tasha smiled. "Danny come in – you are long awaited."

Danny muscled his way to the shop counter, amid the flurry of boxes and setting three cardboard cups in front of the girls.

"So, how's my favourite girls?" Danny asked, taking the lid off his coffee and settling on a stool, ready to have twenty minutes of shop-keepers break.

Danny was like another member of staff. Even though he worked at the coffee-shop next door, he had known Tasha for years, and enjoyed having a coffee break with her now and again just to break up his working day.

"Good, Good," Tasha smiled, and then with a cheeky grin added, "a bit pissed off that there's no double chocolate marshmallow brownies to go along with this hot chocolate … but however, we will forgive you."

Danny smiled and held up a defensive hand. "Now, now, what were your words to me only yesterday?" He cocked his head and put on a girlie voice, "Please Danny – STOP with the brownies – I am becoming the size of a house because of you!"

Tasha sighed. "I did say that, didn't I?"

Danny and Sarah both nodded.

Tasha groaned. "Yes – but that was yesterday – and today is today – and I can't help it if the bambino keeps asking for brownies – it's not my fault."

"Tell bambino he/she can't always get everything he/she wants," Danny said authoritatively. "You don't want the child to turn into a spoiled brat."

They all laughed.

"That is very true," Tasha agreed. "Remind me to promote your advice and services to Great Dad's of the World weekly magazine."

He laughed. "Yeah – me with the no experience of it!"

"Well… " Tasha went on. "It IS a good thing that you didn't bring brownies – Sarah and I are going to a function tonight and I have a horrible sinking feeling that my dress – which is multi-plus – max – size – maternity wear – STILL won't fit me."

"Oh, don't be daft," Sarah smiled. "You'll look gorgeous."

"Want me to give you girls a lift tonight?" Danny offered. "I'll be working for a bit yet so I can drop you there on my way home?"

Tasha looked to Sarah with widened eyes and back to Danny,

"Actually – that would be fabulous! Tom can't drive us 'cos he's working tonight and it would mean Sarah could have a few drinks. And as you know, I don't like driving at the mo – my tummy would nearly get friction burns off the steering wheel."

"No problemo," Danny answered. "Name the time and I'll be here – your carriage will await you."

"Yippeee!" Tasha smiled, and Sarah nodded in agreement. An evening of glam and champagne ahead. What more could a girl ask for?

Well, a whole pile actually, but it was a good start, and miles away from the sneaking Stephen up the stairs scenario.

Stephen… Stephen. Had it been possible that she'd actually forgotten to think about him for a couple of days in a row?

First it was an hour that had passed with no thought of him.

Then a day. Then a couple of days. He'd no longer become the pressing, all-consuming, raw, painful thought that had dominated her existence. How had that happened? By simple replacement? A preoccupation with work, and getting to know a new colleague, and starting to climb a career ladder? A ladder that was shaky and blowing in the breeze no doubt, like a rope ladder hanging from a tree, but her foot had found a place on the first rung, and that was a start, and a million miles away from her clock-watching, envelope sticking days.

And sometimes, somehow, it was possible to put her head on the pillow at night, and realise that a whole day had passed, where she didn't have to obsess about the man with the "shared a bed with a woman but they didn't sleep together" excuse.

Sometimes it was possible to believe that maybe she deserved more than that.

"So what do you think of Danny?" Tasha asked her, pointedly, when they were sitting in their glamorous dresses, awaiting his arrival.

Sarah shrugged. "Nice bloke."

"Would ya though?"

Sarah laughed. "What do mean? Would I fancy him?"

"Yip"

Sarah groaned. "Oh god. Are you trying to match-make?"

Tasha distractedly pulled a lipstick out of her make-up bag and re-applied it for the millionth time. "No... I'm just saying... he's single... you're single... you're the same age... you're both nice people.. he's cute... you're cute...he's looking to be in a relationship... you're looking to be in a relationship... you'd be a MATCH MADE IN HEAVEN!"

Sarah laughed. "Oh God, you're hilarious Tasha!"

Tasha clicked her lipstick shut. "Yes – but you're not disagreeing with me". She winked. She stood up and began the process of smoothing down her dress and fiddling with her straps.

Sarah sipped back a glass of white wine that she had decided to treat herself to, having had a brief guilty moment where she thought she shouldn't be drinking in-front of Tasha in case it would seem unfair. To which Tasha had poured the glass for her and said, "Drink up – enjoy yourself!"

Sarah appraised Tasha from the comfy pink sofa she was reclining on.

"Are you nervous or something?" she asked her.

Tasha viewed herself through the full-length, pink rimmed mirror on the wall.

"Yeah, a bit", she groaned. "I look like a whale."

"Oh don't be so daft," Sarah scoffed. "You look fantastic – positively glowing."

Tasha gave her an amused stare. "Ha! This coming from – Misses – 'Maybe I should eat two Ryvitas a day' – even though she has a gorgeous figure."

"Okay, okay," Sarah conceded. "We're both a pair of silly moanies."

Tasha nodded. "Yeah, we really are." She smoothed out her dress. "Here I am, blessed with a baby inside me, and I'm yamming on about my size."

"Yeah," Sarah joked, "Ya big yammy moanie!"

"Ha!" Tasha picked up her coat. "Oh look – our prince charming awaits."

There at the doorway, standing, waving, was Danny. Cheeky grin, big wave, and happy face. And, if Sarah was not mistaken, a give-away flick of his eyes. A look that flicked down to her legs and up to her cleavage and back to her face.

No, don't be so silly, she told herself. *Just Tasha filling my head with notions.*

Tasha was nearly as bad as herself when it came to match-making, Sarah thought. But that was different, Sarah was attempting to match-make Amy and Jamie, and that was meant to be. Jamie was besotted with Amy. But Danny was just Danny. Coffee shop boy. Boy next door. Literally, boy next door.

It was too obvious. And Sarah didn't want to just jump into the next pool. This time she wanted to wait. Besides, there was still the small matter of Pete, the "I don't want you working on Saturdays" man. Metaphorically, she had far too much on her plate already.

"Sarah," Danny smiled, looking her up and down and giving her a low whistle. "You are looking great."

And with that, he turned, leading the way to his car, with Tasha winking at her, making a thumbs up sign behind his back and mouthing the words, "GET IN!"

Chapter Twenty-Nine
<u>SARAH</u>

"Danny has invited us to his birthday," Tasha announced, as she and Sarah sat with their coffees one morning.

"Oh right, cool," Sarah replied. "Where's it at? When?"

"It's at The Little Swan ...You know...that cute little pub down the cobbled alleyway near the river? It's so cute."

"Oh lovely."

"I think he's reserved the conservatory. Should be a cool night."

"Great."

"So what are you gonna wear?"

Sarah laughed. "God, I haven't even thought about that yet."

Tasha sipped her coffee and stared out the window at the passersby.

"Just cos.. you know... Danny's invited you... and it'd be nice to look nice and..."

Sarah tutted playfully. "I hope you're not trying your matchmaking again...?"

Tasha shook her head. "Who me? Noooo. Trying to make two beautiful friends happy...? Nooooo..."

Sarah laughed. "Whatever." She sipped her coffee. "Anyway, whatever's meant to be will happen. I don't believe in forcing the hand of fate."

Tasha raised an eyebrow.

"Okay. I believe you."

Danny's birthday fell on a crisp autumnal night. Tasha had cancelled due to "agonising stomach pains and extreme hormonal imbalance." Her words, not Sarah's. And Sarah knew that what she really meant was, "I need to go home, have a bath, and cuddle up in bed with my gorgeous husband."

So instead Sarah found herself crunching along the crisp grass of Richmond green with Danny's co-worker Ben. A young, good-looking chap, with a chatty outgoing personality. A guy, Sarah noted inwardly, that she would not kick out of bed.

"So, Danny will be pleased you could make it," Ben said, and later, "Yeah, Danny's really good at the guitar." And later still, "Yeah, Danny's such a dead-on chap."

Hold on here one moment, Sarah thought. *Something is going on here.*

All of a sudden, all of Danny's mates (well, Ben and Tasha), were becoming personal spokesmen for Danny, as though trying to promote him, as though trying to sell him to Sarah...

No. Really? Could it be?

Could it really be that Danny had a thing for her?

She pressed rewind in her head and played back through her catalogue of memories.

The day that he turned up on the doorstep of the shop, all toothy grinned and holding hot chocolates in hand, welcoming her to the 'neighbourhood'.

The time that Tasha said, "He never used to come in here so much for coffee breaks. It was once in a blue moon. Now it's almost every day. Put two and two together Sarah. Why would he want to be having coffee breaks with a humongous pregnant married woman? He's clearly in to see you."

The times he'd say, "Do you want me to nip out and buy you a sandwich? Cheese and onion? Okay. Don't worry, give me the money later."

The times he'd 'just happen' to have the same shifts as her and same coffee-breaks as her.

The times he'd give her and Tasha lifts and look her up and down – and there would be this look in his eyes – regret almost – as though – *I wish I were going out with her.*

No. No that's just silly Sarah. Don't be so arrogant. It's just co-incidence that's all. He's just a nice, friendly fella.

"Sarah!" Danny announced loudly as she walked through the door.

He seemed quite tipsy.

As though they'd already been there for a few hours and they'd all had a head-start. Either that, or his mates had challenged him to birthday shots.

"Sarah!" he repeated. "I'm so glad you could make it."

He hugged her, then gently swayed towards the wall, a drunken grin on his face.

Sarah smiled, soberly. "Thank you for inviting me," she said, politely. As though she were a ten-year old at a classmate's birthday party. As though she was standing there in a cute party frock about the play 'pass the parcel' and 'musical chairs'.

Ben, the good-looking young chap said, "Want a drink Sarah?" He had pulled a wallet out of his back pocket and his body language said, "Come and sit with me at the bar."

So Sarah did. She followed him, and they sat on bar stools, and Danny returned to his birthday circle, and Ben had hijacked her for an intense one-on-one chat at the bar.

They drank wine, and played catch-up and Sarah wondered why Ben was intent on devoting all his time to her. She wondered, hopefully, albeit unconvincingly, if Ben had a notion on her. She wondered lightly that she could imagine it. Her, him, her toy boy, a bit of fun, a time to wean herself off Stephen. A night of flirting, him coming back to hers, making good use of her bed, shagging the regret and pain clean out of her.

But then a girl appeared. A six-foot girl, with long blonde

hair, and legs up to her armpits, and an amazingly defined mid-riff on show. The six-foot blonde legs, approached Ben at the bar.

"Hey."

Sarah could have sworn there was a curl of her lip and an aggressive glint in her eye.

"Oh hi Amanda!" he grinned, all friendly, pretending to look surprised, when really he had probably spotted her the moment he walked in the door.

"How've you been?" blonde legs asked.

She asked this question as though she hadn't seen Danny in aeons. As though he'd been off on a hike around a desert for a year and they had had no means of communication.

"I've been good, yeah, I've been good."

Blonde legs seemed to flinch at this, as though it was the wrong answer. As though she would have preferred it if he'd said, "Agonising. Been stuck in a torture chamber for two months – hands and feet in shackles with only one meal of bread and water every day."

Blonde legs glanced at Sarah at this point, as though she'd only just noticed her. The look was an up and down one of near-disgust. As though to say, "What on earth are you doing with this full-figured curvaceous older woman with unruly hair when you could have me?!"

Sarah shrugged her shoulders helplessly with a smile. As though saying, "Hey, I can't help it if I am amazing company."

Blonde legs turned on her heels, aggressively, off to get drunk and moan to her friends about how much all men are bastards and yet secretly and painfully wonder what was wrong with her.

"Feck," Sarah whistled. "What happened there?"

Ben shrugged. "I dunno. I fancied her an' all... but... I just don't want to go out with anyone at the moment". He took a sip of his drink. "I did tell her that at the time – and she seemed to be okay with it – but then... I dunno... when a relationship didn't materialise – she just seemed to want me even more."

Sarah nodded, fascinated.

"And why don't you want a relationship?"

Ben set his drink down. "Honestly?"

"Yes, honestly."

"Been there, done that, it was shit. So much aggro. Having to answer to someone all the time. Her being pissed off if I stay out a bit later with my mates. Her being angry if I so much as say hello to another girl. Feckin' really draining."

Sarah nodded. "Maybe you've met the wrong girl."

"Hmmmph." He shrugged his shoulders. He took a sip of beer. Sarah took a sip of wine. There was a silence. A contented, intoxicated silence. Where it didn't matter that here they were, two nigh-on strangers, sitting in silence.

During the course of that silence, Sarah watched as Ben eyed up the bar-maid. The way that her black uniformed shirt was too tight for her generous chest. The way that her trousers had been ordered a size too small so that they skimmed across her back-side.

And then – whoa – his gaze switched to the other end of the bar – where a woman with blonde shoulder length hair was waiting to be served. He stared at her while her hair fell forward in front of her face and her hand reached up and swept it back.

Then there was the girl coming down the stairs whose reflection he'd caught in the mirror above the optics. The girl was wearing a short skirt and her skinny legs brushed effortlessly down the steps.

This guy just has an insatiable appetite.

This is the type of guy I would have gone for.

This is the type of guy I would have been trying to prove myself to. The type of guy that I would have thought – 'if he fancies me, that means I'm up there with the best of them'.

Rather than just realising that he would have fancied anything with two legs.

"So what about Danny?" Sarah asked, deciding to turn this encounter into a useful experiment.

"What's the story with him? With someone? Seeing someone?"

Ben scoffed. "Danny? No! Mister romantic? He hasn't gone out with anyone in ages. Far too picky that bloke."

Ker-ching!

"The trouble with Danny…" Ben went on, "is that .. when he's on a night out – he finds the most gorgeous girl in the room and goes for her. Then discovers she's with someone or not interested.. and he doesn't bother with anyone else."

Ben took another sip of his beer. "Any feckin' wonder he's always single that one."

Sarah swivelled round on her bar-stool. She was half-hoping, half-praying that Danny wasn't positioned next to blonde legs.

But blonde legs had seemed to disappear. Sarah hoped – desperately – that blonde legs hadn't gone home to cry herself to sleep over any-woman-would-do-Ben.

Danny was sitting, mid-circle of all his mates, happily drinking away, chatting, and laughing.

Sarah noticed for the first time that Danny had a rather lovely build. That his chest was quite big – as though he might go to the gym often. That he had a fine army of hair that was creeping up under his neck collar and promising a manly rug underneath that might reach down in a fine line to his navel. That he had a laugh that was infectious – a face that spread open and grinned and a head that fell back as his laughter escaped from his throat.

It was an hour later or so when she bumped into him in the hallway. She was coming out of the ladies toilets and he was on his way to the gents.

"Sarah!" he exclaimed with a grin.

"Hey Danny," she smiled, suddenly overcome with a

nervousness, a *flutterby* in her tummy.

"Thank you so much for coming," he said. It was at this point that his hand rested lightly on her arm. A slow-motion moment. A moment when everything else drowned out, and she was just fully aware of his hand on her arm.

"Thank you for inviting me," she smiled.

She noticed then, that he had dark brown eyes. Eyes that were deep and dark, as though she could stand at the edge of the diving board and just jump in.

She knew that was corny, but it was oh-so-true.

In that split second of time, Sarah performed a quick red flag test in her head. The red flag test could have been tempered by his deep brown eyes and the gentle swilling of alcohol in her stomach, but the test went like this:

Wedding ring? No.

Girlfriend? No.

Girl at home that he shares a bed with but doesn't sleep with? No.

Commitment-phobe? No.

Player? No.

Lay-about? No.

After a quick shag? No.

Relationship potential? Yes.

Give him a run for a while and do not shag him but date him for a bit and see how it goes? Okay.

Her? Romantic? Not one bit.

Chapter Thirty
JAMIE

Jamie arrived home. Monday morning. Amy had booked her Monday off work, and he'd wished now that he'd done that too. He was tired and hungover. What he really needed to do was crawl into bed and sleep. His meeting was at 2pm. He consoled himself that the meeting would probably last until 5pm – or 6pm at the very latest – and then he'd come home and sleep.

Mike, his flatmate, was out – probably at work.

Jamie spotted the remnants of ongoing life around their flat – a pair of shoes here, a TV mag there, a few dishes in the sink.

He was looking forward to seeing Mike. He thought, guiltily, about how he hadn't been in touch much. Too wrapped up in Amy-land. He dumped his bag in his bedroom, which had clearly been untouched. Good old Mike. The one thing he could rely on – he wouldn't have people trampling through his bedroom. He jumped in the shower and felt the cool rays breeze through his body.

Just get this meeting over with and get some rest – you'll be back to normal tomorrow.

He slurped a mug of coffee down for extra energy.

Just tell them about all the wonderful work done in London. Think positive thoughts.

Walking past The Pavilion, he was reminded of how much he loved Brighton. The song of the seagulls chirruping away to themselves. People said he'd grow to hate it, but he hadn't yet.

There was something vibrant about them. Show-off-ish even. As though they were saying, "Look at me! Look at me! I can make as much noise as I want! I can do what I want!"

He loved the cobbled streets along The Laines, the people walking aimlessly, the relaxed air, the young crowd, the vibrant colours, the young ones who thought nothing of sitting around smoking blow all day and drinking pints – and just living for pure pleasure.

It was a nice change from the sea of suits in London.

Yes, he was glad to be back. He'd missed this. Perhaps his London chapter would just drift behind him effortlessly, and he would settle into his old life again, and it would have all just been a passing phase.

Because that's what happened in real life, wasn't it? Oh, it would be great if life *could* be a black and white movie. If things became wrapped up nicely – a firm beginning, middle and end, with the hero triumphant and the villain defeated, but real life just wasn't like that.

Sometimes real life was just a mix of blurred stories, hazy edges, chapters drifting into nothingness, people with whom you just lost contact with and all of a sudden, one day you'd ask yourself, "Whatever happened to…?"

And so it would probably be with Amy.

She would just keep banging her head against a brick wall with Gav, until it petered out 'til nothing.

And Jamie? What would he do?

He knew he had to call things off with Stacey, for a start. It was unfair of him to keep things going. It was only messing her head up, and he didn't feel comfortable doing that.

So he would meet her. He would have a good chat with her. He would tell her,

"It's not you, it's me."

He would tell her that she had so much love to give while he was such a commitment-phobe waste of space.

No, correction, he wouldn't call himself a waste of space.

That was far too negative.

Instead, he would say things like, "There are just people for people" and "You will meet someone with whom you click with", and, "No, of course there's nothing wrong with you" (an answer prompted by her tearful questioning).

And he would tie things up nicely with her. He would have her walk away feeling good about herself. And it would be the first time, in real life, where things got tied up nicely. Where the chapter finished in a nice, rounded-off final way.

Yes, he would do all that later. First though, work.

The meeting went well. The boss seemed happy with the outcome of the London work – his job was safe for another while yet.

But when he went home, his living arrangements seemed to be less secure.

In the brief period that he'd been away, his flatmate Mike, Mister bachelor Mike, the biggest slut in Brighton Mike, appeared to have fallen in love and was contemplating moving in with Miss big boobs.

"What do you mean, you've 'fallen in love'?" Jamie asked, standing almost accusatorially in the kitchen.

Mike shrugged his shoulders and accompanied it with a blissful smile. "We're in love", he shrugged again. "She's hot!"

Jamie narrowed his eyes.

"In Love or In Lust?"

"Love," Mike replied, determinedly.

This, from Mike, was like hearing him speak another language.

Mike – pool player, beer guzzler, woman lecher – Bachelor Mike - does not fall in love. It's just not in the script.

"And when did this happen exactly?" Jamie asked, with one hand on his hip, as though they were a couple having a tiff.

Mike looked mock-bruised. "While you were off

gallivanting around London, leaving me here on my own."

Jamie nodded, a slow, deliberate nod, as though an angry parent to a disobedient child, trying not to explode at his misbehaviour.

"She's great," Mike shrugged simply. "You'll have to meet her."

Jamie nodded again, suddenly seeing his life flashing before his eyes, suddenly seeing the rug being pulled from underneath his feet, suddenly seeing his Brighton chapter whizz by far too quickly.

Yes, he was being selfish. Yes, he should be happy for his mate – but that would have to come in time. Right now, he felt tired. Exhausted, in fact, and far too much was changing.

And added to that, he had a needy text from Stacey in his inbox.

"You home babe? You want me to come round for a cuddle? X x"

Turning to Mike, he said, "I'm knackered mate – I'm happy for you - really I am – but I'm just exhausted – too much partying in London…"

Jamie met up with Stacey on Wednesday after work. They met in one of those little pubs beside Churchill Square – the ones with the beer gardens out the back and friendly bar men.

She had made a lot of effort to look nice. He knew this because she had her hair all piled up in an arrangement above her head – as though she'd been at the hairdressers for ages. She also had fancy false nails on, a tight-fitting outfit, high heels, and a strong aroma of perfume, which caught at the back of his throat and made him stifle a ticklish cough.

"It's soooo lovely to see you," she gushed.

His eyes flitted downward to his lap.

It was an unconscious, quick gesture, but it happened, and it spoke volumes.

It spoke of an uncomfortable air, of awkwardness, of something to hide.

Remember, A nice final chapter, he told himself. *Have her walking away being happy in herself. Have her thinking we're still friends. That there is good karma.*

"So how have you been? How is work? Is it nice to be back?" her questions began. The questions were laced with all her news, "That girl Mags at work is still being an out-and-out bitch, I'm not sure I can stick the place much longer . . . oh, and Tracey O'Sullivan is getting married! We all guessed she was pregnant, so this comes as no surprise really and…"

"Stacey, I'm really sorry," Jamie blurted out, "..but I can't do this anymore."

He hadn't meant to say it like that. He had meant to chat for ages. He had meant to share jokes and tell anecdotes and carefully lace the sentence in gently with all his other news, but it just blurted out, like a tell-tale fart.

The look of horror on her face was awful.

"What…? Why…?" her face actually began to crumple, as though it might fold in on itself, and produce deafening cries.

"I'm sorry…I …" Jamie began, floundering about, as though looking for a rip-cord, as though hoping an emergency button would eject him from his seat, and he would disappear, effortlessly.

"It's not you, it's me," he blurted out. He had planned to say that, yes, but when it actually came out, it just sounded crass, vulgar, wrong.

She groaned, confirming his thoughts.

He could almost hear the calculations in her head:

Pointless amount of money spent getting my hair done at the hairdressers: ninety pounds

Pointless amount of money spent getting my nails done: thirty pounds.

Pointless use of annual leave time taken today in preparation: eight hours.

Pointless amount of money spent during the last few weeks on condoms, morning after pills and pregnancy tests: lost count.

He felt like an utter bastard.

Never again, he resolved. *Never again am I going to get myself into this situation. Should I be single and celibate for the rest of my life, I am never going to put myself through this hell ever again.*

"The trouble with you, Jamie McMahon," she said, her nostrils flaring and a thunderous look appearing in her eyes.

Uh-oh, a second name situation.

"The trouble with you is that you're selfish."

She nodded again, her eyes widening further.

"And you're a commitment-phobe," she tapped her chewing gum box on the table as though she wished it the box was his head.

"After everything I have done for you…You can't see a good thing under your nose if it were to hit you on the face…"

His face reddened, not just with humiliation – humiliation at being spoken to like a child – but also anger…

"And you are going to end up like a very old and lonely man Jamie McMahon…"

The anger started to bubble furiously now.

"An old and lonely man with no-one to love him…"

Who did she think she was? The Flippin' Fortune Teller of Brighton Pier? Why didn't she just shove herself on down there and make a few bob while she was at it?

"I'm sorry you feel that way," Jamie said, calmly, repeating inwardly to himself,

She is just hurt, she is just angry, she'll calm down in a few days..

"And to top it all off…!" she cried, her voice rising, other people in the beer garden looking around at them now, Jamie wishing a small circle in the ground would peel back and swallow him up.

"…. You weren't even that great in bed!"

She said this in full crescendo now, her voice lifting to high proportions, as her chair screeched back and she stormed out, toppling a chair behind her, in her haste.

Jamie sat, open-mouthed. The other people in the beer garden sniggered a little, and one drunk fella even laughed, "Oye! Tiny dick!"

Jamie resisted the urge to take Stacey's half-empty glass of wine and smash it over drunk boy's head.

Chapter Thirty-One
SARAH

They say love happens when you least expect it. That it'd just creep up on you and hit you right smack on the face, be there waiting under your nose all along.

Sarah thought she'd never heard such bollocks in all her life.

All those blokes she'd met and all those missed opportunities. All those times with Stephen that had seemed promising at the time but had inevitably crumbled to nothing. All that pain.

Sarah marvelled at the women who met their future husbands at the age of seventeen.

A courtship of two years, an engagement, and then marriage. All those years saved from the pain and heartache. All those years where they didn't have to sob into their pillow, eat gallons of ice-cream, drink copious amounts of wine, and harass their friends on a regular basis with tales of woe.

"It's not fair," Sarah had said to Tasha one day. "It's not fair how people like you just effortlessly find your Mister Right, and people like me have to go through so much pain."

"I know," Tasha agreed, diplomatically. "However you can take responsibility a bit."

Sarah looked up from the display she was arranging. "What do you mean?"

"Well," Tasha explained, "it's true you don't know what fate will bring you – or what's in store … but you can take responsibility by not entertaining the likes of Stephen or any other fella with a similar mind-set. You could try to be more open to meeting a relationship-orientated guy. Rather than these guys who are only out for a shag".

So perhaps this was the mindset that Sarah had adopted on the night she went to Danny's party.

Perhaps it was just all a case of timing. Of two people being ready for the same thing at the same time.

It was the end of the night when Sarah began to think there was something going on. Danny had followed her upstairs, to the balcony area, where a few people had gone to sit and smoke.

When he followed her up the stairs, she just *felt* something. He didn't touch her or even say anything, but something hung in the air.

Chemistry is what they call it, even though chemistry is such a clinical scientific word for an atmosphere that felt full of fizz and promise and she didn't know what.

They were both quiet, and the air felt heavy with excitement and seriousness and inevitability. And she didn't know how that could be so, when nothing was even said.

They talked then, about inconsequential stuff – the weather, his work, her work, birthdays, getting older.

And all along there was a sub-text conversation going on. All the external words said, "nice weather, bit of rain recently, busy at work, staff helpful," but the undercurrent words were; "I fancy you. I like the look of you. I like spending time with you. You are easy to chat to. I could imagine spending more time with you."

Sarah knew that that was the undercurrent conversation. She knew this by the way that his eyes flicked from her eyes down to her lips and back again. A quick, unconscious gesture, but he had done it. She knew this also because when he raised his hand up to his head to smooth back a piece of hair, she copied him. She hadn't meant to, and her hand almost froze mid-way when she realised she was doing it.

"Mirroring his actions," she could almost see the magazine

article, "is a sure-fire sign that you fancy him."

She felt that she was brazenly obvious. She felt that that one single gesture was like a bold flashing neon sign; "I fancy you."

He said something about going out for Tina's birthday on Saturday night and asked if she'd be going. And she said that yeah, that would be nice, she'd definitely go.

He said that he could pick her up beforehand and they could go together and maybe grab a bit of food somewhere on the way, and she said yeah, that would be nice.

He almost gulped out loud, although no sound was made, and there was an unspoken question of "Is this a date then?" except neither of them said it.

They went back downstairs again and joined the rest of the birthday party crowd, which was now starting to thin out, with only the hardcore party animals left behind. They sat in the cosy bar, with the candles burning in old wine bottles and quiet music playing in the background.

And as the night wore on, and Sarah drank more drink, and Danny went off to have another smoke, Sarah went into a quiet mood. Perhaps it was the drink. Perhaps it was relaxing her too much. Perhaps it was the drink that was making her think that if she were to go home now, it would be like walking away from a magnet. Because that's what it felt like. As though, no matter where Danny was sitting or standing at the party, she was conscious of his presence. He was there, in the corner of her eye, all the time, and she felt happiest when he was by her side.

She suddenly felt frustrated and upset, knowing that they'd never get together at all, that this was some silly figment of her imagination, and he was only wanting to be friends, that's all he wanted.

She was quiet and despondent. The night was nearly over. Soon they would be trickling out and she'd be going home. And that frisson of atmosphere or chemistry or she didn't know what, would be gone forever.

Perhaps he sensed her mood, perhaps he wanted to break the ice, because he sat down beside her and said, "Do you want to come back to mine? Everyone's coming back for a party."

Shortly after, she was sitting cross-legged on his living-room floor, enjoying the chat and the laughter with him and his mates.

The night had only just begun.

She sat on and sat on, until she attempted to phone a taxi and said, "Uh oh, all the taxis are booked up."

And that's when Danny said, "It's okay, you can stay here if you want."

And bingo, her plan had worked.

Chapter Thirty-Two
SARAH

Danny said he really did expect to sleep on the sofa and for Sarah to sleep on the bed – that really was what he expected.

But he had patted the sofa and said, "Come and chat to me for a bit," and she had moved from her cross-legged position on the floor and joined him.

Everyone else had gone home by then. The sun was creeping through the pale blue curtains, already promising a new day while Danny and Sarah were still in last-night mode.

The inebriation helped. A cotton wool fuzz coated any potential nerves or self-consciousness. Sarah had rested her hand on Danny's leg. It was an unconscious gesture, but he neither flinched nor seemed awkward. She liked the feel of his muscles under his jeans. He, in turn, took her hand, in a playful way, half-stroking, half-tickling her arm, as though it were a friendly thing to do, as though it wasn't just a prelude to wanting to kiss her. Because that's what he wanted to do. Her full, plump lips, sitting so close to him, the only barrier being fear of rejection; fear of "What the feck are you playing at?"; fear of "oh no Danny – I'm sorry I've given you the wrong impression – we are just mates".

He considered the barrier. A flimsy one at best. Had she just wanted to be friends, would she still be sitting here at silly o'clock? Would she not rather be wrapped up in her own bed?

Yes. But she couldn't get a taxi.

She is drunk.

I have no evidence to suggest she fancies me.

She leaned back on the sofa somewhat, as though she were about to fall asleep. Her eyes started to drift closed. Outside, seagulls squawked, signalling a new day.

Danny's heart sank. She would sleep, and that would be that, and another birthday would have passed, and he would have had an eight-hour drink-fest, still being unable to summon up the courage to kiss her.

Her eyes were closed, and she had wrapped her arms around herself, and she had pulled her legs up to her chest, as though curled up in the womb.

Danny found a blanket, and covered her with it, tucking it around her, making sure she'd be warm and snug. He turned the light off. All there was now was the gentle stream of light that was casting a ray in through the window.

She was asleep. Her lips looked pouted. He couldn't help it. He kissed her.

He pressed his mouth on hers, softly, just covering her lips with his. Half-expecting her to wake up flustering and aghast, shouting something like, "Get off me! You cheeky brute!" But she didn't. She responded.

And all of a sudden, her hand was behind his head, pulling him closer to her, and they were kissing. Fiercely, passionately, all-consuming.

Her and him. On the sofa.

"Oh God," he was saying, between kisses, and then he was up, lifting her, carrying her into the bedroom with whatever combination of adrenalin and strength he had suddenly surging through his body.

And then they were on his bed, kissing for what seemed like ages, to the sound of seagulls rejoicing outside.

The next morning he took her for a walk up the hill, to the place that looks out over the whole of Richmond and the River Thames running along underneath.

Sarah's self-consciousness had snapped back into place and she could hardly quite believe that here they were, one of the smug couples, walking along hand in hand, with a night of passion behind them, and a day of cosy coupledom in front of them. She wondered if she deserved it. If she should pinch herself to check if it was really happening. She couldn't help but have the tiny fear that one day it would all get snatched away.

The night of passion had not ended in sex. She learned enough not to do that. But there had been passion, and there had been chemistry, and that surprised her. Because she'd always associated passion with emotionally distant strangers, rather than a male friend she felt relaxed with.

He knew what he was doing, that was true, and anyway, it didn't matter. Because he looked at her like she was the most sexy woman on the planet, and that was an aphrodisiac enough.

Back at his flat, he cooked her a roast dinner, juggling pots and pans, all with the ease of an aspiring chef. He told her to relax on the sofa and listen to whatever music she wanted to listen to, and so she did. Sitting at the window, watching the world go by, and wondering how this had happened. How had she ended up relaxing on a sofa while a gorgeous man was cooking her dinner? Had she done something wonderful in a past life to deserve such super karma points?

To work he delivered flowers. A huge bunch of flowers that must have cost a fortune and which swallowed up Tasha's head when she held them in front of her.

"To S. From D. X"

"Hmmm… What do you make of the note?" Tasha asked.

"I like it."

Tasha raised an eyebrow. " 'From?' Don't you think he could have managed a 'Love' ?"

"Ugh. No. Too soon."

"Hmmm…Okay…" Tasha conceded. "Well, I for one, am

very happy for you both – and it's a long bloody time coming."

Sarah laughed. "You think?"

"Yup," Tasha nodded.

And so it was with Sarah and Danny; Sarah staying over at Danny's one night at first, and then another, and then another, until it became a regular pattern. Sarah and Danny turning up at work together, giving her a peck on the lips, and her going into the shop, carrying her over-night bag, with Tasha and Tina knowing that that was her dirty laundry, knowing what she'd been up to.

It seemed too idyllic, too perfect. As though everything had just slotted into place in one neat jigsaw, and Sarah didn't know how that could be so. It seemed as if something was at her heels, constantly wanting to snatch it away from her.

Danny didn't have that mindset.

Danny picked her up and spun her around. Danny tickled her until she was squealing. Danny said things like, "Do you have to stay at yours tonight?"

She'd laugh and reply, "I need to get clean clothes."

And he'd pout and say, "Well, make sure to bring enough clothes next time."

It was effortless with him.

But not so with Sarah. She didn't have that same ability to shut off her nagging head and believe that things would work out just fine, thank you very much.

It was actually Tasha who broke the bubble.

It was a Saturday afternoon like any other. The shop was busy, but not overly so. Tasha and Sarah and Tina had had their ten o'clock rotational coffee breaks. A hopefully busy day was ahead. It was warm, and bright, and a good passing trade was expected. Tasha seemed jittery, on edge, as though tense. Sarah put it down to pre-baby nerves. Tasha was due to pop any day. She was round and swollen, and looked uncomfortable when she walked. She was impatient now to just push the baby out and get on with it.

"Can you stay behind for about half an hour after work today?" Tasha asked her. "I just need to discuss something with you."

"Oh …right…okay…" Sarah gulped. "Is everything okay?"

"Oh yes…yes…it's fine," Tasha nodded, but her eyes said something else. Her eyes were shifty, nervous looking, as though really she should be biting her lip and saying, "No actually… something's wrong and I need to break some news to you… and I really don't know how to go about it."

"Everything's fine – swear to God," Tasha replied hurriedly. "Please don't panic – I'm just letting you know I need a chat – in case you had to rush off home early."

"Okay," Sarah nodded, but her head swam, all day. Suddenly it really didn't matter about pink fairy lights and girlie household accessories. Suddenly Sarah had visions of Tasha exposing Danny for who he really was – a big two-timing lying ball-bag. Perhaps Tasha had heard something? Perhaps she needed to break it to her gently? She knew Tasha would rather tell her, as painful as it would be, rather than keep her in the dark.

She took a deep breath and braced herself.

Please God, help me to deal with whatever this is all about….
Please God, help me to deal with whatever this is all about….
Please God, help me to deal with whatever this is all about….

Sarah repeated to herself, like a mantra, as she walked towards the small staff room, trying to ignore the weakening effect that had taken over her knees.

"Have a seat," Tasha smiled, as she sat on one of the office chairs at the table.

Sarah's limbs sat themselves down, even though she was not

aware how they had done that, because she was sure she was no longer in control of her bodily movements, especially as her heart was pounding.

"Please..." Tasha persisted. "Please don't look so worried. It's only me, Tasha."

Sarah smiled, in spite of herself. "Yeah, sorry, can't help but think the worst."

"Well," Tasha lifted her papers and straightened them, even though Sarah was pretty sure the papers were blank, and Tasha was, in effect needing a comforting prop.

"I have had to sit down and have some thoughts about the business..." Tasha began.

This was when it seemed like a blur of words all escaped from Tasha's mouth in one long, endless stream. Words like, "Business expanding...recession...Brighton branch... management...good staff on board...what would you think if..."

That was the jumble of words, but really all Sarah heard was...

"BLUR.....BLUR.....BLUR.....BLUR.....BLUR.....BLUR ....."

She realised at first, that this 'chat' was absolutely nothing to do with Danny and absolutely everything to do with work.

Her brain was fuzz.

Had she always been this slow?

"BLUR...BLUR....BLUR....BLUR...BLUR....BLUR..." Tasha went on, her bangles jangling as her hands did a merry little dance in front of Sarah's face.

"Expanding...new manager...Brighton branch... experienced...trustworthy...calm....reliable... able to take on a challenge..." Tasha went on.

And this was when it was starting to become clear.

"You're asking me if I'd like to be manager of your new Brighton branch?" Sarah asked.

She sat back in shock, letting the words settle out there in the thin air surrounding them.

"Yes," Tasha nodded firmly. "Yes, that is what I'm saying."

Another silence then. As Sarah's mouth dropped open, and she unconsciously, and rather unattractively, began a fish impersonation. It went like this:

Mouth open. Mouth closed.

Mouth open again. Mouth closed again.

Hand on mouth.

Eyes widening.

A little squeal.

An "Are you for real?!"

An "Oh my goodness, that's not very professional of me.. I mean…. Yes!!... Of course… YES! I would LOVE that!! Oh my goodness! I am so touched! Touched! I'm honoured! You trust me with me with that? Oh my goodness!!"

She grinned. Her face nearly exploding all over the place with the length of her grin.

"Yes, of course I trust you with it," Tasha said firmly, smiling. "That's why I've had you here working – to train you up and make sure I'm really happy with your work before I send you down there."

"Wow!" Sarah grinned. "Wow!"

"I'm so pleased that you're happy with it," Tasha sighed. "I was worried you wouldn't fancy it – what with the move to Brighton – and you just getting together with Danny an' all."

Danny. Danny.

Sarah *had* temporarily forgotten about him for all of two seconds.

Danny. What would happen now?

Surely that would be the end of her little fling?

Surely a move down south and dating between Brighton and London would not stand the distance?

Perhaps it really had all been too good to be true?

216

Chapter Thirty-Three
BETH

It was sitting by the riverside that Beth found her solace. The lapping waves, the ducks bobbing along in a little line like a family, one of them trailing behind on her own. The birds circling in the sky, being carried by the wind, trying to struggle against it at times, and then giving in, letting the strength of the wind carry them wherever they were supposed to go.

Beth sat on the concrete steps which led down to the water. She used her coat to sit on and she sat there, a solitary figure, thinking.

That was the trouble, she was doing far too much thinking these days. She felt like her head might explode with the amount of thinking she had been doing. She longed for a simple life. A life of drifting along, effortlessly, without a care in the world.

Perhaps she was getting bored of the pain now. The thought of that gave her hope.

It had been some time now since the running away from Jake incident. She had been cowardly, she knew it.

The "I'm busy, go away" sign had hung on her door ever since. The only person she had spoken to was Roxanne, who was delighted to see that Beth was producing one drawing after the other. Beth was sure that Roxanne knew about the Jake incident. But she had the decency not to pry about it. That was the thing about Roxanne. There was a sympathy from her, an empathy. Probably the result of her own suffering, Beth mused. Maybe because Roxanne had been hurled through her own passage of pain, perhaps it made her a softer person. More sympathetic.

So Beth produced one drawing after the other, and kept her sign on her door, and heard the footsteps outside, and heard Jake's voice, "Beth, are you there?"

"Beth, are you ready to talk?"

"Beth, I'm sorry if I was too pushy."

"Beth, I'm here if you change your mind."

And then nothing. Perhaps he had given up, Beth thought.

The thing is, there was too many "What if's?" surrounding Jake.

What if I only kissed him back because I was feeling vulnerable?

What if he only kissed me because he knew I was vulnerable?

What if he only kissed me, hoping that in my weak emotional state, I would jump into bed with him, there and then?

What if he's just another Karl?

And added to the "What if's?", there were a lot of "Can I's?"

Can I really put myself through all this pain again?

Can I really recover from heartbreak for another time?

And that was why Beth hid herself away.

Because inside her studio, she was safe. No-one could touch her, and she could mend her heart again. Sew it back up again like an old woollen teddy-bear whose eye had fallen off and then sewn back in a haphazard manner, so that it looks the same, but it's just a bit battered. That's what Beth felt like.

But the thing was, that even though Beth was tucked away, she *still* saw the couples strolling along the riverside and she still had to admit to herself that that *was* what she wanted – a relationship. And the relationship didn't live, and her loss was great, because it had been her dream. A dream that she was tempted to bury, like a big shiny pebble under dirty sand.

It was Sarah who talked sense into her in the end. Of course it was Sarah.

"Right. I'm sick of this!" Sarah said abruptly, at their next

Break-up test meeting.

"What?" Beth winced.

"You. Mincing around like it's the end of the world. Hiding yourself away. Wrapped up in your own fear and self-pity."

Beth felt tears threaten to pop out.

"Look – I'm sorry," Sarah continued. "Truly I am. I don't mean to be so harsh – but there is a reason for the 'It's cruel to be kind' statement."

Beth nodded quietly.

"You're ruining yourself. You're letting Karl ruin you. Jake seems like a perfectly nice fella. He has knocked on your door trillions of times and shown extreme patience and understanding. This does not sound like a fella after a quick shag."

Beth nodded again.

"Don't feck things up Beth. Please. Don't hide yourself away."

So Beth decided not to.

She returned to her studio.

She changed her door sign to "I'm in! Pop in!"

And then she sat down.

And she drew.

Her hands were shaking and her heart was thumping and she couldn't concentrate, but she drew.

Or at least, she pretended to draw.

She had her fingers wrapped round a pencil and she spent more time staring out the window than focusing on her easel, but she sat there, expectantly, with her door sign welcome and her heart breathtakingly open and she waited.

And waited.

And waited.

The clock hand rotated around from early morning to lunchtime to early afternoon.

Not a soul trekked down her corridor. They had probably given up on her. They had probably said, "Shame about that new girl – a bit intense. No chat out of her whatsoever. Oh well, I suppose you get these artists types from time to time. A bit reclusive, aren't they?" And they would have forgotten about her, and got on with their own thing, and she would have become a distant memory.

Except that Roxanne never forgot her. Roxanne was the only one who seemed to really understand her. She seemed to know why she was hiding away, why she was so withdrawn, why she was so quiet. Maybe they had that secret bond – that common experience of grief – of losing someone, and losing a bit of yourself.

"It makes you stronger you know," Roxanne had blurted out once. "You think you're going to wilt under the pain of it all, but time heals you, and you begin to realise, "If I can get through this, I can get through anything, and it makes you stronger. You begin to have a quiet confidence in yourself, and an independence."

"Thank you," Beth nodded quietly, knowing exactly what Roxanne meant, grateful that she had shared this hope with her.

"So! Where are we going to hang these wonderful drawings of yours?" Roxanne asked chirpily, changing the subject, keeping the atmosphere light and airy.

"Oh, you can put mine in the back somewhere – I don't want to detract from your exhibition."

"Nonsense. My paintings are all overly colourful – I like your black and white drawings to even it out. We'll put them here", she said, pointing to a front panel that people wouldn't miss on their way in.

"Are you sure? Thank you so much!" Beth gasped gratefully.

"I'm very sure," Roxanne said, decisively. "Now, let's go and treat ourselves to a nice cup of tea and a big feed. Tomorrow is a big day."

The exhibition began at 7pm and was due to proceed until 10pm. A huge vase of lilies were delivered and graced the table on the way in. A young man with a charming smile and a bow-tie stood behind a small table of glasses of wine and bowls of nibbles. Roxanne looked amazing – a red Chinese style dress that came up to her neck and down to her toes, snugly fitting with a long slit from toe to thigh. She also had a red feather head-piece in her hair making her jaw-droppingly stunning.

Beth was in black, which seemed non-existent in comparison, but her many tanning sessions had given her a healthy golden glow, so that she felt radiant. Roxanne and Beth waited, next to smiley bow-tie man, nervously wondering if their invitations were enough, wondering if anyone would bother to come. And Beth wondered more importantly, would Jake bother to come?

Of course he would, she told herself, for Roxanne's benefit more than anything else. She had thought of inviting Karl, for some reason. Maybe in a last ditch attempt to show him how wonderful she was? In the hope that he would reconsider his feelings? In the hope that he would suddenly redress the whole relationship and start over? And then she realised that was ludicrous, futile, fruitless. There was nothing she could do to change anyone else. If she'd learned nothing else, she'd learned that.

The door opened and a person appeared. Two people in-fact! Two absolute strangers who had seen the flyer and came along of their own accord, simply because they loved art. Beth felt like kissing them and thanking them for their very presence, and then she remembered to be cool. And in fact, *they* were the ones saying "Did you draw this? Did you really draw this?"

And Beth had to stop herself from bursting into relieved tears right there and then in front of them. To stop herself from saying, "Oh thank you so much for even saying that!"

She overheard the woman saying to the man, "I just love

that drawing of that kitten. It's so innocent and beautiful. I would love that for our lounge. Can we Ken? Can we buy that?"

"Of course darling. Of course we can."

Beth saw Roxanne look over at her and wink knowingly and it was all Beth could do not to run to the toilets and pinch herself.

The evening galloped on, with more and more people arriving, and people chatting about texture and definition and meaning and symbolism and Beth smiled happily, not realising that her work said anything at all, just knowing that she had drawn, just to make herself feel better.

The door opened again and this time Mary and Paddy arrived but no sign of Jake.

Mary was wearing bright yellow and her voice was heard the moment the door opened.

"Oh! It's so nice to see you!" Beth grinned, accepting the crushing embrace that Mary pounced on her.

Beth gave her an inquisitive look as though to say, "Is Jake not with you?" but no words came out, even though she was sure Paddy picked up on it.

The night was wearing on then and Beth was exhausted but happy. All of her drawings but one had sold – an incredible result. She was sad at Jake's lack of appearance but she chided herself that it was understandable. She *had* avoided him for weeks – no wonder he had failed to turn up. However she was disappointed for Roxanne's benefit – she was sorry that her behaviour had prevented one less supportive friend for her exhibition.

"All sold but one! I can't believe it!" Beth grinned, after most of the people had gone and the exhibition was nearly closing time.

"An incredible result!" Roxanne smiled. "And I'm sold out completely. It's brilliant!"

"I'll buy your last drawing," a voice said.

Jake's.

"If I can."

Beth twirled to see him standing in the doorway. He looked so handsome. A slight stubble. Black trousers, black shirt, a few hairs poking up from under the nape of his shirt.

"Hi" Beth smiled, signalling that all was okay, that her hibernation period was over.

"So can I?" he asked.

"Can you what?" she asked, flustered, her face reddening as his intense stare, the way his eyes crept over her face, her lips, was making her feel self-conscious.

"Can I buy your last drawing?"

There was a pause then, a silence.

"It's very precious," she replied finally. "It needs a lot of looking after. It needs care and attention."

"I know, I'm aware of that," he smiled.

"And you're prepared to look after it?"

"Of course I am. I will cherish it."

"Well then, it's yours," she gulped.

"Good," he replied, with finality. "Now, can I walk you home?"

They walked along the riverside, hand-in-hand, like one of those couples Beth had spotted and been truly sickened by. But this time, it was her. Walking hand-in-hand with her man, and it didn't feel so impossible, or out of reach, or unobtainable.

In fact, she never dreamed it could be so easy.

Chapter Thirty-Four
SARAH

Tasha and Sarah went out for a celebratory glass of wine and bite to eat. Well, Sarah had wine, Tasha had sparkling water.

"Don't you miss drink?" Sarah asked.

"No, not really," Tasha shrugged. "If I was to drink now, I'd be far too sick anyway, so it wouldn't be worth it." She sipped her water. "Anyway, I'm feeling celebratory enough as it is – I have now bagged myself a wonderful manager for my Brighton branch – what more could a girl want?"

Sarah grinned. "Well, I'm on cloud nine."

"And what about Danny?" Tasha asked, biting her lip.

Sarah shrugged. "I really don't know."

She took her knife and fork and sliced the piece of meat on her plate. "I'll just have to see what happens. Whatever's meant to be an' all that."

Tasha nodded, and pretended to agree with Sarah's forced confidence, but her eyes betrayed a secret doubt.

Danny was at a stag party. The first night he'd been apart from Sarah in a while. Of course, it would have to co-incide with her big news. She decided not to phone him or text him, and instead just wait until the next time she saw him to tell him the news.

When she arrived home, there was a figure sitting on her doorstep.

At first she couldn't make out who it was. It was dark. She

was walking up the street in a half-drunk, half-tired manner. The light from the lamp-post was casting a dim view of the figure. It was a male, that much she could tell, but was it Danny? Surely he wouldn't have left the stag party early to come and see her? Surely they weren't that inseparable already?

But no, the figure sitting on her doorstep, waiting patiently for her, like a latch-key kid, was Stephen.

"Hi", he said, simply, as though this was the norm. As though it was perfectly normal to go off, get someone else pregnant, and then turn up on her doorstep.

"What are *you* doing here?" Sarah asked abruptly.

"I came to see you. We need to talk."

"Hmmmph!"

She pushed past him, putting her key in the lock.

"I have *nothing* to say to you."

"Sarah, come on, please," he pleaded. "I've come all this way up from Brighton to see you and I've been sitting here waiting for three hours…"

"So? No-one asked you to."

"Please. I've tried calling you and texting you, but you've obviously blocked my number…"

She was silent.

"Please just let me talk to you for ten minutes. I need to explain things."

She pushed the door open, and allowed him to put his foot on the door to stop it from swinging closed in his face.

She climbed the next set of stairs and opened the door of her flat. Again, he caught the door.

I can't believe I am letting him into this flat. How thick am I?

A five minute chat. That's all he gets. Tell him I want nothing more to do with him.

The flat was quiet. She went into the kitchen, picked a small bottle of beer out of her fridge, flicked the top off and made her way into the lounge.

She collapsed into the armchair and kicked off her shoes, sighing as she did so. It had been such a long day. A long, yet happy day.

She noticed how he had picked himself a bottle of beer out of the fridge too.

What a cheek.

He set the beer on the carpet and sat on the sofa. He rubbed his hands together, as though trying to warm himself up. As though trying to say, *"Look at me. Poor fallen hero that I am, waiting outside for hours for you."*

She sipped her beer and ignored the gesture.

"The wedding is off," he announced.

Sarah looked at him. She *was* shocked, that much was true, but she didn't show it.

She realised, despite herself, that inwardly she felt something, and that something was relief. And she was annoyed at herself for feeling relief, because that would mean that she cared in the first place, and she had been trying her best not to care.

But the relief was about the wedding dress. No more would she have to worry about bumping into Kat and Stephen, emerging from the church, with the wedding dress lifting and swallowing her up, the way it had been happening in her nightmares.

At least she wouldn't have to deal with that.

"What happened?" Sarah asked, a hint of sarcasm in her voice. "Did you get another girl pregnant?"

He did that sigh thing again, as though he didn't want to argue, as though that would be the waste of a perfectly good night.

"No, no I didn't," he replied, simply.

"Then what happened?" Sarah asked. Asking, and yet annoyed at herself for even asking, annoyed at herself for even pretending to care.

"It wasn't right," he shrugged. "It didn't feel right." He hung his head and looked at the floor. "It was for all the wrong reasons."

Sarah nodded, sharply, as though she were the judge and the jury.

"And what reasons were that then?"

He shrugged. "For the children."

Sarah's eyes widened and she lifted her eyebrows. "As good a reason as any."

"Yes, but it's not enough of a reason," he stared at her, fixing her with an intense gaze that she would have found unnerving, if it had been months ago.

"I love *you*, Sarah," he said. "It's *you* I want. You know that. You know it's you I wanted all along."

Sarah found her heart pumping despite herself, and her fingertips had gone cold. She hadn't expected this.

"I *never* knew that," she choked. "You *never* told me that."

She shook her head, as though trying to straighten out her thoughts.

"This is all totally new to me. You've never told me this."

"But I've thought it Sarah. I thought you could tell." He was sitting on the edge of the sofa now, fixing her with an intense stare. "I tried to tell you so many times but you kept running away – the minute I got close – you'd run a mile."

Sarah sat back and sighed. She closed her eyes. This was too much. Much too much. First the news about Brighton. Now Stephen declaring his love. Was it a sign?

Stephen lives in Brighton. I'm being sent to Brighton. Is it a sign?

She was too drunk. Too tired.

She thought of Danny, out at a stag do. Probably surrounded by pole dancers shoving their buttocks in his face. She thought of telling him her news. About moving to Brighton. She thought of his reaction. He would probably say, "Oh dear Sarah… well, I'm happy for you but … I guess that's the end of us… We can't really keep this going if we're living in different towns."

She would nod, understandably, and accept it. Because after all, wasn't that what she'd had to keep doing all her life? Just accept things?

And then here was Stephen. Sitting in her lounge. Finally declaring his undying love. While her head was spinning with drink and tiredness.

Wasn't this what I had wanted all along?

"Any wonder I always used to disappear," she said, testing him. "I had so much to contend with. Kat. Your child. That blonde photographer…"

"The photographer?!" Stephen spluttered. "You mean H?" He screwed up his face as though to signal his disgust. "Don't be so daft! I don't fancy her! Did you think I fancied her? Oh come on, there was no chemistry whatsoever."

"Chemistry?!" Sarah exclaimed. "Since when do you have to wait for chemistry in order to shag a girl? You'd shag anything that moved!"

He signed. And there was a silence. A long silence.

After a while he whispered, "That was the problem wasn't it? You never trusted me."

Sarah laughed then. Her head spilling back into a big sarcastic, angry laugh.

"You're a fecking joke. Coming in here and telling me about trust when you were the one off getting Kat pregnant."

Stephen pursed his lips then. And in between pursings, he half said/ half spat, "We. Were. On. A. Break."

"Hmmph," Sarah exclaimed quickly.

"We were," he persisted. "You had walked away. Again. Kat and I – well, we were just drunk – it just happened."

"What? Like you just accidentally ripped her clothes off and thrust yourself inside her?" Sarah said, too loudly.

Stephen held his head in his hand and took a deep breath.

"It just happened," he said, quietly. "She was drunk, I was

drunk, it just happened."

Sarah *wanted* to believe him, really she did. If only to wrap her tender self-esteem in cotton wool and nurse it better. If only to say, "There, there, there is nothing wrong with you really. You are an attractive, good-looking girl, and the only reason he chose another girl over you was because of a slight accident. Just accidentally Kat's clothes fell off and Stephen entered her and then a baby was born. It was all just a big accident."

She *wanted* to tell herself that it *could* have happened on a break. It *could* have been an accident. She wanted to tell herself "Well Sarah, you did know what you were letting yourself in for.

She wanted to tell herself all that, if only to feel that the whole big painful experience hadn't been a complete waste of time.

But then she suddenly realised that it hadn't all been a waste of time. If it hadn't have been for this experience, she wouldn't have had the get-up-and-go to get a new job. She wouldn't have had a re-think about the type of guys she was attracted to. She wouldn't have been open-minded enough to give a nice guy like Danny a chance.

She wouldn't be sitting there, with a promotion behind her and a new life in Brighton ahead of her.

"I'm sorry for you," Sarah shook her head. "Really I am. I think you just want what you can't have. I wouldn't be surprised that if Kat met someone else, you'd suddenly want back with her."

Stephen's eyes shifted at her comment.

And then the realisation hit Sarah.

"Oh God. This is what this is all about, isn't it? Kat's met someone else – and now you're back trying to hook up with me. How very convenient."

"It's not like that…" Stephen began.

"Just get out," Sarah announced firmly. "Please – just get

out. Go home, sort yourself out."

"I have nowhere to go…" he began. "I can't go back to Kat's … please .. let me stay here."

"No. Go." Sarah said firmly. She walked him to the door. He stepped outside it. And she closed the door, very firmly, behind him.

Chapter Thirty-Five
JAMIE

"Stacey said what?" Mike let out a low whistle. "I'm really sorry to hear that mate."

Jamie shook his head dejectedly. "I'm never gonna be able to step foot inside 'The Western Front' ever again."

"Ah!" Mike laughed, grabbing a beer from the fridge and flinging it in Jamie's direction. "What's that saying – 'Today's news is tomorrow's fish and chip wrapper...'"

"Yeah," Jamie sighed. He was going to lunge into a big explanation of how he had hoped to be Stacey's friend. That he really did hope it was possible to be friends with an ex – but obviously that was just a silly notion – an impossibility.

Except, Jamie didn't talk about it. Jamie felt talked out. In fact, he felt he'd had enough drama to last him a lifetime. He grabbed the controller, flicked over to Top Gear, and put his feet up, preparing for a relaxing evening of chill out time with Mike.

This is how it should be, he thought. *Relief. Stress-free. None of that drama central anymore.*

"Listen mate..." Mike began, before his bum had hardly even touched the sofa. "There's something I need to tell you..."

Jamie raised his eyes from the TV and looked over at Mike. *Uh oh. This did not sound good.*

"I know now's not really a good time to tell you this but ..."

Why is he making this sound as though he's splitting up with me?

"But, well...there's never really a good time to tell these things and well..."

Jamie gulped. He knew what was coming.

"It's Jenny, I'm moving in with her."

And there it was. Like a bullet.

Jamie scrunched his face up and ran a hand through his hair.

"What...? But...like...you've only been going out like...two minutes..."

"Well, it's more like a month actually..." Mike defended himself. "...and we have known each other longer as friends..."

Mike took a swig of his beer, as though gulping back courage.

"So...when...where..." Jamie found words coming out of his mouth, words that were asking for details, words that were trying to make arrangements. He knew he was still at level one – shock. It would take a while before he moved through the barometer to level ten – acceptance and finding a new flatmate.

Okay, don't be so selfish Jamie. Be happy for him.

"Are you out of your mind? One month?"

Mike seemed to wince at this, as though mortified, as though caught red-handed by the bachelor police.

"I dunno," Pete said quietly, "It just feels right, that's all."

"Feels right?! At one month? That's cause you're shagging night and day. Wait til it's a year. Wait til she's putting the lock on the door and not allowing you nights out with the lads."

Don't be so selfish. This is not all about you. Be happy for him.

"She's not like that mate," Mike persisted. His words were warm, but his tone, not so. In fact, Jamie could've sworn he practically *spat* the word 'mate' out.

Jamie laughed, a sarcastic laugh.

"I'm sorry – I'm just in shock – really I am – I mean – what's wrong with dating for a year first..." Jamie held his hands upwards. "Sorry – I'm just sayin' – it's just not like you – that's all – I mean – think about it Mike – it's moving in first – then it's marriage – then it's screaming kids – are you *sure* you want to be stuck with the same woman for the rest of your life? I mean – you're *never* going to sleep with anyone else ever again."

Jamie could tell he'd dealt a low blow with that last comment. Mike actually seemed to physically recoil at the thought of it.

There was a silence then.

Jamie felt convinced he'd won the argument. That Mike would sigh a deep breath and say, "Shit man! You're absolutely right! What was I thinking of? Look what happens to me when you disappear for a few weeks! I totally fall apart! Good job you're here to put me back on track!"

Jamie thought he'd say all that, but instead Mike narrowed his eyes and looked at him accusatorially.

"The trouble with you, Jamie McMahon…." he said loudly, as though he were about to explode. "The trouble with you, is that you're selfish."

Uh oh, why did that speech sound familiar?

"You're just annoyed because things aren't slotting in with your plans! Well, I've news for you – tough shit!"

Jamie winced.

"At least Jenny won't leave her crap lying all around the place! I'm sure she'll be a lot easier to live with!"

You, Jamie McMahon, are going to end up a very lonely old man!

"I'm outta here!" Mike spat, grabbing his coat and keys, and slamming the door behind him.

And then there was one.

To: Jamie_mcmahon@hotmail.com
From: Stacey_sullivan@gmail.com
Subject: Hello

Hello Jamie, it's me. It's late at night and I couldn't sleep so I just thought, 'to hell with it, I'll just email you'. You probably don't want to hear from me, but I've nothing to lose so I thought I'd just write.

I miss you Jamie. I know that sounds silly, but I do. I really, really, miss you. I honestly thought there was something very special between us. And I wanted you to know that if you ever reconsider – well – I'm here – waiting for you.

I love you.

Yes, I really do.

I love you.

There, I've said it.

I love you, I love you, I love you.

Stacey x o x o x o

Ps. You weren't bad in bed really – you were very good in fact x x x

From: Jamie_mcmahon@hotmail.com
To: Stacey_sullivan@gmail.com
Subject: re: Hello

Hi Stacey. Thanks for that.

I'm not really sure what to say except that I'm sorry I hurt you – and I really do hope you find someone really special.

Jamie.

To: Jamie_mcmahon@hotmail.com
From: Stacey_sullivan@gmail.com
Subject: re: re: Hello

Well, that's it then? I tell you I love you and that's all the response I get? I am mortified. You have as much emotion as a brick. I am blocking you now. Don't ever contact me again. Don't email me. Don't message me. Don't even say hello if you bump into me in the street. I despise you.

S

Ps. You were shit in bed. I was faking it.

"Yo mister!" A pleasant voice greeted him on his mobile. "How're you doing?!" There was a smile attached to the voice. A lovely, warm, pleasant, smile, and Jamie wanted to put his arms down the receiver and hug the recipient.

Sarah.

"Sarah! Bloody hell! Great to hear from you? How are you?"

"I am great! Just great!"

He could even hear her beaming down the other side of the phone.

"And it's all thanks to you, Jamie McMahon!"

At last, someone using a double name situation for a nice reason.

"To me?" Jamie asked. "Are you sure?"

"Of course I'm sure! Break-up test, remember?"

Jamie nodded. "Oh yeah, that."

"Listen," Sarah went on, "I've so much to tell you.. and I'm actually planning to be down in Brighton on Saturday. Any chance you could meet up?"

"Chance? Of course! Wouldn't miss it!" he grinned.

"Good," she sounded as though she was nodding in satisfaction.

"Now, get those drinking goggles ready – we're gonna have fun!"

Jamie grinned. He was about to hang up when he added. "Um.. Sar..?"

"Yes Jamie?"

"Is Amy coming down with you?"

"No Jamie," she sighed, "...I think she's going to Gav's on Saturday night..."

"Oh right... okay..."

"Okay, two things…" Sarah began, as they sat in the beer garden of 'The Devil's Dyke' pub.

They had ventured up in the steep hill in the big green open-top bus, Sarah gasping with excitement at the amazing views. Fields stretching for miles. As much greenery as she would spot if she was back home in Northern Ireland.

"Wow! This is amazing!" she cried. "I could get used to this!"

"Hmm," Jamie grunted, "It's amazing how much I never bother coming up here. It takes a tourist to come along before I'd venture out of my own doorstep."

They walked along the grassy hills for all of about fifteen minutes, before Jamie said, "Lunch?"

"Yep"

"Two things…?" Jamie repeated.

Her hands were on the knife and fork on either side of her, as though this gave her more authority somehow, as though she was a judge in a high court holding on to a gavel.

Jamie nodded and grinned. "Why do I feel like I'm at a business meeting?"

"Because I mean business!" she grinned.

Jamie took a long look at his friend. She had certainly come on in leaps and bounds during the last couple of months. She had a new air of confidence. A 'devil-may-care' attitude. A security about her that said, "take it or leave it."

"Okay," he grinned. "Shoot."

"The first thing is…" she grinned, "is that I've got a new job!"

He widened his eyes.

"Not a new job as such – but a promotion!"

Jamie grinned. "Oh Sarah – that's fantastic! Doing what?"

"Marketing manager!" she grinned. "For Beauty Select – they're a branch of Angel House…"

"Oh yeah… I've heard of them.. Beauty Select…" He

looked like he was combing through his brain, trying to locate where he had seen them.

"They're based in Brighton, silly," she patted his hand lightly. "You probably pass them every day – their main shop is in The Laines."

A look of recognition now spread itself across his face. "Oh yeah! Isn't that the bright pink shop – with all the feather thingies..?"

Sarah nodded. "That's the one."

"Oh cool! So I'll be able to pop in and see you on your lunch breaks?"

She nodded, grinning.

"And you'll come out in Brighton for nights out..?"

She nodded again. "Of course!"

"And you'll bring Amy down...? ...and Beth..?"

She rolled her eyes playfully and nodded again.

There was a brief silence then, followed by a look of puzzlement spread over his face.

"Wait... are you going to commute to Brighton every day? ... From Richmond? That'll be quite a journey?"

Sarah rolled her eyes again. "No silly. I'm going to move to Brighton!"

He raised his eyebrows.

"So I..." she put a hand on her chest, "...will be your new Brighton friend!"

He grinned. "Oh Sarah – that's so cool!" He grinned again. "Wicked! That has so made my day!"

He grinned again, and then, finally, the light-bulb went off in his head.

"Wait... have you found anywhere to live yet...? Don't suppose you'd want to be my flatmate, would you...?"

"Well! That was a productive morning if ever there was one!" Sarah grinned, looking around Jamie's apartment and smiling contentedly. "Nice, very nice indeed. And I can move in in one month's time?"

Jamie nodded. "Yep. Or sooner if needs be. I could speak to Mike, see if it's okay with him." Jamie crossed his fingers and made a mental note to make amends to Mike.

"Oh Jamie, this is just perfect," Sarah smiled, looking out the kitchen window to the little decking area outside. "Just one thing though…"

"Yes."

"Well… Amy says you're messy…"

"Oh, did she now?" Jamie raised an eyebrow, oddly happy that Amy had been discussing him at all, never mind the fact that it was about his bad habits.

"Yes," Sarah nodded, with finality, as though she was still in meeting-mode. "So, we'll go halves on a cleaner, okay? Just once a week – someone who could come in and give it a good clean?"

Jeez, why didn't I think of that before? This woman is a genius…

Jamie outstretched his hand for Sarah to shake it.

"That, my lady, sounds like a plan…"

"Good," Sarah shook his hand firmly. "Now, about point number two…"

"Oh yes?" Jamie had forgotten there was another point, he was just so happy to get his living arrangements sorted.

"You and Amy… when are you going to sort it out?"

Chapter Thirty-Six
<u>BETH</u>

Beth was walking along Richmond River when she bumped into him. It was a glorious day. The sun was shining through the trees, the birds were swooping in the air, the ducks were bobbing along, peaceful and happy, like her.

She had a 3pm appointment for a massage followed by a tanning session. She had had her hair cut and coloured the day before. She knew which outfit she would be wearing for her night out – a red backless dress with red heels.

She planned to stop for a coffee and read a book for a while. Jake would be picking her up at 7pm. She would meet his friends and family. Was she nervous? No. Just honoured. Very, very honoured. She knew there was nothing to be nervous about. She knew the first "hurdle" (if that was what it was) was over – <u>he</u> wanted <u>her</u> to meet <u>his</u> friends and family – that spoke volumes. All she had to do was turn up and be herself and be agreeable and smile and laugh in all the right places and they would love her. And Jake would be there, holding her hand, making her feel welcome, making her feel wanted, making her feel included. And she would gaze across at him, with his hand in her hand and she would think to herself, "That's my man."

Just as she had turned to look at the ducks, she heard her name being called.

"Beth! Beth!"

She turned, and saw a tall figure galloping towards her. Karl.

Her stomach did that familiar lurch. A nervous, shaky feeling came over her, where her heart pounded and her fingertips felt cold, and there was this pulsating feeling pumping in her.

"Oh, hello," Beth said, "Blimey, what are you doing up at this time of the morning?"

He grinned, that same familiar grin, with his mouth lop-sided in a lazy smile.

"Ah, you know, things to do, stuff to get on with…"

She wondered if he'd got off with some girl the night before. She wondered if he was on his way home from a session. She wondered if he'd given the girl the grace to lie with her all night with his arms around her, rather than disappearing immediately.

She nodded.

"Am… actually.. do you want a quick coffee?" he asked.

"Sure," she found herself saying, not knowing why he'd want to talk after all this time. Not now that their "friendship" had deteriorated to nothing, ever since sex was off the menu.

There was a bar nearby that sold coffees. They sat on the chairs outside, very cosmopolitan looking, as though they were on holiday. As though they had gone abroad. As though they had packed up their bags together and ventured out on an expedition. Which of course was miles away from reality. They had had a shag, two or three times, and he ran away straight afterwards, and she was lucky if she got the crumbs of a measly text a week later.

"So, how've you been?" he asked.

He was all chirpy and breezy, as though he needed to clear his conscience.

"Yeah, I've been good," she smiled. "I've been good."

They talked about small talk – the weather, work, going out, friends, hobbies. As though they were just two mates, on holiday, chatting.

And then something softened in her. She didn't want to

forget everything and turn the clock back and start all over again. Nothing as silly as all that.

But suddenly her resentment eased away. Perhaps resentment for herself eased away. For after all, hadn't it been all her own journey? Hadn't it been her own discovery? Hadn't it been her who'd wanted to sleep with him even though there hadn't been one single mention of the "L" word or the "R" word or any other word that indicated love or relationship?

Wouldn't he be forgiven for thinking she just wanted casual sex?

Because after all, wasn't that what she had pretended she wanted? Hadn't she covered up how she'd really felt? Hadn't she failed to be honest with herself, never mind be honest with him?

Suddenly she saw that the person she needed to forgive wasn't so much him, but herself.

She had wanted the experience, and she got it.

She had fancied someone, and she got to have sex with him.

On having sex with him, she realised she wanted more.

She wanted him to be exclusive to her. She wanted to be the only one he was sleeping with. She wanted to get regular texts from him. She wanted to meet his friends. She wanted to be part of his life.

She wanted to be in a relationship.

The "R" word! The word indicating commitment and responsibility and pain and pleasure. She wanted it. The whole package.

And Jake wanted it too.

And as she sat there, on her cosmopolitan seat with her ex-fuck-buddy, under a sunny Saturday sky, suddenly she realised that he had been part of her journey.

Part of her journey to lead her to Jake.

And for that, she was grateful.

"Well, I suppose I better crack on," she got her bag together and made to go.

"Hot date?" he grinned.
She smiled, "Yes, actually!"
"Enjoy your night."
"Thanks," she smiled. "Yeah, yeah I will."

Chapter Thirty-Seven
<u>SARAH</u>

Stephen retreated down the steps and out the front door. Sarah felt guilty for all of about two seconds – the thought that he would have to find a B&B somewhere, at this time of the night. But the guilt quickly disappeared; right around the time that she remembered that she wasn't a halfway house. That he couldn't just turn up on her doorstep when Kat had gotten fed up him.

She, Sarah, was no longer going to take sloppy seconds.

Which led her to think about Danny. Out there in the big bad world of the stag party. Where anything goes. Tequila, pole-dancers, lap dances and general debauchery. A girlfriend's nightmare. Could she trust him? That was the thing. This was the first night they'd been 'apart', where he'd been 'on a night out' without her. She supposed she should be sick with nerves, that she should be pacing the floor, worrying about what girl's buttocks would be gyrating in his face. But actually, she felt wonderfully *calm*.

Oh my goodness! Could I possibly have found someone I trust? Could I possibly be secure in myself?

She thought back to what Tasha had said – about how if she and Tom were ever to split up, it wouldn't be the end of the world. It would be painful yes, but she would have her friends and family around her to support her – that she'd be okay.

Strangely, Sarah felt the same way. If there was some reason for Danny to call things off just because she was moving down the road to Brighton, well then she would have known that it wasn't meant to be in the first place. And she wouldn't let it dampen her mood.

She would set off to Brighton, happy in the knowledge that she was starting a fantastic job and living with her fabulous friend Jamie, and she would have tons of fun, and meet lots of new people, and who knew what would be around the corner?

But all the same, she wondered how she would broach the subject to Danny without sounding needy.

Hey Danny…. You know the way we've been seeing each other for all of two minutes?

And you know the way we haven't even had a big heart-to-heart yet about how much we like each other?

And you know the way we are playing it cool and going with the flow and taking each day as it comes?

Well, here's the thing…

I'm moving to Brighton.

And I'm wondering if we can keep this 'relationship' going? (And by the way, are we having a relationship'?)

And I'm wondering if you'll be able to take the train down to Brighton every other weekend to see me – and I can take the train up to London every other weekend to see you?

And can we chat on the phone on Mondays and Wednesdays?

Oh, and while we're at it, I'd really rather prefer if there's no other girls on the scene whilst you're living in London either. Yes, I know London is full of beautiful girls, but you'll just have to resist.

Now, how about that?

That's not too much to ask is it?

It was hardly the kind of thing she could just drop into the conversation.

And yet, she knew she *had* to have that conversation.

If she'd learned anything from Stephen, it was that she couldn't pretend to be someone she wasn't.

So how could she have this conversation exactly?

Over dinner perhaps?

She could cook a lovely big feast (hopefully not a Last

244

Supper) and she would drop it into the conversation, right after the dessert and before they'd collapse on the sofa, fat and happy.

He would cuddle up to her on the sofa and tell her that everything was going to be okay, and they would make love, and that would be their happy beginning.

And that all sounded perfect, except that just as she was mid-cooking, a text arrived.

"Waters have broke. We have lift-off."

Tom.

"OH MY GOD!" Sarah squealed from the kitchen, making Danny rush in, worrying that she'd burnt the food.

"It's Tasha – she's gone into labour early – can we go to the hospital?"

And so they did. Off to the hospital, far too early. Because really, there was nothing they could do, but just sit there and wait, for hours, in the hospital café.

They sat next to the lady in the wheelchair; next to the elderly man with the small cardboard bowl in front of him, in case he was sick; next to the drunk girl, with the greasy hair and the jeans slouched down around her crotch.

They sat with their polystyrene cups of weak coffee and their choice of magazines: Runners Weekly, Knitting Monthly, Stop Smoking Guide.

In the midst of Sarah's weak coffee and the Knitting Monthly magazine, she spotted a face she recognised.

Bright red hair. A mass of curls. Walking down the corridor.

Stacey.

Sarah found herself leaping up from her seat and hurrying in Stacey's direction.

Even though she had no idea what to say to her. Even though the very last thing she could say would be:

Oh yeah – you know your man Jamie – the one that didn't treat you very well? Well, I'm moving in with him… .Oh no, not in that way – just as friends…"

Somehow Sarah thought the last thing Stacey would want to talk about was Jamie.

"Stacey?! Stacey?!" Sarah called, as she caught up with her in the corridor. Stacey turned round to face her.

"Stacey!" Sarah exclaimed, looking her up and down. "Wow! You look great!"

Stacey had lost a bit of weight, was wearing lovely clothes, and had picked up a tan from somewhere (bottle or otherwise).

Finishing with Jamie suited her.

"Oh hi," Stacey said. "Sarah – isn't it? Goodness me, fancy seeing you here."

"Yes," Sarah breathed, suddenly wondering why she'd wanted to catch up with Stacey this way. After all, they'd only been at one dinner party together a while ago, and Stacey was probably still feeling wounded by Jamie.

"I'm here to visit my friend Tasha," Sarah rambled. "She's having her baby – a bit prematurely – so we're just hoping everything will be okay…"

Stacey nodded. "I'm visiting my aunt." There was no further conversation from her.

The awkwardness was painful.

Sarah suddenly kicked herself inwardly.

Why had she run after Stacey like this?

But there was something about Stacey – something nice – something vulnerable – something that made Sarah want to help her.

If Sarah and Stacey could have had an *honest* chat – a *real* chat without any inhibitions or fear or pride in the way, they might have said this:

Stacey: Oh yeah, you're Jamie's friend. God he was such a user. I was so heart-broken. I still am if I'm honest. I mean – what's wrong with me?

Sarah: Nothing! There's nothing wrong with you! You're

246

lovely! So much love to give! There are just people for people! And Jamie's head was just somewhere else. It was bad timing.

And then Sarah would tell her all about the Break-up test, and Sarah would tell her that she was moving to Brighton, and that they could set up a Break-up test in Brighton, and Stacey would say, "I'd love that."

That *would* have been the conversation, if fear and pride weren't in the way. However instead the conversation went like this:

Sarah: It was so lovely to meet you that night at Amy's.
Stacey: Yeah, it was lovely to meet you too.
Sarah: I'd love to keep in touch with you. I'm moving to Brighton – so we could meet up for coffees and things:
Stacey: Yeah, I'd love that.
Sarah: Great – well are you on Facebook? Add me on Facebook and we'll keep in touch that way.
Stacy: Yeah, let's do that.

And off she walked, with Sarah vowing to herself to actually follow up on it.

Then it was back to sitting with the polystyrene cups. And the waiting. And the more waiting. Whilst meanwhile the mid-wife upstairs would be saying to Tasha – "Come on now! One final push! One final push!"

Tasha would be screaming, "You said that the last time!"

"I know, I know, but I mean it this time – One final push!"

And there, next to the woman in the wheelchair, next to the drunk girl with the half-exposed crotch, Sarah blurted it out.

"Danny, I've got something to tell you."

He looked up from the Runners Weekly Magazine. "What's up babe?"

She blurted it all out. Tasha. The promotion. Managing the Brighton shop. Having to move to Brighton.

She looked at him, expectantly, waiting for the cogs to turn in his brain, waiting for him to mull things over, waiting for him to give it a good long think before he committed to anything.

He smiled.

"So…" she asked tentatively. "What do you think?"

"I'm very proud of you."

She smiled, shyly, and then persisted, "Yeah but, what about us…? Can we still…?"

He looked at her smiling. "Of course babe. That goes without saying."

She looked across at him, over the hospital table, over the polystyrene cup, and smiled.

She shrugged her shoulders lightly. "Cool."

He lifted up his polystyrene cup, and she lifted hers, and they clinked their cups together, silently.

"Cool."

Tom appeared in the corridor hurriedly saying, "Come on!"

They followed him, up in the lift, up fourteen floors, emerging out of the electronic doors to a wall lined with windows from floor to ceiling.

The morning sun was starting to shine through – a soft warm red and orange glow.

There in the bed, was Tasha, sitting with her little baby in her arms.

"Ooooh! Look! How cute!" Sarah cried. "Look at the little feet!"

Lots of 'oohs' and 'ahhs' followed, with Tasha sitting proud and happy but exhausted.

"What's her name?"

Tasha and Tom looked at each other. "We like the name Eve."

"Eve – that's gorgeous."

"Okay," Tasha put on her authoritative manager's voice. "The shop is staying closed today – you go home and get some sleep. Thank you so much for waiting. But I'm okay and she's okay. So off you go home."

And so they did.

And Sarah and Danny walked out of the hospital, hand in hand.

Chapter Thirty-Eight
AMY

The black dress with the slit up the side or the short skirt with the woollen tights?

The black dress was sexier – definitely – but it also spoke of trying too hard. It was also a bit over the top for just a Saturday night round at his house.

Amy wondered, briefly, if for once they could just go out for the evening instead of being tucked up in his house like in a nest. Couldn't they venture out to a restaurant? One of those nice ones down by the river? The ones with the candlelight, and the bucketful wine glasses and the waitress' heels click-clacking along the marble floor as her pony-tail danced behind her?

The restaurants with the bar men in bow-ties, polishing glasses and shaking cocktail makers, like something out of a Tom Cruise film.

Wouldn't it be nice if he treated her to that once in a while? As though taking her out and showing her off? Rather than hibernating her away in his love-nest, away from inquisitive eyes.

Perhaps he has something to hide. Perhaps he has a secret girlfriend tucked away somewhere, one that he pulls out of the closet and takes out now and again, like a dog on a lead. Perhaps she gets the restaurant treatment while she, Amy, gets the bedroom treatment.

Amy caught herself in her train of negative thoughts and told herself off.

This is what happens when I hang around with Sarah and Beth too much, she told herself. *This is what happens when they spend all evening scolding me and feeding me with negative thoughts about Gav.*

Sarah had *actually* pointed the finger at her, as though she were a school-teacher, telling off a child.

"Three times," Sarah had said. "Three times you've sat here tonight and told us about what Gav wants – you've not once said about what you want."

Amy had felt herself wince further back into her sofa. She was sorry she'd opened her mouth in the first place. She was sorry she'd even told Beth and Sarah about Gav coming home.

She'd wished, desperately, that she'd just kept her dirty big secret to herself.

"Gav is what I want," Amy had replied, helplessly.

It had been another Break-up test meeting, held at Sarah's house. Amy hardly saw the point in the meetings anymore. Beth was so wrapped up in her art, and Sarah was all biz about her job, that there hadn't been any talk of Stephen or Karl for ages.

It was just Amy, still blabbering on about Gav.

Hoping that they'd understand.

Hoping that they'd realise, that some people are just *meant* to be together, like Romeo and Juliet, or Adam and Eve, or Harry and Sally.

"I just wonder how much more pain you'll have to take before you get sick of it," Sarah had announced sternly.

That was the thing that irked Amy about Sarah sometimes. She was just so forceful, so aggressive, so "in business meeting" mode.

"Well anyway, tell me what's happening with the job... and the drawing..." Amy had desperately hoped to change the subject, wishing instead that she could just grab her coat and run away, and hide under her duvet for a while, re-emerging on Saturday morning, in preparation for her date with Gav.

Beth had talked about the art studio and her drawings, and all the artists she was meeting. She had talked about her exhibition, which made Amy cringe with guilt for not being able to attend.

Sarah had talked about her work, and the different marketing ideas she had pitched to the boss, who seemed genuinely pleased with her initiative.

The girls, it seemed, were climbing their own career ladders, leaving Stephen and Karl effortlessly on the bottom rung.

How come they seem to just 'not care' anymore? It wasn't as if they still loved him or loathed him, there was just an indifference, a lack of emotional angst. As though the pain had been lifted out of them and turfed to one side.

"So do you think of him anymore?" Amy blurted out, to either Beth or Sarah, whoever wanted to take the question and run with it.

It was Sarah who answered.

"No. Not really. Oh I'd be lying if I said he didn't pop into my head now and again, like an unwanted tennis ball flung into my garden," she chuckled. "But it's not such an over-riding, all encompassing thought."

Beth nodded. "Yeah, I agree – and I suppose the only way for me was to replace it with something else – which I've done with my art."

Amy had nodded, as though she understood. But she didn't. Not really. She didn't have an art studio to tuck herself away in. She didn't have an interest in art. She didn't even have a career ladder to climb up. She knew she was on a plateau now, with no going forward and no sliding back. Just comfortably numb.

She thought, briefly, that the only distraction she'd had recently was Jamie, and she wondered if that was wrong. Was it just replacing one fella for another? Was it wrong that she'd spent the last few weeks, nay months, acting like a girlfriend to someone, without the actual sex? Living together, strolling around Covent Garden together, sitting in the park together, talking rubbish?

Spending more time and energy and chat with him than with the object of her affections?

She wondered about the balance of attention. One night in a blue moon with Gav versus weeks of living with Jamie and hanging out with him. Wouldn't it be fair to say that Jamie was the equivalent to a boyfriend already?

And there *was* that moment in the kitchen, and quite possibly, that moment in the pub. What would have happened if they had just leaned in and kissed each other, just to see?

Just to see if X + Y = Z?

"And what about you and Jamie?" Sarah had asked, as though reading her mind.

Amy had spluttered, choking on the sip of wine that she had just tipped back.

"Me and Jamie?" Amy had repeated, as though buying more time.

"Yep. You and Jamie. What's going on there then?" Sarah had asked.

Beth was smiling, impishly, as though this was the best piece of gossip she'd heard in ages.

"Nothing… " Amy had stammered. "I mean… he's a mate.. he's with Stacey.. there's nothing happening…"

Sarah had tutted, as though Amy was talking rubbish. "I'll give Jamie and Stacey one week, tops", she had said, decidedly. "And as for you two..well, I've never seen more chemistry flinging out of two people, ever."

Amy had found a smile creeping over her face, despite herself. A big, full-blown, teenage-like grin.

"Really?" she had found herself asking.

"Oh my God yes. He fancies the pants off you. It's so obvious."

And somehow, Sarah, together with her assertiveness, suddenly went up in Amy's estimations.

"Amy. Any chance you could pop round today. News for you."

Amy's mum's way of texting. She had yet to learn that no "x" at the end of the text made it sound abrupt. No exclamation marks either. No smiley faces. A very sombre message. If Amy didn't know her better, she'd be worried.

"No probs. I'll be round about 4pm. Can't stay long though. Going on to meet someone x o x"

"Ok."

Amy crunched over the grass on Twickenham Green on the way to her mum's house. She loved this time of year, when she had to wear full-length boots and wrap a scarf around her neck. When she got to pull on a woollen hat and not worry about what shape her hair was in. When there was a cool fresh breeze whipping through her lungs making her feel fresh and alive.

"Hello honey," her mum smiled as she opened the big green door and let her inside. Amy wiped her feet on the mat and pulled off her boots. Her feet sunk into the thick carpet as she padded after her mum, pulling off her coat and hat.

"Wow! You look nice mum! What's the occasion?"

Her mum was dressed in a dark red expensive looking suit, one that looked as though its recent home was a hanger in Karen Millen. Her false nails were on, her hair was coiffured to perfection and she even had a satisfied smile on her face to finish the look.

"Stevie and I are heading out to dinner," she grinned.

Stevie was the latest in the Tom, Dick, Harry line, although to be fair, he *had* lasted a good while longer than most.

"Ooh where to? Dinner with the Queen?!"

"Ha! Dinner at the Canyon restaurant – you know, the one beside the river in Richmond?"

Oh yes, that one. The one she was hoping Gav would take her to.

"Any particular reason? Is the business going exceptionally

well or what?"

"Oh yes, the business is going brilliantly. We have a new range of jewellery coming in now.. but that's not the point.. the point is, there's other news…"

Mum stood at the fridge, pulled out a bottle of champagne and ushered Amy to sit at the kitchen table.

"Crikey. Bollinger champagne. None of the cheap plonk for you missus."

Mum waved her hand a little as though to say, "Quiet, I need to tell you something."

She pulled two champagne flutes from the kitchen cupboard and sat down at the pine table.

"So…" she said, twisting the silver foil and loosening it from its grip around the cork.

"Stevie and I have been chatting …"

"Um hum.." Amy prompted quickly.

"And…" Mum held one hand around the cork, one hand around the bottle and began a slight twisting movement.

"… and we've decided to get married."

"What?!" Amy shrieked as the cork popped noisily and flung itself across the other side of the room.

"Yes. Married. Imagine." Mum's eyes filled with tears.

"But… you seemed to never want to get married again.. not after dad.. not after the divorce came through…"

"Oh darling.. I know…"

"And do you know something?" Amy re-arranged herself in her seat, as though settling down for a good discussion. Champagne flute in hand, mum's emotive face, an announcement, as good a time as any to talk. "We never really talk about this.. we never really talk about dad.. you never tell me anything about anything…"

Mum seemed to fluster around for words then, as though this script wasn't going the way she wanted. As though there was just supposed to be a happy and joyous "fantastic!" and that would be that.

"No seriously.." Amy persisted, as her mum hovered the bottle at an angle to Amy's glass and let the bubbles fizz and dance merrily.

"Why did we... why don't we.. ever talk about what happened with Dad? Why did he leave really? Was it something I did wrong?"

"Oh Amy.." Mum closed a hand over hers. "Don't be so silly…" she said, in a gentle voice. "You never did anything wrong. How could you? You were only six years old."

Mum took a sip of her champagne. She shook her head then carried on.

"No, he had an affair."

Amy's mouth dropped open. "What?"

Mum nodded apologetically.

"Yes. And I wanted him to go away and never come back."

Amy shook her head. "But why? I mean how? How could he do that?"

"I know. I'm sorry I could never talk about it. It was just too painful for me."

"But why? Why would he do it? Who was she?"

Mum took a deep breath. She wasn't expecting this. She was expecting good, celebratory times. She was not expecting to delve into the past. Like clearing out the cupboard under the stairs and finding cobwebs galore.

"I found him in bed with the next door neighbour."

Amy's mouth dropped open.

"It was horrible. Painful. Excruciating. The most vivid and real nightmare of my life ever. I can still see it in my head at times."

Amy nodded, sympathetically, wanting her to go on, wanting to finally discover the reason behind the great disappearance.

"She wasn't even that great shakes either, I can tell you," mum laughed, ruefully. "If she'd have been a six foot model, I might have understood, but no."

Amy just sat and listened.

"Of course, I was in shock. It's not the sort of thing you expect to come home to. Your head is thinking 'I must get the spuds on for the wein. I must take the washing off the line'. You don't think you'll come home to that."

Amy shifted in her seat. "But why…? How…?"

Mum shrugged. "Oh I don't know. I asked myself that many, many times. It was almost as though he *wanted* me to find him. I came home half an hour earlier than normal and …. *Wham!*"

"But why have you never told me before?"

Mum sighed, "Well for a start, at the time you were far too young to understand. And I couldn't bear him kicking about the place, so I agreed with him that he should just go. I wanted to close the door on him. I wanted a closed chapter."

Amy nodded. She understood that much.

"You can't start a new chapter unless you close the old one you know."

"That's true."

"So I asked him to go and he did. Fecked off I don't know where. As long as he left Northern Ireland, I didn't really care", Mum sighed. "And then we were free to get on with our own lives. And it was just us two. And I liked that. We were safe. No-one could hurt us. And it was just us two. Having fun."

Amy nodded. "Yes, we did have fun at times."

Mum chuckled. "All those day trips. Ness Wood picnic park. Up to Belfast for shopping. Portrush for the rides in Barrys. Castlerock for the beach. I did try to make sure you had as much fun as possible."

"You did," Amy replied quietly. "Thanks Mum."

"And you were loved. Very, very much. You still are."

Amy smiled. "I know. Thank you. I love you too."

"And we can track your Dad down some day if you really want to," Mum told her quietly.

"I know. I'll think about it."

They sipped their champagne and let the bubbles fizz to their head.

"So, now what?" Amy asked. "Stevie? To be really honest with you, I'm surprised you're letting someone in now. I mean.. god forbid.. but what happens if…"

"He won't do that," Mum interrupted.

"How do you know?" Amy was persistent, yet softly spoken.

Tom. Dick. Harry.

One after the other.

Being in control.

"What makes you trust this one?"

"Because…." Mum said, a faraway smile in her eyes. "Because he was a friend first… Because he chased me for ages… Because he's kind… Because he's trustworthy.. Because if I need as much as lozenges for my cough, he's off in the car like a flash to get me them… Because he's always there for me… Because he's dependable, trustworthy, kind."

Boring?

Crap in bed?

No passion out of him?

"But do you fancy him?" Amy blurted out. "Or is he more like a mate?"

You know, the carpet slippers and pipe type?

"Oh goodness yes," Mum swooned. "Of course I fancy him. Sure have you seen the shoulders on him? He can pick me up and whisk me up the stairs any time he wants.."

"Okay, okay.. I get the message… too much information!"

"So," Mum changed the subject, "How would you feel about being my bridesmaid?"

Amy clinked glasses with her Mum. "I'd love to," she said. "But there's one condition…"

"What's that?"

"No meringue dresses. And no throwing the bouquet in my direction!"

Mum smiled, a glimmer of devilment in her eyes.

"We'll see."

Amy decided on the black dress with the slit up the side.

To hell with it, she thought. *If he won't take me out, I'll take myself out.*

His house was exactly the same. The same smell – a hint of his own manly scent, mixed in with his aftershave. The same sofa, the same rug draped over the sofa, the same wooden coffee table, the same photographic book positioned strategically on the coffee table. The one with the pictures of the naked ladies.

I wonder how many other girls he's used this on, Amy caught herself thinking.

"You look really nice," he said, appreciatively, eyeing her up and down, the long black dress, the cleavage showing, the slit up the side, nearly as far up to her panty line.

"Thanks."

"No, really, you look... wow!" he held her hands and stared at her, as though drinking her in.

He's such a flirt, she thought. *Such an ability to chat up women. Such a natural flirt, with everyone, probably.*

"Thanks," she repeated again.

"Glass of wine?" he asked, padding into the kitchen. He was wearing flip-flops and tracksuit bottoms, and an old t-shirt that was faded and grey and looked as though it had seen several years in his wardrobe.

"Yes thanks." She followed him into the kitchen, and stood, awkwardly, in her high heels and in her long dress, with the slit up to her panties.

"You look... amazing..." he said, tracing a finger up her leg until it reached the tip of her skirt.

She felt that familiar tingling feeling, the one that travelled to her groin and made that happy dance in her private places.

"Thank you," she answered again, stiffly.

259

In the door, finger on thigh, happy dance in private parts, only ten minutes in.

This guy's stats were getting better.

They retreated to the sofa, and sat side by side.

"So!" Amy began, more brusquely than necessary, more brusquely than she had intended. "Tell me everything! What have you been up to?"

It was an attempt at conversation. It was an attempt at an evening being not just about sex, but it was a fruitless attempt.

"Oh, you know…" he savoured her with his eyes, letting his eyes run up and down her body, as though she were a sports car in an exhibition, a thing he wanted to purchase. "Missing you." His hand travelled up the slit again, and she thought, *See Amy.. this is your fault .. this is why you should have worn the woollen tights.*

"Oh really?" she asked, chirpily. "Missing me? Well, that is promising – that is good stuff – that is positive."

She knew she was rambling. She knew she was talking rubbish. She knew this because he cupped a hand behind her head and drew his mouth to hers, silencing her with a kiss.

The kiss was not good. Sloppy. Forceful. Too much tongue. Too much licking around her mouth, smearing her lipstick.

Has he always kissed this bad? she wondered.

Suddenly Beth and Sarah's situations popped into her head; *"It's just not such an over-riding thought anymore."*

Amy pulled away. "Sorry," she said, embarrassed. She took a sip of her wine.

"You okay?" he asked, one eyebrow raised, as though there was something wrong, as though she were a pet who wasn't performing.

She nodded. "Yeah…just.." She sipped her wine again.

There was an awkward silence then. And then he made another lunge. As though a circus performer having another attempt.

"Just two seconds," she grabbed her bag and made a bee-line

for the bathroom.

She sat on the toilet with her head in her hands, wondering what exactly had just happened then?

Had she not given him all the signs? The dress with the slit, the cleavage showing, the high heels... and yet, she didn't expect this.

It was like he wanted the grand finale without the warm-up act. It was everything she had wanted and yet nothing she had planned. She did not want this. She was not a wind-up doll for ready-steady-go use.

She found herself pulling her mobile phone out of her bag.

"Hello," she texted. "How are you? X"

It was an experiment. A silly experiment, granted, but it was an experiment just the same.

"Hey! I'm good! Good to hear from you! How are you? J x"

You see? His text bouncing back effortlessly. No games. No pain. No messing about.

She paused, took a deep breath, and then replied.

"I'm at Gav's. I've just suddenly gone off him. And I think I might have to escape out the bathroom window. ps. re. the Break-up test... have I won? x"

Chapter Thirty-Nine
JAMIE

"You and Amy. When are you going to sort it out?" Sarah had announced, abruptly.

Jamie's face glowered. "I don't know what you mean…?"

"Oh Jamie!" Sarah waved her hand impatiently. "Don't be so silly – it's blindingly obvious."

"What…?"

"You? Amy? Flirting with one another? Fancying the pants off each other?"

Jamie raised his eyebrows.

"You think she fancies me?"

All of a sudden, this conversation was getting interesting.

His face flushed red with embarrassment.

"Well, that much is obvious," Sarah drawled. "The pair of you are like love-sick teenagers."

"But what about Gav? What about her obsession with Golden Boy?"

Sarah tsked, and swatted her hand, as though waving away a fly.

"She'll get over it. She'll get bored of it. She thinks she likes him – but she's probably just lonely. It's probably been something for her to cling on to."

Jamie picked up a pen and rolled it around his fingers, as though contemplating.

"But what am I supposed to do? Just wait around until she gets fed up with him?"

Sarah lifted her eyebrows. "So you *do* really like her then?"

Jamie grinned. "You're crafty. Making me walk into your trap like that."

Sarah shrugged her shoulders. "Sorry. It was obvious. But I was just checking."

Jamie sighed. "So what do I do? I think this thing with Gav is just going to go on and on and on…"

Sarah shook her head. "No. I think she'll get bored of it. I think, when Gav's back for good .. and he's still only inviting her round once in a blue moon… I think she'll realise that nothing's changed."

"You think?"

"Yep. I think at the moment she's hoping that once he's back for good, things will be different. I think she's hoping he'll suddenly turn into mister call-her-everyday. I think when she realises that nothing's changed, she'll tire of him."

"And then what?"

"Just ask her out Jamie, for God's sake."

But what if it's a complete disaster?

"What have you got to lose?" Sarah went on, as though reading his thoughts.

My pride. My ego. What if she knocks me back?

"You've fancied her for ages, why don't you just go for it?"

But what if I'm a complete commitment-phobe with her too?

"If it doesn't work out, well, at least you know you've tried."

And if I mess things up with her, then it'll just be another bastard to add to her list.

There was a silence then. Where they just sat. Where time stood still. Like an egg timer, where all the sand had run to the bottom, and there was just nothing left. And Jamie knew it was up to him. It was up to him to pick up that egg timer and twist it around and set the wheels in motion. So that the sand would trickle down, and time would start again, in a new chapter.

"Or you could just do nothing," Sarah shrugged her shoulders. "You could just forget all about it, and not try anything because of fear."

He knew she was playing devil's advocate with him, testing the waters, giving him the option to walk away, to pretend there was no attraction, to let the opportunity slip by, like a passing train.

"Okay, what to do?" he thought.

A big grand gesture? Like spelling her name on the beach? Or tracing a line of pebbles at her front door – "Amy I love you. X "- Something like that?

No, too corny. She'd run a mile.

Something casual, like, "Amy, what about it?"

No, not appropriate.

Something simple.

Perfectly simple.

The train pulled up to the platform. Jamie stood at the edge, trying not to have a stupid grin on his face.

She emerged from the train door, clutching an overnight bag and a smile. An anxious smile – nervous perhaps?

He grinned and held out his arms to hug her. "C'mere you", he pulled her into a bear-hug, digging his nose into her hair, breathing her in, holding her tight. As though she were a prodigal daughter who had returned.

She was the first one to break out of the hug.

"So, you," she smiled, giving him a playful hit on the arm. "Where are you taking me?"

"What about the pier?" he asked. "Fish & chips. The 2p slot machines. Get our fortunes told?"

"Sounds like a plan," Amy grinned.

They walked off, side by side, falling into their usual comfortable chit-chat.

"Of course I know what the fortune teller will tell me," Amy grinned.

"What?"

That you and I will finally get it together? That after all this faffing about and our merry dance, we'll get it on?

"Oh, you know… that I'll be rich and famous…hugely successful.. company car.. that kind of thing…"

Jamie nodded. "I can see that," he said, in earnest.

On they walked; past the shops, down towards the pier, along the stony beach.

The place where I thought of writing "I love you Amy" in pebbles.

Thank God I didn't.

On up the pier, the fish and chips, sitting side by side on a park bench, like an old couple, Amy squealing every time a seagull circled near her.

He wanted to lean over and take her hand, cradle it in his and sit there, like a couple. But he didn't.

Not now. Wait.

There was playing time on the slot machines. A few rides. Eating candy floss and looking over the sea.

There was flirting, chemistry, the prolonged looks, his eyes flicking from her eyes to her mouth to back to her eyes again.

There was the walking past The Pavilion; it lit up at night. Romantic. Attractive. Special.

There was Amy draping a casual arm through his; linking arms, half friendly, half romantic.

There was her comment; "I love it here in Brighton. There's a nice atmosphere, isn't there."

There was his inward interpretation; "I could consider coming to visit you all the time. I could consider living here."

And then, there was the taxi home.

Here, in the taxi, just grab her. Just take her hand and snog her, here in the back of the taxi.

No, not right either.

And then they were home. In the door. Him showing her the bedroom where she would sleep. Telling her to make herself comfortable. Saying, "It's so good to see you again."

She walked into the room and looked around.

"It's nice," she announced. "Very nice."

She set her bag down.

"So this will be Sarah's room?"

"Yeah"

"And Sarah isn't here tonight because…?"

Because she's pretending to look after her gran. Because she's trying to fix us up.

"She had to look after her gran."

Amy nodded. And then she sat down on the bed. On the blue duvet.

There was a silence then. Jamie hovered in the doorway, as though rooted to the spot. He wanted to say something but he was gripped by fear. He knew he should say, "Night then", and walk away, yet he remained hopelessly rooted to the spot, as though stuck in sinking sand.

Amy patted the blue duvet and said, "Sit here and chat to me for a bit Jamie."

In her eyes, there was something. Longing? Impatience?

Jamie sat, facing her, his heart thumping in his chest.

"I really like you Jamie," she said.

And there it was. Five words.

Five words that were like a key opening the door.

I really like you Jamie.

"And I really like you too, Amy."

And then he kissed her.

A long, soft, sink-down-to-your-knees kiss, as though they were sitting on a cloud and just hanging there.

And it was just her and him, alone on the blue duvet.

THE END

Fantastic Books
Great Authors

Meet our authors and discover our exciting range:

- Gripping Thrillers
- Cosy Mysteries
- Romantic Chick-Lit
- Fascinating Historicals
- Exciting Fantasy
- Young Adult and Children's Adventures

Visit us at:
www.crookedcatpublishing.com

Join us on facebook:
www.facebook.com/crookedcatpublishing

2330382R00140

Printed in Great Britain
by Amazon.co.uk, Ltd.,
Marston Gate.